THE ZAMINDARS BRIDE

BY

ADRIANA GIROLAMI

Cover by Adriana Girolami

ABOUT THE AUTHOR

Adriana Girolami — an accomplished writer of historical fiction, and the author of the beloved historical romance series, The Templar Trilogy: *Mysterious Templar*, *The Crimson Amulet*, and *Templar's Redemption*.

The Italian-born author seduces readers with her gorgeous visual style—both on the covers of her books and on all the pages in-between. Her love of history and the arts was encouraged by her parents who were avid readers, since books were always available while growing up, besides being influenced by the historical appeal of her birthplace, the Eternal city of Rome.

Because of the premature death of her father, as a child she immigrated with her family to the United States where her mother originated from, and later attended *The Art Students League* in New York City.

A successful portrait artist, Adriana created the covers for all of her books. As the illustrator of her book jackets, she paints intricate, visually rich characters that match the complex personalities she creates with her equally well-drawn words.

She is a world traveler, and accompanied by her husband was privileged to visit many beautiful places in the world. As a lover of history she is particularly attracted to the fascinating beauty of exotic India and the splendor of ancient Egypt, her visit to that country was an experience she especially cherished.

Adriana loves to jog in her favorite park, surrounded by trees, and with the sound of nature. Her creativity is especially stimulated in those surroundings. She favors physical activities because her work is so sedentary. Playing racquetball is one of her favorite pastime, and is proud of having achieved a black belt in Kenpo Karate. She always looks forward to new experiences to broaden her horizon, new places to discover in our world, and many new exciting novels to write.

Timber Creek Press
Imprint of Timber Creek Productions, LLC
312 N. Commerce St.
Gainesville, Texas 76240

ISBN-13: 978-1-7363220-0-0

Published by: Timber Creek Press
timbercreekpresss@yahoo.com
www.timbercreekpress.net

ACKNOWLEDGMENT

The author gratefully acknowledges the multi talented Mr. Ken Farmer for his invaluable help in the publishing of *The Zamindar's Bride*. Special thanks to Mr. Buck Stienke for support of my work,

A very special acknowledgment to my friend Dr. R.K.Das.This for his gracious, most relevant and inspiring support of my writing.

The Zamindar's Bride is an amazing cross cultural novel full of intrigue, adventure, and romance. Most books have a single hook that pulls the reader in. Adriana Girolami has once again, in her masterful non-stop style, crafted a story that keeps you engaged with every single sentence.
Bravo!
DR. MICHAEL ADAMSE

I wish to express my congratulations to the talented Historical author and artist Adriana Girolami, for the publishing of her latest novel, *The Zamindar's Bride*.

This exciting, passionate story explores the privileged world of "Zamindars", who were fabulously wealthy land owners, (Feudal Lords) whose power flourished during the British rule in Colonial India. (Zamin in Hindi language), the root word for Zamindar, originated in Persia, since their influence was spread by the Mughals in north India. The Zamindar's Bride depicts the passionate love between an Indian Zamindar and a beautiful European Countess. We enter the glamorous royal courts of 19th Century Europe, and the splendor of exotic India, exploring the many intrigues that flourish in those privileged worlds. The protagonists are challenged by their different cultures, although mysteriously connected by the possibility of reincarnation.

Award winner (Indian) Author and Poet
Former journalist of Khaleej Times

WILLIAMSJI MAVELY

DEDICATION

In grateful and loving memory of my beautiful aunt Molly, who always inspired me with her generosity and kindness, she will always be in my heart.

A special dedication to all my wonderful readers throughout the world, whose support and dedication inspire me to create more exciting novels. I hope you will enjoy my latest offering, *The Zamindar's Bride*.

CHAPTER ONE

THE ELUSIVE DREAM

The sun began to set, and the shadows of dusk spread-out like a heavenly veil upon the lovely province of Orissa under the British Raj during the Indian summer of 1880. This picturesque region of Eastern India was one of the most prosperous ancient Kingdoms of Bharat-Barsh, called Kalinga, with a vibrant cultural and artistic heritage.

The community thrived by the riverbanks of its largest river, the Mahanadi of Orissa, which had been the lifeline for this ancient province since time's recorded history. The waterways flowed through the outskirts of the coastal town of

Kendrapara, which encompassed thousands of acres of land, reaching far into the horizon.

Kendrapara, the oldest municipal town of Orissa, is replete with a rich heritage and surrounded by a cluster of villages with a treasure trove of historical, exotic temples built in honor of the many Hindu deities worshiped by the people.

In this predominantly agricultural community, the inhabitants of this region enjoy the bliss of pastoral life and a collective sense of pride in this culturally vibrant and spiritually rich place that brought honor to the land.

As the day was coming to a close, Vanya and Kyra, two young peasant girls, were merrily splashing in the refreshing waters of the mighty Mahanadi River.

After a long, arduous day nestled in this unique and ancient world, they looked for respite from the oppressive summer's heat. They had given in to the magnetic lure of the flowing waters of the river, which sparkled like diamonds in the sun, and caressed their skin like the cool breezes of the northern wind

The deserted stretch of beach was their special hiding place. It was far from the usual crowds of farmers who tended cows and water buffalos in the thriving agricultural community.

Vanya and Kyra seemed oblivious to the late hour and impending darkness. The girl's silvery laughter resonated happily in the peaceful, pastoral surroundings. Their freshly washed laundry was now left unceremoniously in a rustic woven basket on the river's sandy bank. It was forgotten for the moment, as pleasure took precedence over duty.

Their revelry continued unabated until Vanya paused abruptly. She was startled by the unexpected sight of a man on horseback who suddenly appeared in the distance. She called out to her friend with some apprehension and pointed to the crimson horizon with wonder and curiosity in her eyes.

"Look, Kyra, a man on horseback is coming in our direction…I think it's rather strange since no one usually rides such a lonely and isolated stretch of beach. Perhaps that person is looking for solitude?"

"Maybe you are right, Vanya, but it's truly unusual for someone to be riding this way on horseback," answered Kyra while placing her hand above her brow to shield the brightness of the sun. She then focused her eyes on the mysterious rider whose presence was suddenly causing some disruption to their pleasant afternoon.

It soon became apparent to the girls that the unknown horseman was riding with considerable speed since he gained ground faster than expected.

"I wonder who that person might be, and what is his purpose for being here?" interjected Kyra with concern in her voice, "I am worried by his presence, considering that we are all alone…especially at this late hour."

She then added almost in a whisper, "I hope it's someone honorable and with no evil intentions since we are stuck in this isolated place."

Vanya felt suddenly uneasy as she moved closer to her friend, alarmed by her words. They both remained very still, almost afraid to move, with their eyes transfixed toward the horizon as the mysterious stranger was fast approaching while sprouting his mount to an increased speed.

They were finally able to see with some clarity that the horse was a splendid thoroughbred with its flowing mane blowing in the wind. A cloud of dust rose in the air as its hooves hit the ground with power and speed.

Suddenly, a look of joy and relief brightened Vanya's face as she grabbed her friend's hand with excitement in her voice.

"No need to worry Kyra, I think I know who the man on horseback is. I can even recognize him from this distance. It's our Zamindar, of course!"

"You think it's the Zamindar?" answered Kyra, stunned by her friend's words and slightly amused.

"You must be joking, Vanya. I truly believe you are a captive of your dreams and overactive imagination."

Vanya was annoyed with Kyra as she placed her hands on her hips to assert herself in front of her doubtful and sarcastic friend.

"As usual, you blame it on my imagination. It's so frustrating to put up with your skepticism about everything I say…"

She paused and glared at Kyra, trying to control her irritation, but ultimately decided it would be best to have a friendlier and more positive conversation.

"Please, Kyra, try not to be so cynical. Do you know anyone around here who could own such a splendid stallion? It's easy to see that the horse runs like the wind and seems to release fire from its nostrils. The best we can hope for are horses, who are usually old, slow, and worn out from manual labor."

"Perhaps I am too doubtful," answered Kyra with skepticism, "but you have jumped to the wrong conclusions too many times. Besides, the man on horseback is riding against the light and without his usual escort."

"I guess you don't know much about our Zamindar," insisted Vanya with glee while standing proudly before her friend.

"I have heard people say that he often rides alone by the river's edge..."

She stopped suddenly and pointed with some anxiety toward the mysterious horseman.

"Look, Kyra, he is fast approaching, while we are wasting time in idle chatter...let's make ourselves more presentable to him."

Without waiting for an answer, Vanya took hold of Kyra's arm with unusual strength. She then dragged her reluctant friend unceremoniously out of the water.

"You are hurting me. Let go of my arm!" bellowed Kyra, clearly frustrated by her friend's apparent obsession with the Zamindar, as she pushed her firmly away.

Resigned to Kyra's lack of enthusiasm, Vanya ignored her friend and focused on her appearance instead. She glanced with distress at her wet clothes and messy, tangled hair. She had dreamed so many times of meeting the Zamindar in her romantic world of make-believe, although it was never in such a wet and unkempt condition.

She had envisioned walking in the splendid gardens of his palace in Cuttack, wearing with elegance and flair her mother's peach-colored silk saree. She admired it growing up when her mom wore it on special occasions.

The girl closed her eyes, forgetting her surroundings, and suddenly, like magic, he was there close to her, gazing in her eyes with admiration and longing, whispering words of love, which filled her with ecstasy and joy.

However, there was little time left for impossible dreams, and Vanya, with great haste, attempted to squeeze the excess water from her clothes. She even managed to entwine her lengthy, black hair into a braid, which unfortunately rested rather limp on her shoulders.

By now, the splendid Arabian stallion, Amir, the Zamindar's favorite horse, was in full view, reflecting in his black, shiny pelt, the sparkling embers of the dying sun.

Kyra's skepticism disappeared, and a sense of regret overwhelmed her for having been so disagreeable to her friend's warning. With haste, she managed to smooth out the wrinkles on her wet, cotton kurta. She then quickly pushed back her messy hair, trying to confront the Zamindar with some measure of dignity and respect.

Meanwhile, Vanya picked up her earthen Kalas filled with water gathered from a well, attempting to hide her wrinkled attire behind the large container. She quickly rested it on her hip and held it safely with her left arm as prescribed by the peasant girls' tradition in the area.

Now Vanya and Kyra stood side by side, excited and humbled by the occasion as they waited with anticipation to meet their beloved Zamindar, who was fast approaching.

A SPECIAL MOMENT

Soon after, his highness, the Zamindar Ramakanta Choudhury of Niladripur, appeared dressed with style in white riding clothes tailored to his well-built, masculine physique. There was a brightness to his persona as if the presiding wind had been unable to diminish its luster.

The light color of the garment emphasized so well his bronzed complexion and luminous, intense dark eyes. He wore a tightly wrapped turban around his handsome face, and a meticulously trimmed mustache adorned his lips, enhancing with sophistication his manly appeal. His demeanor was dignified, befitting his high station in life. Yet, a benevolent, friendly aura exuded from him and gave it a touch of accessibility.

The Zamindar was a man of considerable status in his country, and his family's fortune had grown in impressive proportions throughout the years. That is partly due to the capable managing of their many land-holdings by the Zamindars that had preceded him.

As a prosperous landowner, his lavish estate in Kendrapara comprised thousands of acres in the best and most fertile land by the Mahanadi river delta. Their bucolic majesty was cared for by the many tenants responsible for the cultivation of the land.

Ramakanta appeared to be in a hurry this day, considering the speed of his steed. He slowed down his mount's pace as he rode by the young girls, who were respectfully standing by the river's edge, apparently waiting for him. They seemed mesmerized by his sight and lowered their heads in a sign of respect as he waved to them with friendliness.

For Vanya and Kyra, it was such a significant moment of being singled out by their Zamindar, considering the existing caste system and their humble station in life.

They were excited but also intimidated by his presence, as they stood silent and erect, amazed by his unexpected appearance.

Vanya was genuinely overwhelmed by the auspicious moment. So much so that she carelessly released the hold on the water-filled Kalas. The vessel suddenly slipped from her arm and crashed to the floor with a loud thud.

The Zamindar noticed the small commotion that followed as the girls visually, distressed, attempted to pick up the pieces scattered all over the ground and beyond repair.

Vanya was distraught by her carelessness since the Kalas had been one of her family's few valued possessions for many years.

"What can I do now, and what will my mother say?" She moaned desperately.

"Don't worry, Vanya, it was an accident," answered Kyra with a calming voice, attempting to comfort her friend's distress.

"I am sure your mother will understand the circumstances and forgive you."

The Zamindar was moved by the scene, understanding that his presence may have caused the mishap.

Without hesitation, he pulled back the reins of his steed, bringing it to an abrupt halt, and quickly guided him toward Vanya and Kyra. He then addressed them with a friendly voice.

"I am very sorry young ladies...perhaps the speed of my horse might have startled you and caused this unfortunate accident."

The girls looked up, stunned by the unexpected attention they were receiving. Also embarrassed by their disheveled appearance and wet clothes covered with sand, they remained still, almost paralyzed with awe and unable to speak.

Realizing that his presence was intimidating to the young women and not wishing to cause them further humiliation, the Zamindar quickly removed a couple of coins from a leather pouch and placed them on the ground while saying.

"I hope this small token will help replace the broken Kalas and ease some of your distress..."

He paused briefly with a smile and then spurred his steed forward into a faster gallop. The young girls held their breath in wonder as the Zamindar quickly rode away and soon disappeared in the distance.

Kyra was the first to recover from their temporary stupor. She leaped to her feet and eagerly searched the sandy ground for the special gift from their Zamindar. The coins were insight. The girl picked them up, with hands trembling with great excitement. She cleaned them carefully, removing all traces of sand, and marveled at how they sparkled so brilliantly in the sun.

Then, at closer inspection, her eyes widened with surprise, and she motioned her friend to come closer with great enthusiasm in her voice.

"Look, Vanya, they are gold sovereigns, the most valuable currency available in India today. These coins are rare and truly scarce among people around here. I recognized them only because four gold sovereigns were part of my grandmother's dowry when she became a bride. My grandparents kept one as a souvenir and prominently display it during celebrations of their anniversary…"

Kyra became silent for a brief moment while holding the little golden treasure tightly in her hands and close to her heart. She then exclaimed joyfully.

"What an amazing, memorable day this turned out to be…I never dreamed of meeting and receiving such a generous gift from our Zamindar, which makes this experience truly special."

But Vanya was deaf to the world at that moment. Her imagination had taken over, and even the lure of gold was not enough to distract the young woman from her fantasies.

"He is so handsome," she gushed as she pushed back her unruly hair, "did you notice how he stopped his stallion to get closer to us? I will always remember the way he smiled at me. I am certain to have made a good impression."

"I think he smiled at both of us," answered Kyra, shaking her head in disbelief in response to her friend's delusions of grandeur.

"As the ruler of the people, he smiles at everybody," she continued while placing the gold coin in Vanya's hand.

"Give this gold sovereign to your parents tonight. I am certain they will not even notice that you have broken the Kalas."

Vanya looked at the coin with surprise and wonder while Kyra walked toward the basket full of clothes and said with amusement.

"Although our Zamindar was friendly and nice, I doubt he was impressed by our appearance since we must have looked like two wet cats."

The young woman laughed while lifting the heavy basket full of washed clothes. She then placed it effortlessly upon her head and held it steadily with balance and ease.

Kyra was the more pragmatic of the two girls and familiar with her friend's endless romantic dreams. She often attempted to bring her back to reality and spare her the disappointments and unfairness of life.

"There is a rumor that he is getting married soon," she finally said, "the announcement should come in a few days."

Vanya was immediately interested and asked her friend with a little apprehension in her voice.

"Who is getting married, Kyra? please tell me."

"The Zamindar, of course," answered the young woman regretting to spoil her friend's foolish dreams of love, "there are rumors among the people that the occasion is imminent."

"He is getting married?" said Vanya sadly, "why can't the lucky girl be someone like me? I guess it can only happen in my dreams. Do you think he is in love with her, whoever she is?"

"I doubt it," answered Kyra, "the family's arranged the marriage, and no one knows who the lady is...I am sure it will become common knowledge when they announce it to the people."

The shadow of a smile brightened Vanya's face as she stood erect for a brief moment. She held the gold sovereign above her head and began walking back and forth gracefully, with a sensual stride.

"You see, Kyra," she finally said, "I am the future Zamandarin, and this is my crown. I believe that the Zamindar will forego the arranged marriage and choose me instead."

They both laughed happily, dispelling latent sadness and regain once again their careless, youthful ways.

At that point, the girls prepared to leave the lonely beach for the long walk back home after the day's exciting occurrences.

"I believe it's best not to aim too high. It can only cause disappointments and sorrow," said Kyra as she accelerated her stride on the sandy banks of the river.

"However, there is no need for sadness since we will rejoice and share the wedding celebration…"

She paused for a moment and touched her friend's arm with some excitement in her voice.

"You are aware, Vanya, that it is traditional to invite the people to the wedding celebration of our Zamindar?"

"Of course I know it," answered Vanya happily, "it will be a wonderful feast for all of us to enjoy, with lots of music, dancing, and plenty of delicacies to eat. I am certain they will serve many delectable sweets and my favorite wedding desserts, kheer, and rasgula."

Vanya's face brightened suddenly, thinking with anticipation of the new saree she would be able to buy for the occasion. She squeezed with delight the little golden treasure that she held in her hand, and a sense of joy suddenly overwhelmed her.

"Kyra," she said, "I will be the prettiest girl at the wedding celebration, as I make a grand entrance in my lovely new saree, with fragrant jasmine flowers in my hair. I am certain I will be admired by one and all..." She paused at this point as a smile of anticipation brightened her face.

"It will be such a wonderful, memorable day for us to enjoy. Let us hope the marriage announcement will come very soon."

"Yes, Vanya," Kyra said with a benevolent, condescending smile, "I am sure you will be the prettiest one of all."

THE ZAMINDAR'S REALM

Meanwhile, The Zamindar spurred his horse with increased speed and quickly distanced himself from the lonely stretch of beach.

He continued galloping toward his ancestral palace, which had housed the distinguished Choudhury dynasty for generations.

The magnificent structure presided in the historical, social, and culturally vibrant municipal town of Kendrapara.

After the exhilarating ride, he finally reached his palace and surrounding gardens, one of the most stately in the region and evocative of his illustrious family's history.

Ramakanta had a strong connection to the land, which was a real passion for the young man. He was following in the illustrious footsteps of his distinguished ancestor, the Zamindar Bhikari Choudhury, the sole creator of his prominent dynasty, which had endured several generations.

Because of his father's premature death, Ramakanta inherited the title of Zamindar and power over thousands of tenants who worked his extensive and fertile land. Unlike leaders who had preceded him and abused their position in the feudal system with crippling taxes, Ramakanta did it with a sense of justice and functionality. He was unusually kind and generous toward his subordinates while enjoying an idyllic and serene life in his privileged world.

Ramakanta, at arrival, was greeted respectfully by his guards, who promptly took charge of his steed at his return to the palace. He walked with a speedy stride toward the magnificent structure and gained immediate access.

The classical Indian style vestibule was impressive at first glance, with grand archways crowned by an elaborate vaulted ceiling whose gilded details glistened like jewels in the many lights. Artistically inlaid floortiles graced the ambiance, depicting intricate mythological scenes and colorful renditions of indigenous flowers, whose delicate beauty enhanced the exotic atmosphere.

An elegant, aristocratic lady stood in the middle of the vast hall, apparently waiting with some apprehension for the Zamindar. There was a look of concern in her eyes, which was immediately relieved as he made his grand entrance, albeit with a bit of haste.

"I am sorry for the delay, dear Maa, namaste." He said as he lowered his head and placed his hands together in greeting.

"Today, I took a longer ride than usual, and unfortunately, I lost track of time…Although I made some effort to get back as soon as possible."

"But why did you leave without your usual escort or any words on your whereabouts, my son?"

She asked with a sound of displeasure in her voice as she began to walk toward him.

"This was the reason it caused me concern. Besides, I was hoping to talk to you in regards to some issues that need immediate attention."

"Is that why you are waiting out here, dear Maa, and not in the comfort of your rooms?"

Interposed the Zamindar with an indulgent smile.

"Besides," he continued with a touch of impatience, "I am certain the matter is not of such importance that it cannot wait till tomorrow…since it has been a long day, and I am exhausted."

A staunch silence followed his words, which was his mother's way of expressing displeasure. He decided it would be best not to upset the lady further.

With his usual chivalry, Ramakanta extended his arm to escort his mother to her rooms. He was resigned to hear about the critical issues she was so eager to discuss.

§§§

CHAPTER TWO

THE IMPORTANCE OF TRADITION

The Zamindar was close to his mother, the honorable Laxmi Devi, a strong-willed, intelligent woman whose wisdom he valued and trusted, especially in matters concerning his people and the estate.

The lady was also a staunch advocate of traditional Indian values and compliance with their teachings. She raised her son with strict rules to follow regarding the guidance of Hinduism. Since in her belief, it was the only way to receive the

Gods' blessings and have a successful, perpetual life.

While growing up, Ramakanta proved to be an adept student, following with aptitude the religious dogma's requirements. He bowed to the will of his elders and embraced the structure of his society with diligence. However, despite his seemingly compliant nature, his rebellious side soon rose to the surface. His desire for more independence caused considerable friction in his structured world and deep displeasure to his unyielding and controlling mother.

Although the Zamindar loved and respected her, he also resented her patronizing ways. He was deeply conflicted between the teachings that had been instilled into him, ever since he was a child, and the overwhelming desire to be free and make his own decisions.

As he escorted his mother through the seemingly endless corridors of the vast palace, he suddenly was beset by a sense of anxiety, which conflicted with his usual calm and reflective nature.

He had only recently experienced those unsettling feelings, and the reason seemed mysterious to him. Perhaps the cause was a strange, recurring dream that had disturbed him for many nights.

It was always the haunting vision of a beautiful lady whose presence was so overpowering and mesmerizing that overwhelmed him.

She seemed to be calling someone, but the sound was far distant and challenging to hear. However, her image was strangely familiar and so sensual that he was drawn irresistibly toward her.

There was an overpowering desire to hold her in his arms and passionately kiss those soft, luscious lips that burned like fire in the recesses of his mind.

He gazed with longing at the curves of her bodacious body, which was shielded only by a translucent gown sprinkled with tiny crystals that sparkled like stars. But a mysterious force always held him back from the seductive image that intoxicated him with her magnetism.

During the unsettling dream, he struggled valiantly, aimlessly to reach the object of his desire, wanting desperately to become one with the beauty and joy she exuded. He finally managed almost to touch the seductive lady. Unfortunately, the image suddenly disappeared in a burst of light as an irresistible sound called out in the distance.

"Please come to me, Rami. I am waiting for you."

The enticement of the invitation and the lure of her voice was overpowering as he attempted to enter the light and reach the elusive vision that had intoxicated him. But the radiance became diffused and slowly vanished into the darkness.

Suddenly a splendid lotus blossom appeared, dispelling with a golden glow the surrounding gloom.

"The Zamindar whispered, "my Padma," at the lovely sight, "where are you, my Padma? I miss you so."

The dream ended abruptly at that point, in the same disturbing way as the preceding nights. The recurring vision had become an obsession and a real nightmare for the Zamindar, as a mysterious force was drawing him in unknown directions, and he didn't know the reason why.

Laxmi Devi had noticed the change in him and was deeply concerned since her son seemed unusually preoccupied as if he was living in a world of his own.

"Are you feeling well, Ramakanta? You are so silent and distracted recently?" She asked anxiously.

. "I am fine, Maa. There is no need to worry, I have a few things on my mind that distract me, and that is all."

Finally, in virtual silence, they reached their destination. On entering the matriarch's rooms, several girls immediately attended to Laxmi Devi's comfort and brought forth her evening tea.

"Would you also like a cup and some butter biscuits?" She asked while walking toward a silver tray filled with a delectable selection of her favorite sweets.

"Its Darjeeling tea flavored with Jasmine...Your favorite." The lady insisted.

"No, thank you, Maa," answered the Zamindar with slight displeasure in his voice.

"I don't mean to rush you, but it's getting late...What is the important issue that you wish to discuss with me with such urgency?"

Laxmi Devi dismissed the servant girls with a gesture of her hand and placed a spoonful of sugar in her tea. To her son's frustration, she took a long sip before answering.

"You are aware, Ramakanta, that preparations must be made for your forthcoming wedding? Since you are the Zamindar, we need your permission and consent. Therefore you must set the date *now*."

The Zamindar remained silent for a brief moment before answering, with displeasure and frustration written on his face.

"Is this the important issue that required immediate attention?" he asked as he walked toward Laxmi Devi and placed his hand on her shoulder with affection.

"I am tired right now, Maa, and do not wish to discuss this issue further...I promise to give you my answer in the morning."

"Why not give me an answer right now?" Insisted Laxmi Devi, "I just need a date to announce it to Aamani and our people."

"We will talk about it tomorrow," said the Zamindar, with an unwavering sound in his voice, "but for now, I bid you a good night."

He bowed respectfully to Laxmi Devi, whose displeasure was evident, and without further ado, he opened the door and disappeared in the darkened corridor with a fast stride.

Entering into marriage had been ordained in Ramakanta's life since the day he was born. A duty he had to face and fulfill according to society's rules and the Hindu religion.

While growing up, he seldom thought about it or gave any real importance to it. That is until the marriage obligation became disturbingly imminent, and his rebellious feelings suddenly surfaced. A sensation of entrapment overwhelmed him, and he wished to be free of the commitment at all costs.

According to Hinduism, marriage concerned the family structure and the need for procreation. The couple's emotional feelings were discouraged for a successful union since it conflicted with the religious dogma. It encouraged rebellion to the basic structure of arranged marriage by allowing the interference of emotions and independent thinking.

The Zamindar began to question the teachings' infallibility as marriage loomed on the horizon, creating confusion in his mind and considerable stress.

During that night, he was haunted once again by the disturbingly sensual dream. The beautiful lady was beguiling as she softly called *Rami* to join her, with a melodic sound in her voice.

Rami appeared to be the name of choice, and she used it often instead of Ramakanta. However, somehow it seemed familiar to him as if he had been called by that name before. But the location seemed to be far removed from the present, shrouded in mystery and, lost somewhere in time.

The Zamindar woke up abruptly from the disturbing dream with his heart in turmoil. His arms were still outstretched toward the image of his desire and overwhelmed by a strange feeling of loss.

Although she might have been only a figment of his imagination, Padma, as he called her in the dreams, was suddenly an undisputed reality to Ramakanta and the center of his world.

"Who was she?" He repeatedly asked, with utter frustration, since he was sure to have met her before.

"But where and when?"

That lingering question continued to disrupt his thoughts, his peace of mind and, even his sleep.

He recalled the mysterious lady in detail, and by her light complexion and manner of clothing, he was sure she must have been a western woman.

Ramakanta was familiar with Europe since he had traveled through many countries on the continent, especially England, during his study at Oxford University. But he had no recollection of ever meeting the mysterious lady since he was sure that he would have remembered it.

There were far too many questions without answers, although there was only one certainty concerning the unsettling mystery. The dreams began when the wedding date was about to be announced to the people.

"Was the lovely lady trying to stop his arranged marriage from taking place?"

Frustration was the only answer to the disturbing mystery, while her identity had become of paramount importance.

It was the dawn of a new day, and Ramakanta knew that his mother would be waiting for him after her breakfast, eager to engage in the marriage issue, which lingered like an ominous shadow in the recesses of his mind.

Obliging to her request, the punctual Zamindar gained access to her grand rooms. He was surprised to see that she was not alone since an elegantly dressed young woman was standing by her side.

At first glance, the girl appeared intimidated by his presence and withdrew slightly at his sight. However, she immediately regained her self-control and bowed with deference.

After the initial surprise, Ramakanta smiled as he greeted his mother and the unexpected guest.

"Good morning, dear Maa, *namaste*. I hope you had a peaceful and restful night. It's a surprise to find you in the company of Lady Aamani, especially at such an early hour…"

"Aamani is here in response to my invitation for an early tea and breakfast," interrupted Laxmi Devi with apprehension in her voice, "I assumed that her presence would be a pleasant surprise for you…especially under the present circumstances."

The Zamindar was angered by his mother's meddling in connection to the arranged marriage, although he managed to control his temper before answering politely.

"The lady honors us with her presence. She is, as always, a welcomed guest at the palace. However, dear Maa, I thought we were supposed to have an important conversation."

He then added with a touch of sarcasm as he prepared to leave.

"Since you are busy with Lady Aamani, perhaps we will discuss the issue some other time."

"No Ramakanta, please stay," answered Laxmi Devi with a deliberate sound, distressed that her son was preparing to make a fast exit.

"We finished our breakfast and, Aamani is ready to leave since her father is waiting in the vestibule to take her home."

The Zamindar was frustrated and felt entrapped by the unexpected presence of the young woman. He assumed that his mother manipulated Aamani, perhaps against her wishes, and had no desire to be rude to her.

Besides, he knew that it was impossible to escape the subject of marriage. Especially as a Zamindar since he needed to honor the existing contract according to the family's traditions.

The Zamindar's Bride

When he was a child, his paternal grandfather used jathakam, the chart/horoscope based on the stars' placement for a proper marital match. The chosen lady was Aamani Nayak, the only daughter from one of the most distinguished families in the area, whose father was the Zamindar's estate overseer.

The young woman was well educated, refined, and fluent in several Indian dialects and foreign languages. She trained in the arts of singing and dancing, which was a necessary requisite for the future spouse of the Zamindar.

Aamani's instructions were to be pleasing and receptive to her husband's every need and entertain him with the graceful dance steps of the Indian folklore, which is a gem of that ancient art. The rendition is almost a prayer in motion, depicting the gods and their interaction with the human world.

Aamani had worked tirelessly for the honor of becoming the future Zamandarin, and she felt entitled to it. With diligence, she followed the rules and regulations required to become the perfect companion to Ramakanta and bring beauty and joy into his life.

The young woman was petite in size, with a soft bronzed complexion, deep dark eyes framed by arching brows which betrayed a touch of melancholy. Long black hair framed her attractive oval face, and her well-shaped lips conveyed a sensual nature.

Although she appeared timid and shy, Aamani concealed a very determined and supremely ambitious nature.

She had taken great care in dressing for the impromptu breakfast in hopes of making a good impression on the Zamindar. Laxmi Devi had advised her that he favored bright colors on the ladies. Therefore, she chose a vivid pink and orange silk saree, which flattered her complexion.

Many golden bangle bracelets decorated her forearms, and strands of pearls graced her neck, which gave a touch of affluence to her attire.

She was disappointed by Ramakanta's reaction when he first saw her. Although he was always polite and gracious, she could sense he was displeased and even uncomfortable with her presence. However, a glimmer of hope flashed in her eyes when Ramakanta announced that he would escort her to the vestibule to join her father.

In reality, it was only a gesture of politeness toward a family friend. The Zamindar was oblivious of her all-consuming passion, hidden so well behind a veneer of propriety. In his eyes, she was a little sister since they had known each other as children. There was no physical attraction for the girl, and he had difficulty envisioning her as his wife.

But even if Aamani was not considered an object of desire by the Zamindar, passion was not a requirement for an arranged marriage.

Nonetheless, in Laxmi Devi's eyes, she was the perfect embodiment of a Zamandarin and daughter-in-law, mainly because she appeared easy to manipulate and control.

After escorting Aamani and greeting her father, who was the overseer of his land, Ramakanta returned speedily to his mother's rooms, ready to face the challenging conversation.

He was conflicted by the desire to please his mother and the demands of his culture. Although unwilling to enter a preordained and loveless marriage, according to traditions.

When the Zamindar reached his mother's rooms, she was waiting for him by the entrance doors, with anxiety written on her face since she feared his unpredictability and independence.

"Are you feeling well, Maa?" he asked with concern, "perhaps it's unnecessary to have this conversation now. We can discuss it later on when you feel better…"

"No, Ramakanta," she interrupted with a sharp sound in her voice as she stood tall and defiant.

"I am well enough, and I think we should settle this situation right now."

"As you wish, Maa," answered the Zamindar, not wanting to upset her further. He then extended his arm with solicitude and escorted Laxmi Devi to a nearby divan.

The lady was distressed and took a long breath to steady the violent beating of her heart. She drank a sip of tea to regain some control over her emotions and then curtly addressed Ramakanta, making sure that he was aware of her displeasure.

"There is no need for long discussions, my son," she finally said, "you only need to set a date for your marriage, and the conversation will be over."

The Zamindar remained silent for a few seconds before answering. He was displeased with the undue pressure placed upon him by his mother while understanding that the issue was of paramount importance to her.

"I am sorry, Maa," he finally said with a sad but determined sound in his voice.

"I know that I will disappoint you, but after much thought, I decided not to marry...at this time."

Only silence was the immediate response to the shocking announcement. The dowager closed her eyes and clenched her fists in quiet desperation before answering her son.

"You decided not to marry?" she asked, overwhelmed by the news, as a feeling of dread and helplessness beset her. She knew that the Zamindar was the leader of his people, and in the autocratic regime in place, no one could oppose or challenge his will in any way.

However, accepting his decision in silence was impossible for Laxmi Devi. She continued her plea unabated while controlling the anger that was rising within her.

"You have always been aware that marriage was an inevitable step in your life, especially as the scion of the powerful Choudhury dynasty…You must marry according to expectations."

"I understand your displeasure, Maa, but this is a subject I don't wish to discuss at this time," answered the Zamindar with a stubborn and uncompromising sound.

"I wish to be free of the commitment, and I hope you will honor my decision without further discussions…I understand that my stance is unusual under the circumstances. However, it's not a matter for debate, even with your difficulty to reconcile with it."

"Do you forget that arranged marriage is the center of the family structure in India?" Insisted Laxmi Devi with frustration in her voice, trying to change Ramakanta's rebellious behavior.

"I understand your disappointment Maa," answered the Zamindar with kindness but also determination in his voice.

"I have respect for my culture, and the decision was difficult to make. However, it will stand, even if I regret causing you sorrow."

Laxmi Devi was truly desolate while facing Ramakanta's determination and resolve. However, the lady's tenacity was second to none as she continued her plea unabated.

"It is important for the preservation of our dynasty that you should marry my son," she said with increased passion in her voice.

"You are valuable to our people and also posterity. You must fulfill your duty without delays. Please recant your word, and set a date for the marriage as soon as possible."

She stood up and walked toward him with a nervous stride while continuing.

"I know that Aamani will be a proper wife and a perfect Zamandarin…The stars have chosen her to fulfill all requirements necessary for so important a role."

The Zamindar remained silent for a moment before answering with a condescending sound in his voice.

"Yes, mother, all the requirements from the stars…"

"What is the problem, my son?" interrupted Laxmi Devi, thoroughly frustrated.

"You have known for years that Aamani was to be your bride? She is a bright, lovely girl who I am certain will bring much happiness into your life."

Then her voice softened in an almost pleading sound as she continued.

"You have been given much by the Gods, my son, and are a favorite of the blessed Vishnu. Your father and I named you Ramakanta in his honor, which is one of his thousand names…"

"Maa, I regret causing you pain," interposed the Zamindar with some impatience," but for the moment, I do not wish to discuss it further."

"I believe we must address the issue, *now*," continued Laxmi Devi, as she moved closer and held on to his hands.

"You are the Zamindar. No one dares to contradict you. I am the only one who can because I am your mother, and that special title gives me the right."

Ramakanta remained silent but attempted to move away, disturbed by her relentless behavior.

"Perhaps it is because you are not in love with Aamani?" asked Laxmi Devi with persistence while attempting to break the uncomfortable silence.

"I don't know, mother, possibly that is the reason," answered the Zamindar, "I respect and care for Aamani, but I cannot pretend to be in love with her."

"Love!" Exclaimed Laxmi Devi with a sharp and deliberate sound.

"This emotion is unnecessary when you enter into marriage since you may develop a form of it in time...Respect for one another and deference for your religion and culture are by far more important..."

She paused in an attempt to take control of her deeply challenged feelings at that particular moment.

"You are the Zamindar, a leader of our people. Your life should be dedicated to governing dispassionately, consistently, without the distraction of unnecessary emotions."

Laxmi Devi moved away suddenly, appearing uncomfortable with what she was about to say.

"I was *not* in love with your father when I first married, and I am *certain* that he was not in love with me...Despite it, we learned to care and respect each other, which I believe it's far more important in a successful union than being in love."

Ramakanta noticed a slight tremor in her lips as she uttered those words. She seemed distressed, as hidden emotions were, rising while revealing private thoughts.

"I was proud to be his Zamindarin, and the respect I garnered from your father and our people was far more important than raw passion or being in love…"

Laxmi Devi's paused briefly before her voice became sharper while continuing the conversation.
"I am an Indian woman, and I know my place in life according to the wisdom and guidance of Hinduism…It was my honor to bring contentment in your father's life when chosen to be his bride. Also experiencing the great joy and privilege of giving him the son he wished for."

The matriarch became suddenly silent as a shadow of a smile brightened her face while recalling that particular time in her life.

"I never challenged him since it was not my place to do so. I bowed respectfully to his wishes and gave my opinion only if he asked for it, and always with respect and deference."

She lifted her head proudly as a determined look flashed upon her face while she continued her passionate recollection.

"You see, Ramakanta. My life has been an unqualified success because of it. I followed the necessary rules and guidance of Hinduism, which is the true keys to a happy and honorable life."
Ramakanta noticed that his mother spoke a little too loudly in an attempt to paint a rosy picture of her married life. At the same time, it appeared that their relationship had been compromised, in deference to an authoritarian man.

However, he chose not to interrupt her since he never heard his mother talk freely about the subject of love or the marriage she shared with his father.

"You are the Zamindar, my son," she continued as she gently touched his arm.

"All that you aspire will be available if it's missing in your bride…There will *never* be consequences for your actions, and no one will dare impede the quest of your earthly desires…"

Laxmi Devi became suddenly silent as a gamut of emotions overwhelmed her. She then stood erect, proud, before continuing.

"You see, Ramakanta. There were no consequences for your father, the *many, many* times he fulfilled his earthly desires, because of inadequacies on my part..."

Laxmi Devi's voice dropped to a whisper as she lowered her gaze to the ground. In an attempt to hide the turmoil that suddenly overwhelmed her, as she continued.

"This should make it clear that there is no need to postpone the wedding...Since Aamani will be the perfect wife to you, as I was the perfect wife to your father...She will be obedient, loyal, and forever grateful to have been chosen as your Zamindarin."

Ramakanta was deeply disturbed by his mother's words because of his fairness toward all people. Also, to hear the servile attitude Laxmi Devi embraced for herself and all Hindu women, according to society's rules.

"I can get as much loyalty from my hounds," he thought with an aversion to his mother's idea of a proper bride.

However, the Zamindar wisely kept those thoughts to himself, not wanting to impose more grief on his mother. Since he realized that despite her denials, there had been hidden pain in her submission to a loveless marriage. However, she had made the willing sacrifice to achieve the coveted title of Zamindarin.

The honorable, Laxmi Devi, always appeared in control and dignified, with a veneer of aristocracy emanating from her persona. Those traits had created an emotional barrier with her son. But for the first time, she appeared vulnerable to Ramakanta, and more human in her imperfection, and perhaps even defenseless. The Zamindar was touched by it and decided not to press the issue further since she appeared frail, and he was concerned about his mother's health.

"This conversation is too stressful, especially for you, dear Maa…I have now decided to fulfill my duties as expected and set a wedding date according to the wishes of my family and also my people."

Laxmi Devi expelled a sigh of relief as Ramakanta continued with a softer but determined sound.

"I will announce my decision after my trip to Italy scheduled for next month. The excursion will also include a visit to my dear friend and Oxford roommate, Prince Louis Amedeus, Duke of the Abruzzi. "

"Of course, I recall your travel plans," answered Laxmi Devi," but they were supposed to take place after the wedding as a honeymoon celebration for you and Aamani."

"I know, Maa, but the schedule has changed in deference to my wishes. The nuptials will take place *after* my return from Italy."

Laxmi Devi said with trepidation, "I hope that you will not change your mind again, my son…during the trip."

"No, Maa, I promise and give you my solemn word as a Zamindar that at my return from Europe, I will enter into marriage, according to expectations."

"I am so happy, Ramakanta," said Laxmi Devi, with great relief.

"Finally, I will have the joy to see you married and Aamani to become the new Zamindarin…"

"Dear Maa," interrupted Ramakanta with a stern and deliberate sound, "I gave you my word that I will marry…and that is all I am willing to say."

Without waiting for a response from his frustrated mother, the Zamindar bowed respectfully and quickly exited the room.

§§§

CHAPTER THREE

JOURNEY TO DESTINY

The journey to Europe, although arduous, was full of hope and excitement for the adventurous Zamindar.

Fortunately, the Suez Canal was accessible in 1869, and it offered a more direct route between the North Atlantic and the northern Indian Ocean via the Mediterranean and Red Seas.

Despite the many difficulties and limited transportation available for long journeys across the ocean, it proved exciting for the Zamindar to explore distant lands with willingness and temerity.

The best sailing ships available to travel from India belonged to the well-established *East India Company*, which dealt mostly with trade and the transportation of the many European immigrants who traveled back and forth in search of work, mainly in the agricultural field. These hard-working people looked for opportunities to improve their living conditions in faraway lands across the globe.

As the Zamindar secured passage on the ship on his way to Europe, superior and more suitable accommodations were made available to the distinguished passenger within the sturdy but modest vessel. He could share his meals at the captain's table, or if he wished in the privacy of his cabin.

Despite the Royal treatment, aboard the commercial ship, Ramakanta often intermingled and enjoyed the company of travelers and sailors, with approachability and respect.

The crossing proved to be challenging at times. Inclement weather and powerful storms disrupted the daily routine of the passengers. The turbulence created more significant work for the crew at hand, as they were engaged around the clock to secure the ship and passenger's safety.

Ramakanta, with impunity, preferred to be out of his cabin during the disruption created by the angry seas. He seemed impervious to the massive waves, which slapped the vessel like a miniature toy, making it difficult for people to retain balance aboard the ship. Many passengers suffered from seasickness and received warnings by the crew to remain in their cabins for safety reasons.

Nature's rage proved to be a stunning and frightening sight. But somehow, the chaos attracted and fascinated Ramakanta's adventurous spirit. During the height of the storms, he walked on the ship's decks fearlessly, as the crew members, surprised and impressed by his daring, whispered to each other approvingly.

"His Highness, the Zamindar, would have made an excellent sailor."

Finally, after many endless, agonizing days, the challenging crossing was coming to an end. Like a beautiful mirage, the Italian coastline was visible for the first time, shrouded by the reddish mist of an impending sunset. There was great excitement at the motherland's sight since most passengers were

Italian expatriates returning home. In droves, they crowded the decks, heart filled with excitement and joy for the safe ending of their arduous journey.

The Zamindar looked on with wonder and interest as some of the voyagers began chanting the Italian national anthem. In contrast, others shouted, "Viva l'Italia." the crew gave little tricolor flags to the passengers, who held on to them with love and respect.

Ramakanta was impressed and joined the Italian expatriates waving the red, white, and green proudly in the wind. It was a joyous celebration of life, and it was infectious.

Suddenly, an elderly gentleman approached the Zamindar and removed his cap in a sign of respect toward the aristocratic passenger. He then pointed to the land, taking shape and becoming progressively more visible each passing moment.

"Your Highness, I am finally home after so many years…Viva l'Italia!" He exclaimed with a voice filled with great emotions as his eyes filled with tears of joy.

Ramakanta was moved by the special moment as he pondered on how far away he was now from his own home. A benevolent smile appeared on his face while gently touching the older man's shoulder with respect and friendliness.

The Zamindar was dignified, proud of his heritage, and approachable as a true man of the people. He knew that the Choudhury dynasty had a surprising and humble beginning since his grandfather, the honorable Zamindar, Nishamani Choudhury, a man he loved and respected, related to him the history of his family in great details.

It was such a compelling story that captured and stimulated his imagination as a child, and he often asked his grandfather to repeat it to him.

The story began with the young Bhikari Choudhury, the first Zamindar and creator of the family's dynasty.

It was pleasant for Ramakanta to recollect his distinguish ancestor and remember his beloved grandfather, who had since passed away.

The family custom was to use word of mouth, related to the dynasty's history from generation to generation.

It all began in the fertile grounds of picturesque Kendrapara, in which Ramakanta's ancestor, Mr. Bhikari Choudhury, and members of this family lived.

The Zamindar's Bride

Their modest dwelling nestled in a small hamlet called Niladripur was near to the famous spiritual temple of Lord Balram, the Hindu God and elder brother of Krishna, an avatar of the God Vishnu.

Sparse evidence is available about the family's history before Bhikari Chaudhury, the first generation Zamindar, appeared on the scene.

There are suggestions that he was the progeny of humble people, whose primary source of income came from agriculture and dairy farming. However, destiny altered the course of history, and the humble farmer's life changed in a blink of an eye.

The tale began during the early years of the British occupation of India. At that time, the British Colonial Administrator sent an English representative to undertake a survey of the land by the Mahanadi River delta, which was the lifeline of ancient Kalinga.

It comprised thousands of acres of fertile land, linked by the Mahanadi River's numerous distributaries, flowing through the delta and merging into the Indian Ocean.

The Colonial Administrator entrusted the English surveyor with measuring and creating maps of the land extensions. During that fateful time, he appointed a young Mr. Bhikari as his assistant for the surveyor's works.

According to legend, the British Surveyor first noticed him on the riverbank, where the strapping youth was diligently tending his cows and buffaloes, a traditional chore with dairy farmers.

The surveyor must have been impressed by his athletic, healthy appearance and knowledge of the surroundings, the reason why he chose the young farmer to be his assistant.

The Zamindar had a great curiosity about his distinguished ancestor and believed that they resembled each other. According to descriptions, he was a tall and well-built young man with an adventurous spirit.

At that time, Mr. Bhikari worked hard to provide for his family, although he was also ambitious and inventive, common traits among people with leadership qualities.

Despite his humble station in life, Mr. Bhikari possessed a bright and inquisitive mind, with an eagerness to learn and expand his horizon.

The Zamindar's Bride

In the early 18th century, the British occupation was in its infancy, and few in India's general population were familiar with the English language. In all probability, the young man had some basic knowledge of the language since he managed to relate his vast understanding of the delta's topography to the surveyor.

The working relationship between the surveyor and the Indian youth progressed remarkably well despite the many difficulties encountered since Mr. Bhikari facilitated the project by providing the necessary logistic and strenuous physical help.

However, the most challenging part of the survey was about to take place during the last leg of the project, and the surveyor faced his greatest challenge.

The British Government had requested a detailed study of the land located on the river's opposite bank. Unfortunately, the only available connection to cross over the Mahanadi River dangerous waterways was an old bridge, which was poorly maintained and notoriously unstable.

Unfortunately, the inevitable happened because of the monsoon season's rising waters, the old structure finally collapsed. When the Surveyor attempted to reach the opposite side of the river, he realized that the bridge had disappeared. The failing system had been mercilessly swallowed by the mighty river inner currents, leaving no trace behind. The British gentleman was now faced with a significant difficulty since there was no other available way to reach the other side, making it impossible to continue and finish the necessary survey works.

The situation was disturbing to the dutiful English surveyor, who took much pride in completing his job as requested by India's Colonial Administration. Failure was not an option to him, as he stubbornly ventured up and down the river bank looking for any possibility of crossing over the treacherous waterways.

The area was known as the *graveyard* by those who dared to confront the river's might. The ever-present danger frightened the Surveyor, who felt helpless and dared not challenge the power of Mother Nature. But he was bitterly disappointed and perceived himself a failure since he had been unable to uphold his duties and bring them to a happy conclusion.

Mr. Bhikari, who had followed him for days in respectful silence, performed all the duties requested of him, finally decided to address the issue to the demoralized Surveyor.

"Sahib, please do not be concerned. Your survey work will not suffer as long as I am your assistant."

The English man was surprised by his words and asked.

"How can you possibly be of help? The bridge is gone, and I see no other way to cross over to the opposite bank without the danger of drowning."

"Because the river is my home, Sahib," answered Mr. Bhikari with confidence, "no one around here is more familiar with the treacherous waters than I am....The mighty Mahanadi is my friend, and I do not fear it."

The young Indian smiled as he stood erect, confident, displaying with pride his muscular body. He then said with his limited English, aided by the motions of his hands.

"I know I can bring you safely across the waterway upon my shoulders, I am familiar with a special place when the river first bends to the East, and it's easier to cross...I will take you there, but you must trust me without question. I promise that you will not drown or even get wet, and no damage will occur to you or you're surveying apparatus."

The British man was stunned by his young assistant's words but intrigued by the possibility since he was determined to complete the job at any cost. Without further questions, he followed Mr. Bhikari to the place he had suggested as a possible way to reach the other side of the river.

At first glance, the area looked just like any other place in the treacherous waterway. Although, at closer inspection, the surveyor noticed that the river's width at that point was slightly narrower and shallower since multiple rocks reached the surface of the water. However, it still looked terrifying and considerably dangerous.

The surveyor was conflicted as the fear of death loomed heavily upon him. But as he gazed into the young man's eyes, he was impressed by the look of confidence and courage they exuded. There was something exceptional about the young farmer that inspired a sense of confidence and trust.

Since there was no other choice for the surveyor, if he wanted to complete the job as requested, he had to put aside his fears and misgivings while allowing his pride and honor to precede.

He bowed his head, signaling consent without further delays, and quickly gathered his surveying apparatus and placed them in a backpack. Still beset by fears but resigned to his fate, he finally appeared prepared for the hazardous journey.

Mr. Bhikari, with confidence and unusual strength, lifted his body with relative ease off the ground and placed him squarely upon his shoulders. Then without hesitation, the young and adventurous Indian commenced the treacherous crossing in the mighty river with skill and unbelievable courage.

The English man questioned his foolishness since he was not even able to swim. He closed his eyes and devoutly crossed himself as a silent prayer rose to his trembling lips.

The journey across was slow and filled with danger. With acrobatic skill and a remarkable balance, the young man managed to walk across the many stones protruding from the waters, which created a rudimental bridge to the opposite bank. At times the youth sank slightly, and the water reached up to his waist, while the ever-present undercurrents created danger in every step. But undaunted, he marched forward boldly, unafraid, until with exceptional skills and effort, he reached the desired destination, the opposite bank of the Mahanadi River.

The surveyor was thrilled and astounded to be still alive. He shook the young man's hand with appreciation and respect. He was now grateful but more relaxed and trusting during the many additional crossings necessary to complete the work.

Finally, the tough job was coming to a close, and the surveyor was getting ready to wind up the last details before leaving Kendrapara. He was proud to have accomplished his difficult task and was very grateful to Mr. Bhikari for his courage and the extraordinary way he had helped him. He expressed his desire to reward him and asked the young man what he thought would be proper compensation for his effort.

Mr. Bhikari was surprised since, as an honorable, modest person, he assumed that it was his duty to help the surveyor in any way possible. The salary he received was, in his estimation, a proper compensation.

On the other hand, he appreciated the offer of a reward but wished to ask his widowed mother's opinion for a reasonable request.

The next day Mr. Bhikari related to the Surveyor that his mother wished the reward to be some acres of fertile land since the family was of modest means without much land to cultivate.

The Surveyor was happy to oblige and asked Mr. Bhikari what measure of land he wanted as a deserved reward.

At this point, the language barrier came into play, and the young man had difficulty explaining what he wished for, which was a modest amount of ten to twenty acres of land as a reward. He relied on the use of gestures to compensate for his limited knowledge of the English language.

Mr. Bhikari pointed his finger toward the horizon and then created a circle to illustrate the amount of land he wished to receive as a reward.

To this day, it remains a matter of conjecture if the Surveyor misunderstood the request since the young man was pointing his finger toward the horizon and demarcating land as far as the eyes could see.

The Englishman assumed that the request was on a much larger scale, but since he was grateful and delighted with the help rendered, he placed no objection to it. Perhaps he thought that it was a well-deserved reward for a remarkable young man.

With the strength of his recommendation to the British Government, he was legally able to record a very vast stretch of land in a place called Garadpur running into thousands of acres of some of the best, fertile land, in the name of Mr. Bhikari.

Like magic, overnight, the young Indian farmer became Mr. Bhikari Chaudhury, the Landlord, a noble title conferred by The British Rulers, and the first Zamindar of the Chaudhury Dynasty.

In a blink of a fateful moment, perhaps caused by a simple misunderstanding on the part of the English Surveyor, Mr. Bhikari and his family's life was forever changed for generations to come.

Ramakanta smiled while recalling the incredible story that always gave him a sense of pride. He felt a great connection with his noble ancestor. Perhaps he was fortunate to have inherited his adventurous spirit and the great love for nature and life. He also realized that Mr. Bhikari was a truly noble person long before receiving the grand title of Zamindar.

Ramakanta was momentarily distracted by the precious memory. Still, he was now engaged in the present and excited to enter the Tyrrhenian Sea on the journey's last leg. The vessel skirted the coastline of Italy toward the final destination, the port of Naples.

The lovely city perched on green sloping hills was a welcomed sight to the Zamindar. He gazed with wonder at Naples' splendid bay and the imposing Mount Vesuvius rising to the sky so majestic and peaceful. It was easy to forget that it was a fatal volcano, which disseminated death and destruction a couple of millenniums before. However, it was so serene and welcoming now, indeed, a vision to remember for the Zamindar.

He felt suddenly happy and at peace in the impressive surroundings. The locale possessed a definite allure to Ramakanta, there was a feeling of belonging as if he was home again, and he had difficulty understanding why.

The disturbing dreams that had haunted him for so long had disappeared during the ocean voyage, and a sense of joy and expectation suddenly overwhelmed him. Ramakanta did not question his feelings or the reasons why. It was just wonderful to feel so alive, full of anticipation, and entirely delighted to be there.

§§§

CHAPTER FOUR

A NEW WORLD

Early the next morning, having been given priority over the other passengers because of his VIP status, Ramakanta, followed by a small entourage of personal guards, was escorted to the ocean liner's exit.

There was a sense of excitement and trepidation as the Zamindar stepped down from the gangway that connected the ship to the pier, and he was finally safely on Italian soil.

At first glance, it was a crowded and tumultuous scene in the busy port, as hundreds of people waited impatiently for relatives and friends to disembark the ship. Ramakanta looked around for a familiar face and was relieved to see his friend, Prince Louis Amedeus, Duke of the Abruzzi, waving at him from a distance, with a bright smile on his face.

The Prince belonged to one of the most distinguished and wealthiest Italian families. A member of the *House of Savoy,* well known in Europe since the 12th century. His father was Prince Amedeo of Savoy, Duke of Aosta, and his grandfather *King Vittorio Emanuele II* of Italy.

The aristocratic friend quickly approached the Zamindar with a speedy stride while several of his attendees began to take care of his many pieces of luggage.

It was a special moment for the two friends to face each other after a relatively long separation. They had become friends while roommates at Oxford University in England and happy for the opportunity of spending time together again.

"Welcome to Italy, dear Ramakanta," said the Prince with excitement in his voice, "may God be praised for your safe arrival from your long and difficult journey."

"Thank you, Louis," answered the Zamindar, moved by the warmth of the reception, "I am so happy to see you again after such a long hiatus."

"It was a special time we shared at Oxford, my friend," said the Prince as he escorted the Zamindar to his waiting carriage.

"I enjoyed the freedom from the responsibilities connected with our titles, and above all, the tyranny of etiquette …"

He stopped and laughed while uttering those words.

"Happy times indeed, dear Louis," answered Ramakanta attempting to smile while saying.

"Unfortunately, the oppressive sense of duty is forever present in our lives…I suppose that we were born with great privileges for which we should be grateful. We have wealth, power, everything but freedom."

The two friends looked at each other, pondering the complex reality they had to face every day.

The Prince was the first to break the uncomfortable silence with an upbeat sound.

"No time for regrets, we are *free now*, at least for the duration of your stay in beautiful, sunny

Italy…I have taken a short vacation, and I intend to enjoy every minute of it."

The friends laughed as they entered the carriage on the way to the Prince's palace located on Naples' outskirts.

"You will enjoy a proper rest after the long ocean voyage," said the Prince, "besides, Naples is a beautiful city, and we will engage in some sightseeing together.

The Prince paused and pointed to the view of the Neapolitan countryside, glistening in the bright sunshine.

"This visit, dear Ramakanta, will allow you the opportunity to visit our varied landscapes and enjoy our diverse architectural structures throughout the regions in the Italian peninsula. I am certain they will be of interest to you…"

"I am so happy to be here," interrupted the Zamindar as he looked on with awe at the splendid view that conveyed a sense of peace and joy.

"It's hard to explain, but I feel so comfortable here…and for some strange reason, it seems so familiar, almost as if I have been here before."

For a moment, the Zamindar seemed to be lost in a world of his own while he looked wistfully out of the carriage's window, enjoying the splendid and welcoming sight. He then smiled and said to the Prince.

"Dear Louis, I am so grateful for your gracious hospitality. I hope one day, soon, you will honor me with a visit to my estate in India."

"It will be a pleasure, my friend," answered the Prince, "I always wished to visit India, with its remarkable history. I am certain that it will be amazing to explore the majestic temples and archeological wonders of your beautiful country."

"Hopefully, it will be soon. I look forward to sharing my beloved country with you, my friend," answered the Zamindar.

The Prince smiled in consent then said with a slight uneasiness in his voice.

"I was wondering if congratulations are in order…since in your last letter you mentioned your plans to be married. I believed your European trip was to be a honeymoon celebration. That is if I remember correctly."

"No…I am not married, at least not yet," said Ramakanta, a bit apprehensive about answering the challenging question.

"Sorry, I guess I was mistaken. I didn't mean to pry in your personal life," answered the Prince, a little uncomfortable with the Zamindar's vague response."

"Forgive me, my friend," said Ramakanta. "It was not my intention to sound evasive. Yes, I was supposed to marry, but at the last minute, I canceled the ceremony since I couldn't go through with it. However, at this point, it's only postponed until my return from the European tour."

"I see," answered the Prince, slightly confused, "are you certain there will be no second thoughts the next time?"

"No, Louis, I gave my word to my mother. The word of a Zamindar, therefore, it's a solid promise."

"I suppose that is a guarantee. There is no backing away from a promise made to your mother," answered the Prince with a smile as he patted his friend's shoulder.

"Was your marriage prearranged, according to the rules in place for a Zamindar?"

"Yes, my marriage was prearranged by my family when we were both children. However, arranged marriages are a way of life for most Indian people, not only a requisite for Zamindars."

"It's not so different in Italy or Europe since prearranged marriages are common but mostly for the aristocrats," said the Prince with some displeasure in his voice.

"You see, my friend, as we speak, my parents are deciding who will be the proper Princess for me to marry." He then added with a touch of sarcasm.

"Fortunately, the choice has been narrowed down to only two—the Princess Dagmar of Denmark and the Princess of Hess from Germany. I have no preferences since I saw their pictures. They both are attractive enough, I suppose."

The Prince smiled as Ramakanta listened with interest since the situation was so similar to his own.

"I have heard on many occasions that love is not important in an aristocratic marriage. A proper union that will benefit the family line is all that matters."

He paused with little enthusiasm in his voice before continuing."

"I suppose in our privileged world. It will be easy to find passion with someone of our choosing, outside the boundaries of marriage."

"I guess our cultures are not so different after all," interposed the Zamindar, "since I have had similar conversations with my own family. But lately, I have been questioning the validity of such beliefs."

"You think it's so important to be in love when you marry?" Asked the Prince, intrigued by Ramakanta's words."

"I guess at this point I do," answered the Zamindar, surprised by his conviction, since for years he had been indoctrinated otherwise by his culture.

"I think it's impossible to have great feelings of love for a woman chosen by someone else to be your wife…"

The Zamindar paused and smiled bitterly before continuing.

"Of course, there is the option of having more desirable females on the side, who are readily available, especially for members of the aristocracy. Unfortunately, it reduces the value of marriage to just procreating children for dynastic purposes ..."   Ramakanta paused briefly before continuing with more determination in his voice.

"Why marry then, to please the family and society? Better to remain single and do whatever you please, with complete freedom of action."

"Is that what you are planning to do, my friend, remain single?" Asked the Prince, with curiosity, "despite the expectation of your family and your people?"

There was only silence as the Prince continued with a bit of sadness in his voice.

"Unfortunately, in our position in life, it's necessary to take a wife, regardless of our propensity to be free...I guess neither one of us will remain single for long, under the circumstances."

Ramakanta appeared a bit disturbed by the stark reality. He decided it would be best to continue the conversation realistically rather than with wishful thinking.

"I was making a conversation about something that I believe now, but unfortunately to no purpose. I guess that regardless of my personal feelings, I will abide by the rules ordained by my society as expected."

At this point, the Prince attempted to dismiss all negative thoughts. His friend was visiting with the expectation of a carefree vacation, and it was best to enjoy the day.

"Look at the sky Ramakanta, it's a bright and sunny morning, a perfect day for your first exploration of beautiful, romantic Italy. Let us rejoice!"

They now laughed happily and in unison, removing unpleasant thoughts from their minds for fear of disrupting the reunion of loyal friends in the historical splendor of Italy.

The sojourn in Naples was more exciting than expected since Ramakanta had the opportunity to visit some of the world's most beautiful sights, conveniently located on the city's outskirts.

He marveled at the splendid Amalfi coast, the island of Capri with the famous Blue Grotto, and the ruins of the doomed city of Pompeii, which used to be the summer retreat of the Roman Emperors.

Although interesting, It was sad to visit this symbol of luxury and privilege, so tragically destroyed thousands of years before, from the devastating rage of the mighty Vesuvius.

The Zamindar was overwhelmed by the fantastic sights and felt an innate attraction to the beauty of Italy. The surroundings gave him a sense of joy, but also of peace and tranquility. There was an aura of familiarity to the place that was conducive to pleasant expectations.

Prince Louis Amedeus was a very experienced guide and gracious host to the Zamindar, a knowledgeable man and quite astute in governing. With his political skills, he had been able to befriend many European rulers and secured several lucrative trades that enhanced his wealth.

The Zamindar was eager to engage in similar profitable trades with the European continent to benefit his people and enhance the Chaudhury dynasty's wealth and power. He was very grateful to his friend, who was willing to introduce him to some of the most influential European leaders who might be helpful in that regard.

A SPECIAL ENCOUNTER

Prince Louis was true to his word, and soon after Ramakanta's arrival, he organized a Ball in his honor. The event was the perfect opportunity to introduce the Zamindar to members of the European Gotha, who would be eager to meet the distinguished Indian aristocrat.

For the occasion, the Prince's palace was resplendent. The stately hall glistened by gaslights with thousand candles resting on crystal chandeliers, Which increased the surroundings' grandeur.

The banquet tables were lavishly decorated and reflected the abundance provided by great wealth.

The food prepared by experienced chefs was delectable and appetizing. The cuisine included exotic dishes from faraway India and wonderful vegetarian selections to counteract the western appetite for game meats and fowls.

However, the Prince requested beef omitted from the menu in deference to his friend's respect for *sacred cows*.

In Hinduism, cows are considered sacred. Also, 'caregiver' or maternal representation to the people.

But since the Zamindar was not a vegetarian, he

was fully expected to enjoy the superb and mouth-watering selection of meats and western foods.

Pheasants stuffed with sweetbread, walnuts, and raisins were displayed on substantial silver platters and artistically decorated with the bird's brightly colored feathers. Coveted hunting prizes, such as wild boar and deer, were particular favorites, roasted to perfection and glazed with honey and precious oils.

Tender suckling pigs stuffed with apples and berries and a great assortment of salt and fresh water fish from the surrounding lakes and imported from the Mediterranean completed the lavish display.

This abundance was decorated with exotic flowers and fruits, delighting the guests who washed down the food with precious Italian wines and imports from all across Europe.

Young servants stood nearby with great silver carafes filled with wine to ensure that the guest's glasses were never empty.

However, the highlight came when the herald announced to the aristocratic crowd the arrival of the guest of honor:

"His Highness, the Zamindar Ramakanta Chaudhury of Niladripur." The imposing name resonated with a loud timber and great clarity in the center hall.

Ramakanta made his grand entrance, accompanied by his host, Prince Louis, and warmly welcomed by the elegant and sophisticated guests, eager to meet the distinguished visitor.

The Zamindar was striking that evening, dressed with sophistication and elegance, in a simple white silk Sherwani jacket and matching pants. The garment was void of jewels and embellishments but showcased his tall and well-built figure. A single diamond decorated his tightly fitted turban and sparkled brilliantly, reflecting the many lights. Strings of precious pearls surrounded the gem, which rested just above his brow.

The light color of his clothes' sharply contrasted with his bronzed complexion and the intensity of his coal-dark eyes. A meticulously manicured mustache framed his lips and enhanced with masculinity the structure of his handsome face.

He was the embodiment of an exotic nobleman, and his allure attracted the ladies, who attempted to capture his attention in many ways. They appeared eager to engage in conversation with the sophisticated guest of honor from the faraway land across the oceans.

However, despite appreciating the warm reception, it was challenging for the Zamindar, who was overwhelmed by all the attention. He favored quiet moments and intimate conversation rather than being the center of attention. However, the small inconvenience did not stop Ramakanta from enjoying the splendid feast in his honor, which the Prince had so lavishly and generously offered.

The sumptuous hall reverberated with beautiful music and dancing. The entertainment provided reflected the multicultural gathering, combining pianos and violins' lovely sounds. But also Indian sitars to give a touch of home to the honored guest.

Graceful girls in their bejeweled, traditional costumes performed Folk and classical dances of India. They also enacted in grand style stories from Hindu mythology.

Suddenly, there was a pause in the revelry because of the striking appearance of a beautiful young woman, who gracefully descended the central staircase.

Her presence immediately attracted the Zamindar's attention and admiring glances from the surrounding crowd as she moved forward, basking in the gleaming lights of the hall.

She was tall, graceful, and elegantly attired in a splendid blue gown with tiny crystals appliqué that sparkled like many stars. It showcased to perfection her slender waist and the loveliness of her figure.

She held herself with dignity, although her face was slightly flushed, and a touch of shyness was evident, caused by all the attention created by her presence.

Ramakanta gazed with amazement and fascination upon the contour of her beautiful face, accented by dreamy eyes and soft, sensual lips. Long, lustrous dark hair framed her delicate features, enhancing her great appeal with beauty.

But it was much more than her loveliness that captured the Zamindar's attention. It was a sense of overwhelming surprise since she was the visual embodiment of the woman he dreamed about in so many disturbing and sensually charged nights.

It appeared now that she was real through some miracle, and her beguiling presence took his breath away.

The Prince was immediately aware of his friend's interest in the lady and hastened to introduce her as she approached them with a bit of hesitance. He smiled as she bowed to him in greeting.

"Please forgive my late arrival, dear Louis," she said with unusual familiarity, "I was unavoidably detained…"

"No need to apologize, my dear," interposed the Prince." I am glad you are here since you always enhance a gathering with your lovely presence."

He then turned toward the Zamindar, who was silent while staring at the young woman with wonder and expectation in his eyes.

"Dear Ramakanta, allow me to introduce to you the Countess Diana De Gautier, who is one of the most decorative additions to any gathering."

In response, the lady stepped toward the Zamindar and, for a moment, stared at Ramakanta's face with an intense look in her eyes while the Prince continued the introduction.

"Dear Diana, it is my pleasure to introduce to you His Highness, the Zamindar, Ramakanta Choudhury of Niladripur, who is my honored guest and a most welcomed visitor from India."

Diana bowed gracefully in response as a smile brightened her face while saying with a soft-sounding voice.

"I am pleased to make your acquaintance. Your Highness, may I extend my sincere wishes for a pleasant and eventful stay in my beautiful country."

The Zamindar struggled valiantly to retain a dignified demeanor while facing the woman of his dreams, as he managed to answer with his usual gallantry.

"My visit to your wonderful country has already surpassed my greatest expectation, dear Countess De Gautier. I am grateful to His Royal Highness for his hospitality and the special privilege of meeting you."

The Zamindar's voice became lower and softer as he uttered those last words, and the Countess appeared a little uneasy in that particular moment.

However, it became evident to the guests that there was a special connection between the Zamindar and the lovely Countess. They appeared oblivious to the public circumstances that brought them together and were in a world of their own.

The Prince was at first surprised by their unusual behavior, considering the formal circumstances. Although he quickly realized that, at least for the moment, his presence was superfluous.

With his usual gallantry, he smiled, bowed, and politely walked away, giving them some measure of privacy, even if amid the crowded hall.

It was a special moment for Ramakanta and Diana. They were apprehensive and perhaps a bit confused at first as they faced each other in silence. There was a measure of confusion in explaining the feelings that suddenly overwhelmed them, without a clear understanding of their emotions.

They were total strangers, and despite it, there was a real connection, which was overpowering and somewhat bewildering. However, the uneasy silence was suddenly broken by the Zamindar as he moved toward the young woman while whispering.

"Padma, you are Padma…"

"Why did you call me "Padma, my Lord?" She interjected, surprised and a bit intimidated by his words.

"Because the meaning of the word "Padma" is Lotus blossom, my lady," answered Ramakanta with a smile as he continued.

"According to Indian mythology, Lotus is the consort of the Sun God. I thought of the beauty of the flower when I first saw you. I hope you will forgive my boldness, but it was my natural and honest reaction to your loveliness."

Diana blushed in facing the intense look of the Zamindar's eyes that seemed to penetrate the depths of her soul.

"No need to apologize," she finally answered while regaining her elegant stance.

"I am truly honored to be compared to such a beautiful and delicate flower. Besides, I am aware that Padma is the Sanskrit word for the Lotus blossom,"

"I am glad you are familiar with it," answered the Zamindar with approval.

"Strangely," continued Diana appearing more relaxed, "the Lotus is my favorite flower. I was always attracted and drawn to it. During my many visits to the palace, I often walk through the gardens and frequently visit the lotus pond. I always find it so peaceful, and it gives me a sense of joy..." "Do you know that the Lotus is the national flower of India?" Interjected Ramakanta, "the lovely bloom is sacred to us. It occupies a unique position in the mythology of my country since time immemorial."

"I was not aware of that fact," answered Diana, fascinated by the subject, "I guess I should have known since the Lotus blossom has always been important to me."

The Zamindar moved closer to Diana and spoke in a softer tone.

"There are many stories connected with the flower. In ancient Egypt, the Lotus was the symbol of creation and rebirth…"

"Rebirth?" interrupted Diana, visually intrigued by the word, "you mean to say that the flower represents reincarnation and eternal life?"

"Yes, life everlasting," concurred the Zamindar.

"It's historically known that the Lotus flower was a symbol of the sun in their beliefs. Because at dawn, it climbs above the water and opens its bloom, while at night, it disappears in its depths. Sunrise and sunset."

Diana pondered on his words and then said.

"If the Lotus blossom is a symbol of rebirth and reincarnation, could there be an eternal life? I sometimes wonder…"

"In Hinduism, we believe in rebirth and eternal life without misgivings or doubts…"

"No, my Lord, I don't believe it's possible," Diana interrupted with a dismissive motion of her hand, clearly disturbed by the Zamindar's words.

"Besides, there is no way of proving that anyone ever returned from death to a new life…There are only strange coincidences that confuse the mind and may create false realities."

"What coincidences are you referring to, my Lady?" Ramakanta asked as he moved closer to her. "Besides, there is nothing to fear, even in the possibility that you might have lived before…"

"I am a Christian, my Lord," Diana interrupted, visually uncomfortable with the tone of the conversation as she slightly recoiled from the man.

"The concept of reincarnation is not part of my beliefs…although I always respect other points of view."

The young Countess was aware of her overreaction to the subject of reincarnation and had difficulty understanding why she was so passionate about it. There was also a sense of uneasiness in the sudden attraction she felt for the Zamindar, a man she had just met. The emotion seemed very strange and contributed to her confusion.

An uneasy feeling overwhelmed her, and Diana wished to escape the disturbing situation. She felt embarrassed about having lost sight of the proper etiquette required in the social environment.

She looked around and noticed that they were the center of attention in the great hall. Practically all the guests were staring at them, with curiosity over the intensity of their conversation.

"I believe it would be best if I leave now, Your Highness," she said with a little trepidation as she moved slowly away.

"All the other guests are eager to talk to you, and I have taken up so much of your time...I sincerely apologize for the breach of etiquette."

"No, my lady, please don't go yet," said the Zamindar anxiously and sincerely disturbed that the mysterious Countess of his dreams was about to leave.

"There is so much more I would like to say. Won't you please stay a little while longer?" Insisted the Zamindar hoping to change her mind. But Diana was determined as she answered.

"I believe it's inappropriate that I should

manipulate all your time, with so many other guests eager to talk to you."

Without further ado and despite Ramakanta's plea, she bowed with grace and elegance and said in parting,

"It has been my pleasure and honor to meet you, Your Highness. May you find great joy in your eventful visit to Italy."

"It has been my pleasure as well, dear Countess," answered the Zamindar with gallantry but openly disappointed by her sudden departure.

Finally, resigned to the inevitable, he bowed politely while saying in parting.

"My dearest wish is to meet you soon again, My Lady. I thank you for brightening my day with the loveliness of your presence."

The young Countess, with determination, distanced herself from the Zamindar, who immediately was surrounded by many of the other guests. However, he followed her with his eyes and noticed that before exiting the stately hall, she turned around, looked at him, and smiled.

§§§

CHAPTER FIVE

A MYTH COMES TO LIFE

After following the proper etiquette and graciously interacting with the many guests present at the lavish party in his honor, the Zamindar was finally free to speak in private with Prince Louis.

He thanked him profusely for the splendid reception and expressed how much he enjoyed it. There was also an appreciation for the connections he had made with influential political and business leaders from different countries in Europe. They seemed receptive to the possibility of lucrative trades with India, which could prove very beneficial, and make his trip abroad worthwhile in a tangible way.

However, he was now finally able to address the issue, which at that moment was most important and closest to his heart.

He wanted to know who the young Countess Diana De Gautier was. Because she so strongly resembled the lady of his dreams and someone he thought to have met before.

Her presence had stirred his imagination, and there was an intense curiosity about her.

The Prince was expecting his friend to ask questions regarding the attraction he had for Diana.

The Zamindar felt a bit uneasy in addressing the subject, but he finally said.

"Please forgive my inappropriate behavior, Louis. It was not my intention to ignore your other guests. But the Countess impressed me greatly since she seemed so familiar to me, like someone I have known somewhere in the past."

"No need to apologize, dear Ramakanta, and no one will blame you for wanting to talk to Diana, who is charming and very beautiful…A great combination, which is hard to resist."

"I thank you for being so tolerant, my friend," answered the Zamindar with gratefulness, "If you don't mind, I would first like to know if she is…"

"Married," interrupted the Prince, with an understanding smile, "no, my friend, she is *not* married…"

He paused as he pondered for a moment.

"However, just a couple of months ago, Diana was planning to marry an Italian Prince. The ceremony was to be attended by members of the European Gotha. But suddenly, and without explanations, she broke her engagement and became a bit of a recluse ever since."

The Prince paused for a moment with a puzzled look on his face before continuing.

"I believe it was about the same time you canceled your wedding plans…Strange indeed."

"I must admit, Louis, that I am happy the Countess is not married," answered the Zamindar, "and for some strange reason, I am relieved about it…"

He paused, feeling a bit uneasy before continuing the conversation.

"This is very confusing since I am not impulsive by nature, and this powerful attraction toward the lovely Countess is unusual and surprising at best."

"Perhaps your feelings are not that unusual," said the Prince, "you have heard of love at first sight? It happens at times, and possibly it happened to you."

"Maybe," answered the Zamindar, "I guess you could call it a form of love, but it's much more than that because I have the unsettling feeling of having known her for a long time...I felt such great emotion and joy when I first saw her, as if someone I loved and lost suddenly, came back to me."

The Prince smiled while questioning the seriousness of the conversation with a dismissive gesture of his hand,

"That is strange indeed, my friend, taking into consideration that I have known Diana since she was a little girl, and I am *certain* you never met her before."

"I guess you are right, Louis," answered Ramakanta in agreement, "these strange feelings could have been the result of my over-active imagination."

The Zamindar thought best to change the subject without confiding Diana's appearance in his dreams and believing in having known her in past lives. The issue would prove difficult since his western friend had no belief in reincarnation.

He began to walk toward the exit door prepared to say goodnight, then suddenly, he stopped and asked.

"Before I leave, Louis, can you please tell me something more about Lady Diana...I need to know all I can about her."

"Unfortunately, there is little I can tell you, my friend," answered the Prince, "she is a very private person who does not share her inner thoughts easily. However, I will be glad to give you some general information if you wish."

The Zamindar bowed his head in consent.

"She comes from a distinguished family and is the only child of the late Count Emil De Gautier and the late Countess Lina De Gaetani. She is a knowledgeable person who is truly kind and generous. Diana is often busy in her charity work, since she is independently wealthy, having inherited her family's title and estate."

"I sensed her warmth, at first glance," said the Zamindar concurring with the description of the lovely Countess.

"However," continued the Prince, she is fiercely independent, unlike the generally submissive women of our time. She has a strong will and mind, which seems to guide most of her actions with very few exceptions."

"Independent?" said the Zamindar with an approving smile, "I suppose that quality makes her even more appealing in my eyes since I have met few independent women in my country, or even in my life."

"I guess we should drink a toast to all the independent women of the world," said the Prince approvingly, "they make life more challenging, exciting, and interesting."

The two men laughed heartily at the unusual subject and prepared to say goodnight after a truly eventful day.

The Zamindar placed his hands together, bowed to his friend in parting, and then quickly walked away.

Ramakanta descended the central staircase with a hurried stride and quickly disappeared into the shadows of the great hall. He slowed his pace as he walked through long corridors illuminated by the brighter lights of gas lamps. This new invention quickly spread throughout Europe, even if mostly available to the well-to-do, because of the considerable cost of installing the gas connections.

The evening had been so exciting and full of surprises. Ramakanta's mind wondered in many different directions as he walked at a brisk pace in the vast palace and finally reached his bed-chamber. The room was designated initially for State visitors and furnished with elegance and style. A large bed with an impressive canopy crowned the area. Precious blue damask wallpaper soothing to the eye covered the walls, enhancing the grandeur of the surroundings. Splendid inlaid furniture rested against the walls, completing with patrician flair the exquisite ambiance.

Ramakanta was by now eager to rest after the long but eventful evening. He felt suddenly tired, but it was more emotional turmoil than physical exhaustion.

He began to remove his clothes with eagerness. But he was suddenly overcome by fatigue, and while still partly dressed, he decided to lie down on the bed.

He found great pleasure in placing his head on the soft pillow and then closed his eyes in an attempt to manage a few minutes of peaceful rest.

Unfortunately, the desired slumber lasted only a short while, and a sense of anxiety awakened him. There was an overpowering desire to get out, as a strong sense of claustrophobia suddenly overtook him.

Since Ramakanta was still partially dressed, he got out of bed and, after putting on his shoes, retrieved the Sherwani jacket resting on a nearby chair and placed it on his shoulders. He then made a fast exit from the room.

A palace guard patrolling the vast residence was surprised by the sudden appearance of the Zamindar, especially at such a late hour. He quickly approached him and addressed the distinguished guest with curiosity and respect.

"May I be of help, Your Highness? Is everything all right?"

The Zamindar realized how unusual it seemed to the guard to see him walking the palace corridors in the middle of the night.

"I am fine, thank you, it's just a bit of insomnia," he added with a smile, "perhaps I am not yet accustomed to the different time zone and decided to take a relaxing walk."

"I understand Your Highness," answered the guard with respect, "insomnia can be very unpleasant at times. However, if you wish to enjoy some fresh air, a stroll through the palace gardens could prove beneficial. Besides, the place is illuminated through the night and patrolled by sentries. Therefore you will be quite safe there."

"That is an excellent idea," answered the Zamindar, "I thank you for the suggestion. The fresh air might do me some good and help me sleep."

"I will be glad to escort you, Your Highness, if you wish…"

"No, thank you," interposed the Zamindar politely but firmly, "I am certain I can find the way myself."

The sentry bowed with respect and quickly stepped aside, giving the Zamindar free passage.

Ramakanta started to walk briskly down the corridor but suddenly stopped as a thought flashed through his mind, and once again, he addressed the guard.

"Do you know where is the location of the lotus pond in the gardens?"

"The lotus pond?" Parroted the guard, surprised by the question. He thought for a moment before answering.

"I believe you can find it in the eastern end of the gardens. There is an imposing statue of Venus in that area, which is quite visual, and it might be helpful guidance in finding your way."

"Thank you, I appreciate your help," said the Zamindar as he waved good-bye and quickly disappeared in the long corridor.

The Zamindar easily accessed the sprawling palace gardens. The manicured area was brimming with trees and many pools with waterfalls that sparkled in the moonlight.

There was a sense of relief while entering the verdant world opening in front of him, so mysteriously alluring by the shadows of night.

The Zamindar's Bride

The ambiance was peaceful and lovely, with only the occasional sparkle from fireflies disrupting the darkness in that perfect world.

Ramakanta felt at peace there, with a sense of joy and expectation. He had a strong feeling that someone had called him, with a lure that was overpowering and yet benign and comforting.

He gazed at the starry sky and the full moon whose silvery light was unusually bright, conquering the presiding darkness.

The friendly walkways gave him easy access to the splendid gardens, as he strolled with confidence toward the eastern direction as suggested by the guard.

His steps became more hurried toward a destination that was not clear in his mind. He also questioned the unknown reason for his overwhelming need to be there.

Suddenly Ramakanta paused and noticed that he was alone since the ever-present sentries were invisible at that moment.

He felt uneasy in the solitude and shadows of night and began questioning his behavior.

"What rational person would be standing there at such a late hour, and for what purpose?" He asked with some frustration.

"Am I losing my mind in the absurd search for a reality that lives only in my dreams?"

He suddenly thought that he had enough fresh air and would be more reasonable if he went back to his room and try to get some sleep.

But he was a captive to his emotions at this point. It was impossible to change directions since he needed to be there.

By now, he was deep within the garden, and the ever-present trees cast shadows in the solitude of the place. The statue of Venus was visible in the distance, and her cool whiteness glistened in the moonlight. It was a lure he couldn't resist, as he quickly reached the seductive Goddess of love.

From that vantage point, the Zamindar was even able to spot the Lotus pond, located at a short distance from the statue.

He could now see Venus's reflection in the dark waters of the Lotus pond that seemed to be calling him with a magnetic appeal that was irresistible.

Unfortunately, there was nothing unusual to see in his aimless search for an undefined objective.

Except for his reflection into the murky waters, he stared into a dark hole, deep and impenetrable.

Disappointed and frustrated, he picked up a pebble from the ground and tossed it into the pond with considerable force.

He then gazed with wonder at the circular symmetry created by his small projectile.

"Suddenly, a familiar, silvery voice broke the silence, dispelling with its tone the static feeling in the air.

"Please, Your Highness, do not disturb the Lotus flowers sleeping deep into the waters. They will soon rise again at dawn, ordained by nature and life's eternal cycle."

The Zamindar remained breathless for a moment, overwhelmed by the magical sound of her voice. He turned immediately around and faced once again the lovely and mysterious Countess.

Lady Diana De Gautier was a splendid apparition in the moonlight, so ethereal that he feared she might disappear.

The reality of that magical moment melted into dreams. Even Diana's name had special meaning since it related to the Goddess of the moon and the hunt, a mythological figure of great stature, not unlike the seductive Goddess of love.

However, the Countess was real enough as she stepped forward, smiling brightly. She curtsied to the Zamindar with grace and style, faithfully following court protocol, as a member of the aristocratic circle.

"Your Highness, it's a pleasure and a surprise to find you here," she said while walking toward him and asking with curiosity.

"Do you usually venture so late at night in the palace gardens, or is this outing in the moonlight an exception to the rule?"

The Zamindar was stunned by her sudden appearance and was speechless for a moment. He finally managed to find his voice and said almost in a whisper.

"Dear Countess, you are here? I dared not hope that my dearest wish would suddenly come true. Please forgive my boldness, but I had the strange sensation that you were calling me and wanted me to be here…"

Diana interrupted him, slightly perturbed by his words, as she asked.

"That is an unusual suggestion, my Lord…You believe that I possess such powers?"

Noticing her uneasiness, the Zamindar reassuringly answered her.

"There are many things we can't explain, My Lady. Perhaps because a superior power might have predestined them."

Diana immediately interjected with skepticism to the unusual suggestion.

"I suppose that anything is possible…However, I find it difficult to believe that you are here because I willed it."

"Perhaps it was only wishful thinking," answered the Zamindar, "driven by a deep desire of wanting you here."

Passion was reflected in Ramakanta's eyes as he continued.

"I remember with great clarity your words during the party celebration, dear Countess, especially about the Lotus pond in the palace garden. I wanted to believe that you extended an invitation for me to be here, even at this late hour…"

"I was speaking about a place I love, without extending an invitation," interrupted Diana with uneasiness, "besides, it would have been very inappropriate to invite you here, in the middle of the night."

The Zamindar moved closer to the young woman while saying with a smile.

"Then, why are you here, my lady? You must admit that your presence at this late hour is also very unusual."

"There is a simple explanation, Highness," insisted Diana, "I had a touch of insomnia, and that is the *only* reason why I am here."

Ramakanta looked deep into her eyes and sensed the confusion, even fear that had suddenly overtaken her. He was very close now, and the young woman stepped back, intimidated by his presence.

Because of the many small pebbles covering the walkway's unstable ground, she lost her footing and balance. The ever-vigilant Zamindar immediately encircled her waist to prevent a fall. He then, suddenly and impulsively, drew her close to him in a warm embrace.

Without warning, a powerful emotion ensued, almost the sensation of an electrical charge as he finally held her in his arms.

Her nearness filled him with desire and overwhelming passion. The depth of his emotions was more profound than anything he had ever experienced in his life.

During that magical moment, surrounded by the gardens' moonlit solitude, an intoxicating, alluring fragrance emanated from her silky hair. The scent was reminiscent of Jasmine's delicate bouquet, which evoked sensuality and passion to the Zamindar.

Beset with desire, he held her closer while caressing the contour of her lovely face. Slowly but deliberately, he placed his burning lips on her nape and reveled in the smooth softness of her skin, which was sensual and irresistibly alluring.

For a few moments, Diana appeared receptive to the romantic overture and nestled happily in his arms that seemed so comforting and familiar.

A special bond and a feeling of mutual attraction unified them in that all-encompassing moment of passion.

Unfortunately, the harmony was short-lived, as Diana attempted to free herself from the embrace, which was tempting, seductive, but deeply disturbing. She felt vulnerable to the exotic lure of the handsome man as he held her passionately in his arms.

"No, Rami, please let me go," she finally said, unable to control her anxiety.

The Zamindar, with his innate chivalry, immediately released the passionate hold he had on her but appeared amazed and stunned by her words.

"Rami…you called me Rami," he asked with great emotions, "why did you call me by that name?"

Diana was surprised by his reaction and remained silent and thoughtful for a few seconds more before answering.

"I don't know why I called you by that name. It just came to me without any explanations for it…"

"No, my Padma…there is an excellent reason for it," interrupted the Zamindar with excitement.

"The name didn't just come to you, for I believe you have been familiar with it for a very long time. It may even explain the connection that truly exists between us."

Ramakanta moved closer to the young woman as he continued speaking almost in a whisper

"You called me Rami in all those beautiful but unsettling dreams I had of you…"

"Dreams? You *also* dreamed about me?" Interrupted Diana as she retreated in shock and surprise.

"Yes, my lady," answered the Zamindar, "there were many dreams about you, which is the real reason I came here...I had to find you for my peace of mind."

The Zamindar moved toward Diana and held her hand with love and warmth as he continued with great emotion in his voice.

"What is most important right now is that you also had reoccurring dreams about me, which proves that we are truly connected, perhaps even from past lives..."

The Zamindar paused as he looked deeply into her eyes before continuing.

"There must have been a great love between us that proved impervious even to death...I feel it's alive right now and explains the powerful need for us to be together."

Diana attempted to move away from the Zamindar. She was deeply disturbed by his words, which addressed a concept she could not accept or comprehend.

Ramakanta understood the difficulty Diana had with the possibility of reincarnation. He spoke to her gently, attempting to soothe her distress.

"Please, my darling, you must not be afraid of those dreams because they may hold the key to the true relationship that exists between us…whether past or present."

Once again, the Zamindar placed his arms around Diana and held the young woman in a warm embrace.

Although still distressed, she relished his comforting, protective arms' about her as she inched her body closer to his.

"Yes, I did have many dreams about you," she finally said, "your presence was enticing, loving, and strangely familiar. You called me Padma and repeatedly invited me to join you. Soon it all became very disruptive, like a never-ending nightmare…"

Diana paused, visibly shaken by the recollection, as she rested her head on the Zamindar's chest while continuing.

"I must admit that your presence was alluring, and I wished to follow. But despite my efforts, I was unable to reach you because an invisible barrier always held me back…"

The remarkable similarity of their dreams moved Ramakanta. Her words seemed to bring needed light to the mystery of their relationship.

He held her closer in his arms and caressed her gently in an attempt to dispel Diana's confusion and distress. He could feel the accelerated beating of her heart as she trembled, overwhelmed by strong emotions and the fear of the unknown.

"I thought I was going mad," she finally said, "with so much confusion and distress. I tried desperately to make sense of it, to find some peace…"

Diana paused to gather her thoughts before continuing.

"This was the real reason I was late attending the party in your honor. I was afraid to meet you because of those strange dreams. But eventually, I gave in, despite my reluctance."

The Zamindar answered her with soothing and comforting words.

"Have no fear, my beloved Padma. You are safe in my arms, and I truly believe that as long as we are together, nothing can harm us."

He smiled and brushed some rebellious strands of hair from her face as he continued.

"You see, my darling, I had the same dreams, and I was unable to reach you as well, despite the enticing invitation and my deep desire to be with you..."

The Zamindar paused and remained pensive for a moment. He struggled to reconcile with all the mental disruptions that seemed to have taken control and changed his life forever. He then said.

"I believe to finally understand the real reason we were unable to connect in our dreams. Because it was only a reminder that we lived somewhere in this world, and we had to search and find each other."

"Then you believe that we are predestined to be together?" Asked Diana with strong emotions.

The Zamindar remained silent as he placed his arms around her waist since their special bond of love was everpresent and undeniable.

"I believe that we have known each other for a long time," he said with conviction, "you are the love of my life, Padma, someone I need to be with to find joy and contentment in my present existence..."

He paused as he looked deeply into her eyes before continuing with a soft sound in his voice.

"You see, my darling, I truly believe that you have been by my wife during several lifetimes."

Diana remained silent and shocked by his words. Her uneasiness was evident from her body's tightening as she moved slightly away from the Zamindar and finally said.

"Rami, you seriously believe that we had been married through several lifetimes? You must admit that it sounds like a mythological fable, an altered state of reality that I will never be able to accept…"

The Zamindar understood Diana's skepticism to his words since he was a practicing Hindu and reincarnation was part of his beliefs. While in Diana's Christian faith, there was only one life everlasting.

He paused for a moment, allowing Diana to ponder on a revelation that was deeply disturbing to her. He then continued with a clear and deliberate sound.

"Please hear me out, my beloved Padma, and don't judge my words too harshly…I truly believe that we lived together in former lives, and you were my wife reigning by my side as my beloved Zamandarin…"

"I am sorry, but I don't believe in reincarnation," Diana protested, "there must be a different explanation for these strange occurrences in our dreams. Perhaps it's some form of telepathy or inherited memories that are pulling us in such unusual directions."

The Zamindar understood her grievances and attempted to soothe her with comforting words.

"I value your skepticism, my love, since this is a premise against your basic religious dogma. However, we both believe in the existence of God, with equal reverence, and that is all that should matter. I only know that I need and love you, regardless of the issue of reincarnation."

The Zamindar paused and looked into Diana's eyes, noticing that tears of emotions were rising to the surface and sparkled like diamonds in the moonlight. He gently wiped them away as he whispered.

"Dry your tears, my darling. There is no need to be upset or afraid since it doesn't make a difference what you or I believe. Please, tell me that you love me too, my Padma, and nothing else will matter."

Diana remained silent. There was a feeling of solemnity and solitude. As if time suddenly stood still and captured them in a magical, everlasting moment.

She felt so alive and happy in that romantic interlude, surrounded by so much beauty and peace. It was an incredible feeling of freedom, void of control, and the ever-present rational-thinking.

"I do love you, Rami," she finally whispered. I love you so much..."

The revelation was decisive for both of them. Only the eloquence of silence could adequately express their feelings in that pivotal moment. They had finally found each other, and all the anxieties that plagued them for so long had suddenly disappeared. There was no need for explanations at that point since nothing could spoil that unexpected moment, not even the uncertainty of the future. Since the joy they were experiencing was a special gift to cherish for a lifetime.

They were standing by the lotus pond, and Venus's reflection was once again dominating the peaceful waters during that magical night. A soft breeze permeated the air, and only the silver sparkle of the moon reflected on the two faithful lovers, whose path had so unexpectedly and yet finally crossed.

Gently, his hand caressed the contour of her lovely face and touched the rosy cheeks, lingering by the outline of her ears, exploring with relish the structure and perfection of her features.

She stood silently transfixed, enjoying the sensual touch that was relaxing but deeply enticing at the same time. Ramakanta continued to draw on the outline of her face as his smooth finger caressed her graceful neck and long silky hair.

He finally pulled Diana closer by the waist, and she responded passionately, feeling his hunger and desire, as the sensual touch of her palms moved upon his chest.

She was there now, more enticing than he ever imagined in her shy but seductive presence. He could feel the warmth of her breath that burned him like fire in that decisive moment of ecstasy and passion.

Diana no longer avoided his gaze as she looked straight into his eyes, suddenly unafraid, and as his lips closed in on hers, warmth spread all over her neck, her chest, her fingers, and the very depth of her being.

Ramakanta touched her lips softly, gently, first exploring her mouth's sweetness, then capturing it more boldly, completely. They were together in the intensity of their emotions as their fingers touched and their hands linked tightly with fervor.

Their smoldering desire conquered that moment of absolute joy and captured them in an inescapable and romantic web of unity.

They were one in that magical moment, forever possessed by their overwhelming passion.

§§§

CHAPTER SIX

A STEP INTO ETERNITY

It was noon, and the Sun-God was now high in the sky, spreading light and warmth throughout the landscape and gaining power in the dominance of a new day.

Suddenly, the Zamindar appeared by the entrance of Prince Louis's study. The room had been their usual meeting place. However, there was a sense of anxiety written on his face as he approached the Prince, sitting comfortably at his mahogany desk.

He addressed the Prince with a sense of urgency in his voice.

"Good morning Louis, I hope this it's not an inopportune time for a visit since I need some information for my peace of mind..."

"As always, I am pleased to see you, Ramakanta," interjected the Prince in his usual friendly way, "there is no need for apologies since I was expecting you...because I believe to know what you are about to ask me."

"You know what I am about to ask?" parroted the Zamindar, surprised by his words but slightly amused. He walked toward his friend, appearing more relaxed than when he first entered the study.

"I suppose you have become a psychic, dear Louis," he said with a smile, "or perhaps my question is too easy for you to guess since it concerns the Countess De Gautier..."

He paused for a moment and took a deep breath before continuing.

"I was upset after learning that Lady Diana departed from the palace earlier this morning..."

"Yes, she has left, my friend, you are correct about that," interposed the Prince as he rose from his chair and grabbed an envelope resting on top of his desk.

"Diana left earlier than expected, but it's not unusual for her since she comes and goes as she pleases. As you know, she is considered a member of the family, and there are no formalities between us."

His friend's words saddened The Zamindar, who muttered softly, almost to himself.

"But she didn't even say good-bye to me."

The Prince overheard him and quickly walked toward Ramakanta. He then placed the envelope in his hand and said with a smile.

"You are mistaken, my friend. If you believe that Diana ignored you, she remembers you above all others and left this note just for you…"

"I guess she favored the unemotional simplicity of a note to say good-bye, instead of doing it in person," interrupted the Zamindar finding little comfort in his friend's words.

"No," insisted the Prince, "Diana does not wish to say good-bye to you…On the contrary, my friend, the note is an invitation to her estate. She hopes you will be a guest in her home at your earliest convenience, and she is eagerly waiting for you there."

The Prince continued the conversation in his usual, friendly tone, albeit with a touch of good-natured sarcasm.

"You are mistaken if you think she is avoiding you. I believe that she wishes to be only with you since she did not extend her invitation to me. As you can see, dear Ramakanta, you are the *only* guest she desires in her estate at this time."

"Lady Diana sent me an invitation to her estate?" Asked the Zamindar with great excitement in his voice while unceremoniously ripping the envelope open.

A touch of anxiety lingered as he read the few words in the note, which replaced his distress with an overwhelming sense of joy. The message was short but to the point.

"Please come to my estate, dear Zamindar. I am waiting for you. Forever Padma."

There was a great relief since, at first, he thought that she was trying to run away from him, perhaps frightened by their mysterious connection and passionate interlude in the palace gardens.

However, for the moment, nothing else mattered except the blessed reality that he would soon reunite with the woman of his dreams.

Prince Louis had remained silent for a while, giving the Zamindar time to absorb the excitement and joy of Diana's surprising invitation.

He finally spoke in a familiar but deliberate sound.

"You are free to go at any time, Ramakanta. My coach and driver are at your disposal and convenience. Our coachman, Gaston Dupree, will take you safely there since he is familiar with the location of Diana's estate, which is at a relatively short distance from the palace."

"Thank you so much, my friend, for all your help and wonderful hospitality. I am sorry to take an early leave from your company. However, the situation is truly unexpected, and the visit to Lady Diana's estate is of paramount importance to me…"

"I know Ramakanta. The visit is equally important to Diana," interrupted the Prince with a touch of concern in his voice as he moved closer to his friend.

"Perhaps it's not my place to say anything. However, I have issues with a situation developed within my palace, and because of it, I feel a sense of responsibility…"

"I understand your concerns, my friend," interposed the Zamindar, "you are free to speak and ask any questions you deem necessary. I will try to answer the best way I can."

The Prince was pleased by the Zamindar's receptiveness to his apparent worries. He continued speaking with a soft but determined sound, attempting to understand better the strong connection that appeared to be developing between Ramakanta and Diana.

He moved closer as he continued with unease and a darker tone in his voice.

"My friend, I have concerns about Diana's romantic connection with you, not only because of the differences in our cultures, which might prove problematic. But of greater importance, concerning your impending marriage back home. I question where Diana fits in your world, and what future can you offer her under the circumstances?"

The Zamindar remained silent but appeared to agree. He touched his friend's arm as he answered with deep emotion in his voice.

"I understand your concerns, Louis, since, in your place, I would feel the same way...I wish I could speak with certainty on this issue. However, destiny is unclear on what is in store for Diana and me since we never addressed a future together. At least up to now."

The Zamindar paused and looked at the Prince with determination before continuing.

"I hope you can believe that even if we just met, I love Diana with all my heart and would not do anything that could bring her unhappiness or hurt, even it was to my detriment. I give you my word of honor to that end."

Ramakanta's words moved the Prince. He valued his honorable nature and did not doubt the sincerity of his intentions. He extended his hand to Ramakanta while saying with determination and respect.

"I understand about your predicament, my friend. However, I have no doubts about your honorable intent toward Diana. Although no one can predict what the future holds, you have my best wishes and full support, if you should ever need it."

Later that afternoon, after taking leave from Prince Louis, The Zamindar was on his way to the Countess De Gautier's estate.

The affable coach-master, Gaston Dupree, proved to be a real asset during the trip, with his vast knowledge of the surroundings and the many historical sites.

The weather continued to be friendly up to that point and made his sojourn and sightseeing in the beautiful countryside more enjoyable.

However, the trip seemed longer than expected because of Ramakanta's impatience. In reality, it only lasted a little more than an hour to finally arrive at the coveted destination, the beautiful estate of Diana De Gautier.

It was a magical moment for the Zamindar as the coach moved with speed in the long, winding road that guided the way to the splendid mansion, now visible in the distance.

It was Diana's world, and Ramakanta could feel her presence in the perfection of the manicured landscape. A fresh pine scent was in the air, intermingled with the aroma emanating from a profusion of Oleander bushes. The Zamindar was familiar with the flower. One of his favorites, although aware of the poison hidden beneath the beauty of their blooms.

The stately mansion glistened in the sun in its marble whiteness and classical Greco-Roman style. There was a sense of elegance and beauty in the area, but also simplicity. It was much more relaxing being there, without the grandeur and splendor of the Prince's Palace.

He could now see a few estate attendees preparing to welcome the approaching coach and the presence of an aristocratic lady waiting by the front door.

"Who is she?" the Zamindar asked Gaston with wonder and curiosity at the sight of the lovely woman.

"She is Lady Amelie, your Highness, the maternal aunt of the Countess De Gautier's. Her favorite, among the few relatives still left in her family.

"I can see a family resemblance even from this distance," answered the Zamindar with admiration as they approached the entrance of the stately home.   He quickly exited the coach and walked with a brisk pace toward the Lady.

As he drew near, he noticed that she had a benevolent smile on her face, and he felt at ease in her presence since her demeanor was so welcoming. Ramakanta kissed her extended hand as she curtsied elegantly in greeting. He then stared with admiration at her splendid blue eyes that matched the color of the cloudless sky. There was a sense of kindness in them besides beauty and the focal point in her lovely face.

"Welcome, Your Highness," she said with a soft but clear voice, "it is an honor to have you as a guest in our house."

"It is my honor, dear lady," answered the Zamindar with gallantry, "and a pleasure to meet you."

"I am Lady Amelie, Diana's aunt. I have the distinct pleasure to welcome you since my niece is presently galloping happily in the countryside, which is her daily diversion. However, Diana is expecting you and should return very soon. I have the pleasure of doing the honors in case she missed your arrival."

The butler stood by the entrance door, and Lady Amelie signaled for the Zamindar to follow her into the neoclassic structure.

The vestibule was an impressive sight as they entered the vast atrium. Ramakanta's eyes were immediately attracted by a beautiful fountain in its middle, crowned by a statue of Venus, with flowing water spewing from its many spouts.

There was a special aura of serenity in the surroundings. The prolific use of white marble was evident, and its luster shimmered in the reflective lights of the open ceiling. There was a sense of harmony throughout the ambiance, and the Zamindar felt relaxed and strangely at home.

He was squired to an elegant salon alive with the house servants, busily preparing refreshment for the distinguished guest.

Lady Amelie invited Ramakanta to sit comfortably in one of the many divans in the spacious area and asked.

"Your Highness, would you like some fresh lemonade made of fruits from our orchard? Or would you favor some tea with biscuits, baked by our talented chef early this morning?"

"I would like a cup of tea, my Lady," he answered. "In my estate in India, it's almost a ritual to drink it at the beginning of the day. Besides, those cookies look delicious and inviting. I would love to taste them."

"I hope you will enjoy more than a couple of our chef's little masterpieces," said Lady Amelie proudly, "would you like lemon or milk in your tea?"

"I prefer lemon with and a little sugar," answered Ramakanta.

"You prefer lemon?" said the Lady, a bit surprised by the answer, "that reflects more of an Italian tradition. I believed that in India, they generally use milk in their tea."

"They do. My Lady, but I prefer it this way. I guess that is just one more thing I have in common with your wonderful country."

As Lady Amelie was about to answer, a small commotion outside of the mansion attracted her attention.

"I believe it's Diana returning from her ride with her usual escort," She said, "I can hear the sound of the horses outside in the courtyard."

The Zamindar immediately walked toward a window as a sense of joy and excitement overwhelmed him. The woman he loved was now visible through the clear glass of the stately window as she quickly dismounted her horse with athletic skill.

Lady Diana dressed in masculine style riding clothes appeared striking in ankle-length boots over black tights with leather inlays. A black riding cap held back her hair, which she removed with haste once on the ground, allowing her flowing, shining locks to fall upon her shoulders.

To the Zamindar, she appeared most alluring in the elegant but unusual riding attire.

In India, no women dared to be so bold as to shun feminine riding clothes, especially during that repressed time in history. Western women as well, especially aristocratic ones who would generally ride more elegantly sidesaddle.

However, Diana's independent and rebellious spirit fascinated Ramakanta, who was more attracted than ever to this captivating woman.

For the moment, the many challenges facing him paled in comparison to the desire of finally being reunited with this elusive and exciting Lady. The one he deemed the most alluring female he had ever known.

Diana was excited about sighting the coach, knowing that the Zamindar must have arrived at the estate. She eagerly looked up at the mansion's facade and was able to see in one of the windows Ramakanta's face, looking on with a bright smile on his face.

The young woman waved happily with anticipation and ran toward the entrance. Eager to be reunited with the man who had captured her imagination and her heart.

She soon entered the salon, appearing much more relaxed than the sophisticated and elegant Countess De Gautier of their first meeting.

Her long, shiny hair was a bit messy. A sudden blush due to the moment's excitement added rosiness to her cheeks and a special glow to her face.

Diana was lovelier than ever in her casualness and simplicity, while her eyes met the passionate gaze of the Zamindar.

For a brief moment, they were unable to speak. However, because of Lady Amelie's presence, they were brought back to reality and a sense of formality, which was befitting to the occasion.

Diana gracefully bowed to Ramakanta with a bright smile on her face while saying.

"Welcome, Your Highness, may your visit to our home be a joyful experience."

"It has already exceeded all expectations, my Lady," answered the Zamindar with warmth and sincere gallantry.

"I am truly honored to be in the company of such lovely ladies."

"You are very gracious, Your Highness...I can see that you have met my dear aunt, Lady Amalie," answered Diana as she kissed the noble Lady on the cheeks."

"Yes dear," interposed Lady Amalie, "we are already excellent friends, and I look forward to his stay in our home."

The noble and intelligent Lady was aware that her presence was superfluous at that moment, with Ramakanta and Diana appearing a bit uneasy and eager to be left alone.

Without further ado, she bowed in parting to the Zamindar and announced her need to attend to some chores. She also signaled the servants to join her.

Finally, alone, they remained silent as they faced each other, overwhelmed by the magic of that moment and the joy of being together once again.

The Zamindar's Bride

The Zamindar was the first to break the spell as he eagerly moved toward Diana and placed his arms around her waist, drawing her very close to him.

"Padma, my Padma," he whispered as he inhaled with delight the pine scent emanating from her hair. The lovely, fresh aroma captured while riding through the multitude of pine trees, which mostly populated the sprawling estate.

He touched with tenderness her smooth cheeks, still cool from the refreshing ride in the great outdoors, and caressed the slender contour of her graceful neck. Ramakanta relished the silky softness of her skin, which was so enticing to the touch. As his lips drew close to hers, he was able to inhale her honeyed breath and beset by an overwhelming desire to capture her soft, sensual lips in a deep passionate kiss.

Although the young woman had remained silent throughout the loving overture, she was a willing participant in the sensual embrace. Their bodies were very close, and she could sense the accelerated beating of his heart while he could feel the rounded, soft perfection of her breasts.

"Kiss me, Padma, kiss me!"

The Zamindar said beset by passion as he reveled in the joy of having his beloved captive in his arms.

She held on to him seductively, caressing his face with her long, elegant fingers while offering her lips to a smoldering, passionate kiss. The sensation lingered on for a long while as if true happiness could only exist in each other's arms.

Suddenly Diana stirred from the seduction of the sensual moment. She gently but firmly pushed him away, having regained a sense of reality from the magical moment of love.

"My aunt Amalie is in the house, Rami. We must show restrain and respect, for she might walk in on us …"

"There is no disrespect, my darling," interposed the Zamindar caressing her hair lovingly as a smile brightened his face.

"I also doubt that the lady will enter unannounced since she is far too insightful and kind…I am certain that she would never cause unnecessary embarrassment to people that truly love each other and belong together…"

Suddenly, in response to his words, Diana moved unexpectedly away, toward one of the windows. She remained strangely silent while staring at the beautiful landscape drenched with sunshine. There was a faraway look on her face, and she seemed preoccupied with some deep thought.

The Zamindar quickly joined her and placed his arms around her slender waist while saying with concern in his voice.

"Why so pensive, my love…Tell me please, is there something bothering you?"

"No…nothing is bothering me. I am sorry if I seem distracted since I am delighted to be with you."

But despite the denial, there was visible sadness on Diana's face, and the Zamindar wanted to know the reason why.

"Please, dearest, I sense that something is bothering you…I felt uneasy when you left the Prince palace, without even saying goodbye…"

"You are unfair, Rami," she interrupted, attempting a smile.

"I sent you a note with an invitation to my estate. There should have been no doubt that I wanted to see you."

The Zamindar placed his hands on her shoulders with a firm but affectionate hold while saying.

"Look into my eyes, darling, and please be honest with me…You know that you could have extended the invitation in person, which could have spared me so much anxiety until I read your note…"

"You must never think that I would leave you," interrupted Diana with a genuine passion in her voice, "since you are the one I love. It's just that I was upset when I found out that you…"

Her voice broke suddenly, filled with emotions, and she was unable to continue the conversation.

"Please tell me, Padma, what is the reason that upsets you so…I have the right to know," insisted the Zamindar, deeply distressed by her words.

Diana stood erect at that point while looking deeply into Ramakanta's eyes. Now her voice was firm, sharp, and perhaps a bit accusatory.

"Very well, Rami, I will answer, but I feel that is not my place to question the situation, although it is disturbing to me…I was informed by Prince Louis that you are getting married at your return home. Besides having given your mother your word as a Zamindar, in commitment to that promise."

The Zamindar's Bride

Ramakanta was startled by Diana's words but not resentful toward his friend. He understood that as an honorable man, the Prince felt obligated to inform Diana and protect her from a difficult situation since she was considered a family member.

The Zamindar was very sorry for having caused Diana distress. He held her hands with warmth and love as he finally said.

"My darling Padma, it is true that I promised my mother to marry at my return home. As a Zamindar, it's my duty according to the traditions and rules of my society. However, in the feudal regime that is now in place in colonial India, no one's will is above the Zamindar or has the power to override my wishes…"

He paused suddenly, taking a deep breath as Diana listened quietly and intently to every word.

He then smiled as he looked deeply into her eyes with passion and love while saying.

"My darling, you must believe that despite traditions, I have decided to marry for love. In that regard, there is *only* one woman whom I wish to have by my side as my Zamindarin, and that special woman is *you*. If you will have me as your husband and give me the honor of your hand in marriage."

There was great passion in his words and a sense of urgency as he added a romantic plea.

"Say *yes,* my dearest Padma, please join me in this exciting and challenging journey through life as my beloved companion...Your consent is all I wish for, and it will make me the happiest of men."

Diana remained silent. There was a sense of joy but also surprise in her eyes as she looked lovingly into his face. Her voice was soft but firm as she finally spoke.

"Rami, I am overwhelmed by your words and hardly know how to express my feelings at this moment...We met only a short time ago, and yet I feel that we have known each other for ages. I am so honored that you wish for me to be your wife..."

She paused to catch her breath, and calm the tumultuous beating of her heart, before continuing to speak with a deliberate sound.

"You know that I wish to marry you and spend the rest of our lives together...However, there is more to consider than the love that we have for one another because it might cause hurt for many people, especially to the girl who was supposed to become your bride…"

Diana paused and moved slightly away from the Zamindar before continuing.

"The Prince told me that as children, you and the future bride were promised to be married. Besides the pledge, you made to your mother to enter into marriage according to traditions. I am certain that she will be bitterly disappointed with your decision to marry a western woman instead of the one chosen by the family."

The Zamindar smiled with indulgence, trying to dispel her fears as he cupped her face in his hands and gently kissed her lips.

"You are so kind and caring, my Padma, and these are virtues, which I greatly admire in you. However, your consent to become my bride it's all that matters to me at this point. I am fully aware that many difficulties are looming our way, but I am certain that we will be able to conquer them if we face them together."

The Zamindar continued the conversation in hopes of dispelling her skepticism.

"You see, dearest, arranged marriage is commonplace in India and not just relegated to

Zamindars. The families choose the couple in question with little deference to their wishes. My future bride was chosen by an astrological chart when we were both children, and we never had a romantic connection."

"But we should consider the girl's feelings as well," answered Diana, still uneasy and questioning the situation.

"Perhaps, she cares about you more than you think, since women are generally more sensitive and emotionally vulnerable than men…Do you know if she is in love with you?"

"It's doubtful," said Ramakanta, dismissing the possibility, "I am only certain that she fancied becoming the new Zamindarin, although I doubt she ever had a real infatuation or love for me."

Despite the reassurance, Diana remained uneasy as she asked.

"Since becoming the Zamindarin, it's such an important position in your society. Won't she lose face in front of the people if you refuse to marry her? It could prove devastatingly painful to the ego of a young girl…"

"No, Padma," interposed the Zamindar with a dismissive motion of his hand.

"Please rest assured that only our families were privileged with the information. Therefore I am certain that she will suffer no embarrassment in front of the people. Besides, she belongs to a very distinguished family and has many suitors. I am certain that she will marry someone else and hopefully find happiness in that union."

"Finally, Diana seemed relieved and convinced by his words and smiled while saying.

"I am happy that she will suffer no embarrassment...It would have bothered me to know that the joy of our marriage could cause so much pain for someone else."

But the momentary relief was short-lived, as she asked the Zamindar a probing question with some apprehension.

"What about your mother, Rami? Please be honest with me. How will she react to your marriage with a western woman of a different religion?"

The Zamindar remained silent for a moment, with a sad look on his face. Since there was nothing positive, he could relate to Diana about Laxmi Devi in that regard.

He was sure that his marriage to a foreign woman would deal a devastating blow to her authoritarian nature. But in deference to Diana's wishes, he decided to be painfully honest with her.

"Dearest, my mother, will welcome you into the palace with her usual dignity…However, since we are dealing with the truth, I will not pretend that she will *ever* accept you as a daughter-in-law."

"You don't think she *ever* will?" said Diana, shocked and disturbed by the answer.

"Her unyielding nature will not allow her to open her mind to a different vision of life," continued the Zamindar with sadness.

"She lives by rigorous Hindu religious beliefs, which are at the center of her life, and she is devoted to them. It hurts me to convey to you the sad truth of my mother's rigid and uncompromising nature."

"Diana was stunned by those words, which cast an ominous shadow to the joy and excitement of marrying the man she loved. She remained silent, unable to find the right words to express her disappointment and sorrow.

"I suppose that my very presence will be a major reason for dissension between you and your mother," she said sadly, "our marriage, instead of joy, could bring tension and even unhappiness into your life…"

"No, my love," interrupted the Zamindar distressed by her words.

"Never think that our marriage would bring anything but joy in my life. Please understand that my mother's disapproval will make no difference in my desire to have you as my bride. Because there could never be true happiness in my life unless I have you by my side."

Diana remained silent but moved by his words as he continued.

"You see, dearest, I had difficulties with my mother long before I met you. She disapproves of my independent nature since she is very controlling. The situation worsened when I became the Zamindar because of my father's premature death, and in my position of power, she has to abide by my wishes without questions.

Diana was still uneasy despite the reassuring words. She dreaded moving so far away from her home and entering an unknown culture with an openly biased mother-in-law.

She moved closer to him and held his hand while saying.

"Rami, how can there be happiness in our marriage, with your mother so opposed to it, and living with us in the palace…In reality, there can be no expectations for joy, in such a stressful situation…"

"No, my Padma," interrupted the Zamindar as he placed his arms about her.

"I will not be torn between two people because my allegiance will always be with you. My mother is welcomed to share in our happiness if she wishes. Or, she will remain detached and lonely in her repressed world of intolerance."

He caressed Diana's cheeks with gentleness and love as he continued.

"You see, dearest, I love my mother, and my devotion to her is unconditional. Nothing will change since the estate is vast, and in many ways, she will be living in place of her own, with her servants to care for her. However, she must be respectful of you as my wife. The same way I know, you will respect her as my mother…"

Diana listened quietly but remained conflicted, "I am worried, Rami," she insisted.

"Your mother's rejection cannot be dismissed or ignored…Although I truly love you, I have real concerns about moving away from my country and enter a different culture where I might not be welcomed…"

Diana paused as the Zamindar appeared distressed by her words while understanding her reasonable grievances. However, regardless of the circumstances, the possibility of losing her was never an option as far as he was concerned.

"I want you to be my bride, darling Padma," he said with passion while holding her in a tight embrace.

"Please remember that you come first in my life, and I will never lose you regardless of the circumstances…Therefore, if you refuse to come to India because you fear isolation and rejection, I will remain here with you instead."

"Diana was stunned by his words and genuinely moved by the measure of his love. She smiled and pushed back a lock of unruly hair from his forehead while saying.

"My dearest Zamindar, you would remain here because of your love for me?"

She paused, beset by strong emotions, and then suddenly, shook her head in firm denial.

"No, Rami, I would never ask that of you because I know how important you are to the welfare of your people…You should never forego your responsibility to them, not even for me."

Suddenly, Diana's fears seemed to have been tempered or disappeared as she continued.

"Your love, my Zamindar, gives me confidence and faith that as long as we are together, there is no reason to fear…Therefore if you are willing to sacrifice everything for my sake, I can do no less with my love for you …"

Diana paused, took a deep breath, and looked into Ramakanta's inquisitive eyes as she continued with a soft but determined sound.

"I know that it will be challenging to leave my country and all the people I love…But despite the difficulties, I am willing to enter this fascinating new world and try to learn your culture and care for the people as you do …"

Diana paused and held the Zamindar's hands while saying with great emotions.

"Above all, Rami, I offer you my loyalty and my heart, for I am honored and joyful to accept your proposal of marriage."

The Zamindar was speechless for a moment as a look of happiness radiated in his handsome face.

"My dearest love," this is the most memorable moment in my life because we have found each other after a long and painful separation...Finally, you are mine once again, and the world is alive with the beauty of our endless love."

Diana was conflicted and confused by his words, but all those lingering doubts and questions had taken second place to the seductive allure of the moment.

She could feel the soft touch of his hands caressing her face gently, moving slowly down her neck and shoulders, and finally capturing her waist with increased strength as he held her closer and closer to his body.

She could feel the tumultuous beating of his heart and the burning power of his breath as his lips moved slowly but deliberately toward hers. A pleasurable shiver overwhelmed her as they melted together in a passionate, smoldering kiss that took their breath away.

For a few beautiful moments, they were locked together in a sensual, passionate embrace, lost in each other's arms in a splendid, magical world of ecstasy that was powerful and all-encompassing.

Diana revealed in the splendor of the moment and the desire to be forever connected to this person who seemed comforting and familiar. Who held in his passionate embrace the magical key to her happiness.

§§§

CHAPTER SEVEN

ETERNALLY YOURS

The dining area in Lady Diana's estate was set with celebratory elegance that evening. The stately room shimmered with crystal glasses, silver cutlery, and precious china, beautifully displayed on an embroidered, antique tablecloth decorated with the De Gautier's family crest. Several servants were at hand to serve a rich selection of food, mostly inspired by Indian cuisine, to honor the distinguished guest.

Reflecting on the formal occasion, Diana was resplendent in a midnight blue silk taffeta gown, with her hair in an elegant updo that beautifully framed her lovely face. She showcased a stunning sapphire pendant, which decorated her graceful neck and sparkled in the chandeliers' reflected lights.

The young woman caressed the precious gem gently and smiled as she addressed lady Amelie.

"Dear auntie, this precious pendant is a special gift from Ramakanta. Presented to me in honor of an auspicious and joyous occasion…"

Diana paused and leaned toward her while continuing in an apologetic tone, albeit with a touch of etiquette.

"Please forgive the secrecy, and if the news I am about to convey might come as a complete surprise…However, with great joy I like to announce that His Highness, Ramakanta Choudhury of Niladripur has asked for my hand in marriage, and the honor of becoming his Zamindarin."

Only silence followed the announcement. Lady Amelie appeared stunned and seemingly unable to speak as Diana continued.

"Because of his responsibilities as the Zamindar, Ramakanta asked me to join him in India and permanently reside there as his wife."

Diana's held the Zamindar's hand while her voice remained soft but determined.

"I have accepted his proposal taking into consideration the many difficulties at hand because of the love we have for each other…However, we hope that you will share in our happiness and give your blessing to our union."

The young woman remained silent while waiting for her aunt's reaction to the startling news.

It was of paramount importance to Diana that Lady Amelie gave her blessings to the imminent marriage. She loved her dearly and hoped for her approval during the exciting but challenging time in her life.

Lady Amelie's uneasiness in response to the announcement was apparent to the anxious couple since she also had difficulties making eye contact with Diana.

"This celebration is on the occasion of your engagement?" She finally asked, almost in a whisper.

"Yes, auntie," answered Diana in an apologetic tone, "I am sorry to have made such a secret of it…"

"We both apologize, dear lady," Interposed the Zamindar. "It was not our intention to keep it a secret, and I realized that it would have been proper to ask you first for Diana's hand in marriage since you are the closest member of her family…"

The Zamindar stood up and respectfully walked toward Lady Amelie as he continued the plea."

"I had to be sure Diana would accept my proposal because of the many difficulties our union may face and her willingness to marry me despite it."

A shadow of sadness flashed upon his face as he continued.

"There will be problems of acceptance from family and friends, concerning differences of religion and culture. But, because of our great love, we are willing to face the challenge. However, your blessing is very important to make our joy complete."

The noble lady smiled as an aura of dignity, but also kindness and warmth were apparent on her face. She then said with an amicable tone of voice.

"I believe the grand occasion of your engagement should call for congratulations and celebration...rather than the need for acceptance of family and friends."

Then lady Amalie lifted her glass of wine in honor of the engaged couple, but a slight tremor was visible in her hand. With her usual grace, she managed to control her emotions as she continued.

"Your engagement is not a complete surprise since it was apparent that the feelings you had for one another were more than friendship."

"Thank you for understanding, dear auntie," Diana said softly, "your approval means so much to both of us..."

Lady Amelie interposed with her usual benevolence but appeared conflicted.

"I am always on your side, dear, you must know it since your happiness means so much to me...However, there are difficulties concerning your decision to move so far away from home. I am afraid that it will be very challenging to leave a world that you are familiar with and accustomed to and enter the unknown of a very different culture."

Diana and Rami remained respectfully silent as the noble lady continued to speak with kindness but concern in her voice.

"You have never ventured outside of Europe, and we must consider your strong, independent nature ...If I recall, you have always been passionate about the unfair treatment of women in the western world. Therefore, I fear the difficulty of your assimilation in the Hindu culture, which is even more male, dominated than ours."

"I know," answered Diana, "there are many difficulties that lay ahead...But although I will move away from my country and the people I love, I will *never* give up my individuality and become someone other than who I am."

Ramakanta concurred with her words.

"I am delighted and grateful that Diana has accepted my proposal of marriage and will join me in my country...Considering her great sacrifice, I will not make any additional demands upon her. She is free to follow her western ways in my country if she so chooses."

At that point, the Zamindar held Diana's hand lovingly as he continued.

"My Lady, regardless of the difficulties that might lay ahead, her happiness and safety are paramount to me, and I will protect her with my life if it's necessary. You have my word of honor in this regard."

"I have no doubts of your good intentions, dear Ramakanta. It's apparent that you love Diana and that she is in love with you. I witnessed the joy in her eyes when you first came into her life. It erased the sadness that was always present ever since the death of her parents."

Lady Amelie paused while taking a sip from her glass before continuing with great emotion in her voice.

"She is like a daughter to me, and I shall feel great pain of separation when she leaves for India. However, above all, I wish her happiness, which is more important than the loneliness I will experience without her loving presence. But I am concern about her safety, as she moves far away from home, in a world that is unknown to her…"

Lady Amelie paused, then stood up from the table, followed by Diana and the Zamindar. At that point, they faced each other as aunt Amelie reached for the young couple's hands and placed them together while saying.

"My dearest wish is for love and peace to always be in the path of your lives…I gladly give you my blessings for a happy future, as husband and wife."

Then aunt Amelie, fighting tears of emotions brimming from her eyes, hugged Diana and Ramakanta with warmth, disregarding the usual etiquette with familiarity. She then said with a happier sound in her voice.

"Have you decided on the date for your upcoming nuptials? There is very little time available to have a proper celebration. since the return voyage to India is scheduled very soon. I will do all I can to help organize the wedding reception and send out the invitations to family and friends…"

"Sorry to cause you so much work, dear auntie, your help is truly appreciated, especially at this time," said Diana with a bright smile, as she placed her arm around her waist with great affection,

"I will let you know about the exact date for our wedding as soon as we make the decision."

"That will be fine, dear, and I am glad to be of help. Please know that you can always count on me," answered lady Amelie as she prepared to leave the room while saying.

"I must excuse myself because there is so much to do, and I like to get started right away."

The lady seemed a little flustered as she hugged Diana and Ramakanta before leaving the dining room with considerable haste.

"Poor auntie," Diana said, "she is always so helpful, trying to make things easier for me. I am fortunate to have her."

"I know, darling," said Ramakanta as he placed his arms around her with warmth and love.

"Today, we should rejoice not only in the celebration but also in the validation that our love survived through several lifetimes."

The young woman was disturbed by his words since it was still difficult for her to accept the concept of reincarnation. She ultimately decided that eternal life's perception was a beautiful and romantic mystery and chose not to question it further. She revealed instead in the sensual feeling that had captivated her ever since the Zamindar entered her life.

"I do believe in our love, Rami," she whispered while finding comfort in the warmth of his arms.

The Zamindar lifted her head gently and placed his lips very close to hers. He could feel the warmth of her breath caressing his face, and it was intoxicating. He never experienced with any other woman the burning desire he had for Diana. She was now in his arms, beautiful, sensual, the way he had envisioned her so many times in his dreams.

But she was real now, and he could caress her soft skin and marvel at the hint of cleavage that emphasized the roundness of her breasts in the elegant décolletage of her gown.

Beset with an overwhelming passion, he kissed her soft, rosy lips with hunger and desire, and she responded with sensuality and fervor.

"I love you so much," the Zamindar whispered as he reveled in the perfection of her body, now captive in his arms.

"It will be an eternity until the event of our wedding. I do not wish to wait a moment longer since I want you to belong to me right now…"

"I love you too, Rami, and I also want to be your bride as soon as possible." Said Diana as she lovingly caressed his hair, deeply moved by the excitement and passion of the moment.

Suddenly, a look of excitement appeared in her eyes as she said with enthusiasm.

"Perhaps there is a way that will even spare aunt Amelie the concerns of overseeing the preparations for a grand wedding celebration."

"What way?" interrupted Ramakanta, filled with anticipation.

Diana moved slightly away from him to regain some control over her emotions as she spoke with a soft but determined sound.

"Rami, You know how essential my faith is to me. And although I wish to be your wife with all my heart, it's of great significance for me to receive Christ's blessings to our union, or I will not feel truly married. Even after the legal ceremony celebrated in front of a judge."

"I understand, my love, and I am willing to marry you in your church and in any way you wish," answered Ramakanta with enthusiasm.

"I know that you will, dearest," answered Diana, "but you are a practicing Hindu and should not change your beliefs on my account since it would be an act of convenience and not of faith."

Diana continued with a serious tone, " therefore, considering that we both believe in God, I wish for you to accompany me to my church and share our wedding vows before Christ. There will be no officiating of the wedding ceremony. It will only be a pledge of love and loyalty to our union shared between the two of us, with his blessings…"

"Of course, my love, it sounds so wonderful," interposed Ramakanta with excitement in his voice.

"It will be the perfect wedding in your favorite church, before the Christ you worship…I vow to enter with reverence in the house of the Lord since I too believe in God and ask the almighty to bless our union and our love."

Diana smiled as a sense of joy and relief appeared on her face while saying.

"Thank you, dearest. I am glad you concur to a private wedding with the blessings of Christ, without all the pomp and circumstance befitting our station in life. I favor the loveliness of the little country church in my estate, where I received my baptism. It will be the perfect setting for our special wedding."

Ramakanta smiled and drew her closer to him, concurring enthusiastically with the suggestion, as she continued.

"If you wish, dear Rami, we could marry tomorrow in the church of Saint Justin, a special, sacred place where I often worship..."

"Yes, my dearest love, we will marry tomorrow," interjected the Zamindar, overwhelmed with joy.

Abandoning all etiquette, he lifted her body off the ground and rotated Diana gleefully in the room.

The sound of laughter resonated happily during that unique moment of true happiness. The young couple felt suddenly liberated from the heavy burden and responsibility of their aristocratic birth. For the moment, they were no longer the dignified Zamindar and the sophisticated Countess De Gautier. But just a young couple in love delighted to be in each other arms and oblivious to anything else.

They kissed passionately, again and again, filled with joy and anticipation of their forthcoming nuptials.

"I am overwhelmed, my darling," he finally said, "tomorrow it will be the happiest day of my life because my most coveted dream will finally come true."

"Mine too, Rami," she whispered, "I never dreamed that such happiness truly existed. A sense of familiarity suddenly overwhelms me, and I wonder if I have known you in the past and perhaps been in your arms before."

"You have been in my arms before, I am certain of it," answered Ramakanta passionately, "you are the one chosen by destiny since it was written in the stars a long time ago."

The Zamindar then whispered.

"This is what I truly believe, my darling. But all that matters is the reality of the present, regardless of what transpired in the past."

Diana was touched by his words and pondered how everything had changed in her life since the Zamindar's appearance. She felt removed from reality in a whirlwind romance, reminiscent of an enchanted fable, which had taken over her life. But whether it was reincarnation or something else, it made little difference because she was sure that he was the man of her destiny and her true love."

Diana suggested after some consideration, "I think our marriage should remain a secret from everyone, including aunt Amalie...I hope she will understand and approve of our actions under the circumstances because it will be a practical solution for all concerned."

"I believe you are right, and she will be happy for us since lady Amelie is such an understanding lady," concurred Ramakanta.

"Then Rami, it's all settled for tomorrow morning, "she said with excitement in her voice as she moved closer to him.

"We will ride to the church with my carriage, and no one will suspect our true destination since I often travel alone through the countryside..."

She paused, a bit overwhelmed by the occasion and her impulsive, almost reckless behavior.

"I guess it's all coming true...and tomorrow will be our wedding day," she whispered to affirm the reality of the situation.

"Yes, my love," he interposed with excitement in his voice, "but there is just one more thing we need to do and make the wonderful day simply perfect."

"What do we need, Rami?" Asked Diana, openly curious.

"The Zamindar answered with a smile while gently caressing her hair as he continued.

"After the celebration, where will we go to spend our wedding night? I know that your palace is a splendid place with many beautiful rooms. But for the wonderful celebration of our first night together, I would prefer to be in a different place. Alone, just the two of us, in a world of our own."

The Zamindar lifted her chin while speaking and reveled in the blush that tinted Diana's cheeks bright crimson in response to his words and made her appear in his eyes even more beautiful.

"We must think of our honeymoon, darling, even if the wedding it's on such short notice....It would mean so much to me if we could share a special place that is only ours and worthy of our love."

Diana smiled as she answered.

"You mean a romantic, lovely place just for the two of us and far removed from everyone else?"

"Yes, my love," insisted the Zamindar, "I admit of having become very possessive of my future bride. Therefore, for a little while, I wish to have her all to myself."

"Just you and I, my Zamindar," insisted Diana with a radiant smile on her face.

"Yes, my darling, just you and I, alone for a few magical days of our blessed honeymoon...Do you know of such a place?"

"Perhaps I do," answered Diana with an enigmatic smile and then remained silent for a few more moments, relishing the suspense created by her words as she whispered.

"I think I know of a perfect place in which to spend our honeymoon night, my Zamindar. It's lovely, secluded, and far away from everyone else, just as you wish..."

"Sound's wonderful, darling, but where can we find this magical place?" said the Zamindar with excitement in his voice.

"Diana smiled but did not immediately answer the question enjoying the little suspense she had created.

"Please tell me, my love, don't keep me in suspense," pleaded the Zamindar, "where is this perfect place worthy of our first night together?"

"The hunting lodge of Prince Louis," Diana finally answered.

"It's a beautiful, secluded place surrounded by greenery and lovely grass flowers, which sprout everywhere like an eternal spring."

She then continued with excitement in her voice.

"This perfect place is not too far away from my estate, and I am free to use it anytime I wish…Since hunting season is now over, the lodge is empty, except for the elderly custodians who live in the surrounding grounds. I am certain that if requested, they could be most helpful in providing to our comfort and privacy…"

"Sounds wonderful, my darling," interjected the Zamindar with enthusiasm and deep emotions.

Everything seems so perfect in every way for our special wedding day. I only wish it was already tomorrow."

§§§

CHAPTER EIGHT

PLEDGED TO LOVE

Early the following day, gardeners were busy at work, clearing the grounds and pathways of fallen leaves and debris collected during the night. They were also tending the many plants and flowers that surrounded the Countess De Gautier's lovely estate.

Diana's carriage was already waiting by the central entrance. The horses' neighs disturbed the peaceful environment, waiting to be spurred on by their lady into a fast gallop.

The Zamindar appeared in fashionable western clothes and wore an impeccably styled light gray suit and white shirt that conveyed an air of aristocratic refinement. But the open collar gave a less formal appearance to the attire while bringing to the fore his striking and well-built body. He appeared at ease in the European fashion, which he wore with an innate style, as a special glow highlighted his face framed by his meticulously arranged, shoulder-length, black hair.

He looked up at the sky tinted in a light shade of blue, with little fluffy clouds that failed to shield the suns' increasing brightness. The morning dew was visible everywhere, sparkling like tiny diamonds above the greenery in the splendid, lush landscape.

The Zamindar reveled in nature's beauty, so plentiful in Diana's country estate. It was reminiscent of his sprawling acres of fertile land, laden with nature's bounty, which he loved, and hoped to share with Diana on his return to India.

A smile brightened his face at the cherished imagery so deeply ingrained in his memory as he murmured.

The Zamindar's Bride

"It's a sunny morning, my Padma, as our two worlds are coming together in perfect harmony. The Gods are smiling at us with the most promising sign of favor, in honor of our wedding day."

The eager bridegroom then paced the ground impatiently, waiting for the appearance of his bride.

A little apprehension and eagerness were visible on his face. However, he knew that he had arrived a bit too early, instead of the agreed time.

He had difficulty sleeping during the night because of all the excitement of his impending wedding. A thousand thoughts raced through his mind and kept him awake as the night seemed to progress at a snail pace.

Finally, as the first light of dawn broke through the gloom of that eternal night, he decided to get up and relieve his restlessness by getting ready for the auspicious occasion of the day.

There was almost a fear that something might spoil the great feeling of joy seldom experienced in a lifetime.

To relieve his restlessness, he looked at his gold pocket watch to make sure of the exact time. He then realized that it was only a few minutes from the last time he checked.

The beautiful watch, with superb engraved details, was Diana's engagement gift to him. It was a precious family heirloom that once belonged to her beloved father.

"Padma, my love," He whispered as he caressed the golden gift, beset with emotions.

"Please come soon. I miss you so much."

Almost in response to his plea, suddenly, the front doors of the mansion parted slowly. Like a vision, Diana came out of the shadows and appeared on top of the stairs, brightened by sunlight.

For a few moments, she looked around with apprehension since the brightness temporarily obscured her vision. However, it was soon replaced by a radiant smile at the sight of her Zamindar eagerly waiting for her.

As Diana walked gracefully down the stairs, she never looked more beautiful in his eyes. A serenity and radiance brightened her face, with a rosy tint visible on her cheeks due to the moment's excitement. Her hair was flowing freely on her shoulders like a shiny mantle and framed her face with beauty. She wore an elegant, white chiffon gown, whose full skirt swayed softly in the gentle breezes of the morning air. The delicate fabric gathered at her waist showcased her lovely shape to perfection. A splendid lace mantilla rested on her shoulders and fell well below her ankles, giving a bridal look to the simplicity of the beautiful gown.

The Zamindar rushed to her side and extended his arm to escort his bride down the remaining stairs safely.

They stared at each other, quietly, beset by strong emotions, but managed to retain the dignity necessary for the solemnity of the moment. The Zamindar was the first to break the silence.

"My darling Padma, your beauty rivals the splendor of the sun, which shines so brightly in honor of our betrothal."

"Yes, Rami, it's a beautiful day," she answered softly, "a perfect day for our wedding, my love. I was surprised to find you here since I came down earlier than expected."

"I arrived even earlier," answered the Zamindar, "I guess we were both so eager for our special day to begin."

Diana lowered her head in a sign of consent as they walked toward the waiting carriage. The Zamindar helped her climb into it, making sure not to disturb her gown's delicate fabric, and quickly joined her taking control of the reins.

But before leaving, they looked at each other with love. Ramakanta leaned forward, attempting to kiss her rosy lips, which were parted in a radiant smile and appeared incredibly tempting.

"Not now, my love," she said in a soft but determined sound while placing her long, elegant fingers upon his lips. "

He grabbed her hand suddenly and kissed it with passion while saying.

"I understand, darling, you wish to wait till we are married...I guess I will have to be patient for a little while longer."

"Yes, a little while longer, my Zamindar," answered Diana with an indulgent smile, "besides, I have something to show you now, which will be useful and important to our wedding."

The Zamindar's Bride

As the Zamindar looked on with curiosity, Diana placed a little velvet box in front of him and opened it with some emotion. It contained two golden wedding rings, one of them covered with sparkling diamonds, which glistened in the sunshine.

Diana caressed the precious jewels lovingly as tears appeared in her eyes while saying.

"They were my parent's wedding rings, the most precious memento I have left of them. I wish to use these rings for our wedding ceremony. It will make me feel that they are close to us on this special day and bless our union."

"It will be an honor, my Darling," said the Zamindar, "Although I was not fortunate to have known them in this life. I am most grateful for the priceless gift they bestowed upon me. My loving and beautiful bride."

Without further ado, the Zamindar spurred on the horses into a gallop through the winding road of Diana's beautiful estate. He soon increased the speed toward the bucolic land expansions that lay ahead as far as the eyes could see.

Suddenly, Diana pointed to a structure that appeared on the horizon, partly shielded by the heavy vegetation. The bell tower and the cross visible on its peak made it evident that it was a charming country church.

"It's the church of Saint Justin, Rami. It has been part of De Gautier's estate for over two hundred years. This holy place is open to all the people that wish to worship, and so many come from the surrounding villages to attend services as well. I go there often for the celebration of Sunday's mass, and of course, I received my Baptism in this special place."

"I feel privileged to enter this church that has such meaningful memories for you, dearest... It's also so peaceful here, surrounded by so many lovely wildflowers."

The Zamindar suddenly stopped the carriage, and with great agility, jumped onto the ground while Diana looked on with surprise.

He walked toward a green patch of soil where a profusion of daisies had sprouted spontaneously from the ground. He gathered a small bunch of the wildflowers, and without delay, brought them back to the carriage and handed them to his future bride while saying.

The Zamindar's Bride

"Beautiful flowers for my beautiful bride on the occasion of our marriage, since I believe they are essential to the circumstances...In our Hindu wedding ceremony, flowers are also part of the ritual. The bride and groom exchange garlands of flowers in the Jai Mala, which expresses the desire for the couple to be married to each other."

"Thank you, dear Rami, but flowers are also important in western wedding ceremonies," answered Diana.

"The bride always carries a beautiful bouquet, and the groom wears a boutonniere on his lapel. There are usually flowers by the church's altar, which lends beauty to the festive and holy atmosphere."

With a smile, Diana removed a daisy from the bunch of wildflowers and placed it on the Zamindar's lapel while saying.

"I regret that there was no time this morning to create a proper bouquet from our greenhouse. Besides, I did not want to raise suspicions about our wedding plans."

She then held the lovely flowers very close to her heart and said with great emotion.

"I love these wild blooms, especially daisies since they were my mother's favorite…"

"I am glad you love them, darling," interposed the Zamindar, "now we are truly ready for our wedding…So let us go without further delays."

Ramakanta climbed swiftly back into the carriage and spurred the horses to a fast gallop toward the church of Saint Justin, and in a brief period, they arrived at their destinations.

In closer proximity, the country church was a lovely sight shining in the sunlight. The Zamindar looked on with admiration at the very picturesque and charming image presented, so manicured and in perfect order.

At first glance, there was no one insight, and the church appeared closed to the general public. Although, at closer inspection, they noticed a man busily working on the surrounding grounds. But it wasn't easy to see who that person was since all the trees and shrubberies partially hid him.

"It must be one of the gardeners," said Ramakanta as he prepared to dismount the carriage.

Once on the ground, he helped Diana

descend with gallantry, taking great care not to damage her lovely gown.

But the little commotion caused by their horse-drawn carriage attracted the worker's attention, and he quickly came out from the shelter of the trees and became fully visible as he approached them.

"It's father, Anthony!" Diana said, recognizing the man as the pastor of the church.

Taken by surprise, the priest quickly attempted to regain the customary dignity and walked toward the unexpected visitors with friendliness while saying.

"Lady Diana, it is such an unexpected pleasure to see you here, at such an early hour…Are you planning to attend services in the church?"

"Good morning, father. We are sorry to have startled you with our unexpected presence since we did not have the time to give a proper announcement of our visit," said Diana in an apologetic tone as she moved closer to him.

"However, I have the great pleasure of introducing to you our guest, His Highness, the Zamindar Ramakanta Choudhury of Niladripur, who is a welcome visitor from India."

"Although we live a quiet life," said the priest with a friendly smile, "I have heard of the eventful visit, and he is most welcome here…We are a small community, and rumors travel fast."

He then turned toward the Zamindar and extended his hand in greeting.

"I am father Anthony in service to the church of Saint Justin. It is my pleasure to meet you. Your Highness."

"I am honored to meet you, reverend Father. I thank you for your gracious welcome," said the Zamindar as he responded to the handshake with reciprocal friendliness."

"I must explain, Father Anthony," interposed Diana while appearing a bit flustered in the presence of the priest.

"You see, our visit this morning is for a special reason…The Zamindar and I are here to be married."

"You are here to be married?" asked the priest, unable to conceal his surprise.

"I received no notice concerning this important occasion, and unfortunately, I was unable to make the necessary arrangements…"

"No arrangements will be necessary, father," interposed Diana, because there will be no formal ceremony to celebrate."

Diana appeared uneasy as her voice became softer while attempting to explain the situation.

"You see, Father Anthony. My fiancé is a man of another faith but a believer in God. Under the circumstances, we plan to exchange our vows beseeching our Lord Jesus's blessings without the clergy's officiation. I believe it will be more honest and respectful rather than have him convert to our faith only for a matter of convenience."

The priest remained silent and a bit perplexed by Diana's words, and then he said.

"I am sorry, my Lady, but if you marry in a Christian church without the officiating of a priest, it will not be considered a legal union."

"We understand the difficulties involved, Father Anthony," answered Diana with a respectful but determined sound.

"We pray that God will bless our union since we enter our plea with all the sincerity of our hearts…There will be a legal ceremony as well, to satisfy the norms of society."

"My Lady," the priest said with benevolence.

"It's not my place to question the wisdom of God or the choice you made. I can only relate to the rules of the church."

"I understand, Father Anthony," answered Diana, "we are sorry to have placed you in an uncomfortable position...I had hoped that the church was empty at this time, and we could have exchanged our wedding vows in complete privacy..."

Diana paused, a little disheartened as she addressed the priest with dignity and respect.

"However, under the unusual circumstances, we will understand your objection to our wedding celebration in your church?"

Father Anthony smiled while pointing to the church's entrance with solicitude and kindness.

"All are welcomed who come to the house of the Lord in love and peace. Please enter without delay and with my blessings."

Diana, moved by the priest's understanding and kindness, kissed his hand with respect and devotions.

In response, Father Anthony walked toward the church's entrance wooden doors to give the young couple access.

Diana smiled and paused for a moment before placing the lace mantilla over her head. The precious fabric flowed almost to the ground, transforming the young woman into the beautiful bride of Ramakanta's dreams.

As he marveled at her loveliness, the Zamindar extended his arm to Diana, and the couple appeared ready to enter the church, with the appropriate dignity befitting the solemn occasion.

"This is our wedding day, Rami," she whispered, overwhelmed with emotions.

"Yes, my darling Padma," he answered, "it's the happiest day of our lives."

Father Anthony firmly pushed the door handles and opened the imposing carved doors of the church. Without further delay and a deliberate stride, the young couple ventured into the holy place.

The Zamindar looked around with admiration and respect. At first glance, the interior was a bit austere but beautiful in its simplicity, with a delicately decorated vaulted ceiling and a white marble altar as the focal point. Although the church was empty, it shimmered in the light of a hundred votive candles, which gave the place a warm, welcoming feeling, while golden sun rays filtered through the stained glass windows.

Diana felt at ease in the familiar place and crossed herself with devotion. She noticed with joy a beautiful selection of freshly cut flowers decorating the altar. Perhaps she thought, Father Anthony placed them there before their arrival, and it seemed a remarkable coincidence and a good omen.

The country priest squired the happy couple to the altar. He first bowed to the image of the cross prominently displayed in front of the communion table. He turned around with a benevolent smile and lifted his hand toward Diana and Ramakanta in a sign of blessing. Without further ado Father Anthony walked away toward the church's sacristy, giving the young couple the requested privacy.

Diana and Ramakanta knelt with reverence by the altar, resting the flowers and the wedding rings in front of them. They closed their eyes in silent prayer, deeply moved by the solemnity of the moment. They finally looked at each other with love. The Zamindar was the first to speak as he took her hands in his.

"Diana De Gautier, I wish to share in this momentous occasion a poem I have written for you, titled - Soul Mate- because that is what you are and will always be to me."

******

"When I was stranded at the crossroads of uncertainty.
In my life's odyssey,
I halted the endless search
of the surface and the core,
of the grandeur of the earth for a coveted scent.
Upon finding you, my fragrant blossom
that spills out benign fragrance
on the confines of the Eden
of my mortal life.
I ended the search
of the soul of the self
and also of the Supreme,
upon meeting you

at a fateful junction
on the winding path of my life.
I also halted my search
for a beam of light,
at the Seat of Enlightenment,
upon finding you, my starlet
that now radiates my inner self. "

Diana remained silent and overwhelmed by the poem's beautiful words, as Ramakanta continued with warmth and emotion.

"Diana De' Gautier, in the presence of God and beseeching his blessings, I take you as my beloved wife in the perpetual cycle of life, as I give you my endless love and eternal fidelity."

Having spoken those words, the Zamindar placed a flower in Diana's hair. He then opened the little velvet box, retrieved the splendid golden ring covered with small diamonds, slipped it on her annular finger, and kissed her hand with love and devotion.

Diana's eyes brimmed with tears of joy. She smiled at the Zamindar and finally spoke with a soft but clear voice.

"I Diana De Gautier, in the presence of God in his holy house, take you, Ramakanta Choudhury, as my legitimate spouse to whom I pledge my eternal loyalty and love."

The young woman then placed the golden ring on his finger while saying.

"Dear Rami, take this small token of my endless love. Let it be a reminder of my faithfulness and devotion to you."

The young couple remained silent for a brief moment, lowering their heads in reverence and respect. They then clasped their hands together while their lips met in their first kiss as husband and wife.

Suddenly, as Diana looked around the holy place with devotion, she was startled and exclaimed with a joyous sound.

"Look, Rami, the sun rays are shining on our hands...I believe it's God's blessings to our union."

They both looked on with great emotions as a ray of sunlight from a stained glass window shined brightly on their clasped hands, bringing life to the sparkling diamonds of her wedding ring.

Gratefulness radiated on their faces from the little miracle that gave so much meaning to their special celebration on that faithful day.

After genuflecting with reverence and respect, they walked out of the holy place, hand in hand with renewed hope for happiness in their future life together.

§§§

CHAPTER NINE

THE SCENT OF JASMINE

With her usual kindness, Lady Amelie accepted the romantic elopement of Diana and the Zamindar. She welcomed the happy couple with open arms, despite her concern, and quickly arranged an impromptu champagne celebration for the newlywed couple.

Only e few close friends, including servants to the estate and their families, were in attendance. It was all in deference to Diana's wishes for a simple celebration void of the expected grandeur.

The bride was radiant and lovelier than ever for the occasion, basking in the beauty of the celebration. Rami shared in her happiness while accepting the many congratulations and good wishes from their guests.

As a special gift, Aunt Amalie adhering to traditions, presented the bride with a beautiful white orchid's bouquet. The rare tropical flowers were grown in the estate's greenhouse, and they became part of the special celebration for the happy couple

As the festivities were coming to a close, Diana performed the traditional bouquet toss reserved for all the single girls in attendance. According to the legend originating in England's ancient times, the lucky lady who would catch the bouquet was the chosen one to become the next bride.

Soon a friendly rivalry ensued among the girls, but the daughter of the estate's chef was ultimately victorious. She displayed a bit of agility, coupled with considerable athletic prowess, leaping into the air to capture the cherished prize. She then squealed with delight while gazing into the approving eyes of her young man while the attending guests applauded enthusiastically.

The Zamindar's Bride

The bridal couple was finally ready to leave, and Diana warmly embraced aunt Amelie, thanking her for the lovely and memorable celebration. Then, without further delay, the happy couple briskly walked toward their carriage, under a cloud of rice, tossed by all the well-wishers in attendance.

They laughed with delight and waved good-bye as they boarded the carriage richly decorated with fresh flowers. A whimsical sign was posted proudly on its rear, with the happy caption of *Just Married!*

On their way to a romantic honeymoon, a small cloud of dust rose from the horses' hooves while spurred on to a fast gallop.

The carriage was now at a considerable distance as they entered the rural countryside while aunt Amelie and guests continued to wave good-bye.

The beginning of dusk was quickly setting in as the sun's golden rays gave way to the impending shadows of darkness. Suddenly a cool breeze spread through to the air, causing Diana to shiver in her delicate chiffon gown. The attentive Zamindar immediately noticed the little discomfort and placed his arms lovingly about her shoulders while asking.

"Are you feeling cold, my darling? It's getting chilly now as evening approaches. You must be a bit uncomfortable with your beautiful but very light dress in the open carriage."

"No, Rami," answered Diana almost in a whisper.

"I love the cool wind caressing my face and hair. It's just a bit of excitement as this wonderful day comes to a close…"

"Not the end of the day, my love, but just the beginning of our life together." Interposed Ramakanta as he moved closer and softly whispered in her ear.

"Do you know what I wish for right now?"

"No dearest," answered Diana with a bit of curiosity, "what is it that you wish? Please tell me."

The Zamindar smiled and kissed her lips with tenderness before saying.

"I wish that time would slow down the eternal rotation, to preserve a bit longer the perfection and splendor of this day."

"I have the same wish," answered Diana, "but there is so much we can look forward to, even as time marches forward in its natural course."

"Yes, my love," answered Ramakanta as he held her close.

"Our honeymoon night is fast approaching, and I know that it will be the crowning glory in this memorable and perfect day."

The Zamindar spurred the horses faster with anticipation and concern that the darkness of night might overtake them.

Finally, the hunting lodge of the Prince appeared in the distance.

The mansion looked impressive, surrounded by greenery and a profusion of multi-colored Bougainvillea, draped on its facade with colorful splendor.

The Zamindar was immediately pleased by the picturesque image of the lodge. He deemed it the ideal, romantic place for their wedding night.

As they quickly reached the front of the mansion, an elderly couple was standing respectfully by the entrance, appearing to be the newlyweds' welcoming committee.

The man immediately approached the couch as the Zamindar pulled back the reins and brought the horses to a complete halt before dismounting with agility and extended a helping hand to Diana.

Once on the ground, the young woman smiled at the man with friendliness while walking toward the entrance. She greeted the lady with familiarity since she knew her to be one of the custodians of the hunting lodge."

"Good evening Emma, I thank you and Luigi for all the valuable help extended to us on the occasion of our wedding."

"It is our pleasure and honor to be of service, my lady. We express our sincere congratulations and the very best wishes for a happy and long life together."

Said Emma with a welcoming smile, while the efficient Luigi, despite his advanced age, removed the carriage's heavy suitcases with little effort.

The man was proud to display his considerable strength as he brought them into the mansion with ease and climbed the many steps to the upper floor and the bedrooms.

Emma squired the bridal couple to the lodge entrance, which appeared to be a beautiful and welcoming sight.

The stately hall exuded a warm glow. The shades of crimson reflected the smoldering embers in the grand fireplace, which crowned the room with rustic elegance.

The atmosphere appeared so relaxing to the happy couple as they inhaled jasmine's subtle aroma, infused throughout the great room. The pleasant sound of cedar logs crackling in the fireplace gave it that unique and intimate feeling of warmth.

The hunting lodge's rustic appeal conflicted with the elegance of splendid Persian carpets and inlaid furniture. An assortment of vintage firearms and hunting prices hanging prominently on the walls completing the surroundings' charm.

Diana was attracted to an impressive collection of shiny swords from different parts of the world, decorating with their striking beauty the patrician environment.

The young bride had always admired the prominent collection during her previous visit to the lodge. Since swordsmanship was one of Diana's favorite sports, she excelled in it, having studied fencing as a very young girl.

Suddenly, the sight of a beautiful bouquet of long-stemmed, white roses attracted her attention. A cloud of baby breath used in bridal floral arrangements surrounded the flowers with beauty. The lovely offering was displayed in an elegant porcelain vase and rested on a nearby table. The enclosed card was a congratulatory message from Prince Louis on the occasion of their marriage.

The couple smiled with appreciation and gratitude for all the generosity and affection displayed by their friend. His lodge's use for their wedding night was a cherished gift, which enhanced their young lives' most memorable occasion.

While Diana was distracted, the Zamindar exchanged a few private words with Emma before she discreetly disappeared into the mansion's upper rooms to make final preparation for their wedding night. In the interim, Luigi had taken possession of the carriage and quickly removed it from sight.

Rami and Diana were finally alone in the privacy of the lodge, eager to celebrate the first night of their wedded bliss.

They remained silent while basking joyously in the warmth and privacy of the vast hall.

Ramakanta walked toward a large silver plate filled with white, oval-shaped candies and offered one to Diana as he indulged in one himself. He was very impressed by the delicious taste and asked the name of the desserts.

"They are called "Confetti," she answered, "and are a special delicacy indigenous to Italy, dating back to ancient Rome...They are considered a sign of good luck, health, and long life, often used for weddings when their color is pure white."

"I think we should have another since they bring so much luck," answered the Zamindar as he placed one more candy in Diana's mouth.

He kissed her passionately before she had the chance to swallow the tasty dessert and whispered in her ear.

"I must admit, my darling, that the confetti's do not compare, delicious as they are to the sweetness of your lips."

Diana smiled in appreciation and unexpectedly invited the Zamindar to sit on one of the chairs, resting against the wall.

She then retreated gracefully in the large area while he looked on with anticipation and surprise.

For a moment, Diana stood erect and dignified. She then bowed and lifted with grace and style the hem of her wedding gown, which dragged onto the floor. Without further delay, she initiated an unexpected dance to the surprise and delight of her groom. The young woman began moving with amazing grace while spinning freely with exquisite skill as the gown's soft chiffon fabric lifted into the air and displayed the beauty of her long, shapely legs. It was a dance of agility as she incorporated the challenging jete' or ballet leaps with the ease and grace of a butterfly.

The Zamindar was captivated by the sensual, artistic beauty of the movements and deeply impressed by her outstanding ability as a ballet dancer. It was a bold fascinating side of his bride, which he never suspected but much admired.

Ramakanta was familiar with Ballet since, during his father's regime as the Zamindar, dance troupes performed at his estate in India, during art exchanges with the western world.

His father had explained that Ballet was an elite form of dancing, which originated in the 15th century during the Italian Renaissance and was regarded as a unique art form.

He was now overwhelmed by the beauty of the dance and Diana's grace and elegance. She was a surprisingly strong woman, and yet so soft and feminine, as she stood seductively before him bowing gracefully.

"I had no idea, darling, that you were such a talented dancer," said the Zamindar overwhelmed by the beauty of the moment."

"Ballet lessons were a compulsory part of my teachings as I was growing up," answered Diana with a smile as a pink glow appeared on her cheeks.

She then moved toward him and sat happily on his lap, and placed her head lovingly on his chest while saying.

"I am so glad you liked my wedding dance since it was dedicated to you, my dearest husband, in honor of our special day."

The Zamindar was more fascinated than ever by his beautiful and unpredictable bride, with her exciting disposition and free spirit.

"I love everything about you," he said as he kissed her ardently, overwhelmed by passion. The repressed emotions kept in check during the celebrations came suddenly to the surface, in the enticing solitude of the lodge.

He knew that the helpful Emma, with discretion, must have made her exit through the servant's quarters, and they were finally, truly alone.

The plush elegance of a carpet by the fireplace suddenly attracted him, which appeared enticing and inviting.

He suddenly lifted his bride in his arms and deposited her by the warmth of the fireplace, then invited her to rest upon the soft carpet, conveniently placed before it.

Diana obliged willingly and stretched with relish her lovely body on the enticing softness of the carpet. She seemed so peaceful and radiant, almost luminous in the warmth of the firelight.

The Zamindar looked on breathlessly at her beauty. The long silky hair framed her face like a shiny halo as the embers of the fire tinted her face with crimson. She waited with a look of longing in her eyes, so lovely in the soft golden light as she extended her arms toward him.

He hastened by her side, burning with desire, and caressed her long, flowing tresses with a sensual touch that brought pleasurable shivers through her spine.

She was supremely seductive in that moment of sensuality with an alluring invitation.

They kissed passionately in their endless desire for one another, which burned brighter than the embers in the fireplace. He caressed with a gentle touch the sensual curves of her body and inhaled the lovely scent of her skin, which intoxicated him.

By now, the gown's light fabric was barely able to cover her body's disturbing perfection and the soft roundness of her breasts.

"I want you so much, my love," he whispered, overwhelmed by a consuming passion, as he began to remove gently but firmly the obstructions to his desire.

He could now see her long, beautiful legs emerging from the veils as he marveled at her shapely ankles and the silky smoothness of her skin. Zamindar was overwhelmed by her sight. It was like uncovering a priceless treasure while feasting on the beauty it presented. She reveled in the seduction of his muscular, manly arms, which were passionate and comforting at the same time.

Although she was equally engaged in their emotional tryst, Diana felt suddenly uneasy and overwhelmed by the moment's burning sensuality. It was a new experience in her young life since she never shared intimacy with any other man.

While her husband's burning gaze now challenged her innate shyness, she blushed violently, but the red amber's of the fire camouflaged the color rising within the whiteness of her complexion. She became uneasy and conflicted.

The Zamindar noticed her reticence and uneasiness to this most memorable moment in her young life. She was excited, willing, and yet still overwhelmed and afraid to give in to such raw passion that seemed somewhat primeval and without restraint to her.

He caressed her face gently to relax her tension and possible misgivings while whispering in her ears.

"Do not be afraid, my darling, you are safe in my arms, as you have been safe in them so many times before. Our love is timeless, precious, and should bring us only joy without any fears on the blessed occasion of our wedding."

She smiled in response since his arms around her felt comforting and strangely familiar, and she suddenly had a feeling of excitement and liberation.

"Yes, my Zamindar," she whispered. "I feel safe in your arms, and I now truly believe in having been in them many times before…"

He interrupted her words with a long, passionate kiss that removed uncertainty and objections with an all-consuming desire that seemed endless. Their bodies were more volatile than the raging fire burning before them in the restraint of the fireplace. Her silky skin, barely shielded by the delicate fabric, intoxicated the Zamindar. He slid his strong arms about her and held her so close that she had to catch her breath. Diana felt an overwhelming warmth and desire taking over her body, as well. Their lingering kiss was more sensual than ever before, as their bodies united in ecstasy on the soft, luxurious embrace of the carpet.

Their burning desire permeated the room as the magnitude of their emotions became so intense that they were overwhelmed by it. They realized that the joy they felt in each other's arms was unlike anything they experienced before. Perhaps a superior, benevolent power had reunited them as ideal soul-mates from lives long past and blessed them with the perfect night of love.

Finally, the sensual turmoil subsided, and their bodies relaxed, exhausted by the intensity of their fiery passion. They both felt satisfied and complete in that moment of unison, as they had become one in their ecstasy. The aroma of jasmine seemed more fragrant to the happy couple in their most magical and memorable moment.

Soon after, Rami and Diana hand-in-hand climbed the central staircase to the upper floor and finally entered their lavish bed-chamber. The room was perfect for marital bliss but had been deferred temporarily to the carpet and the fireplace's romantic allure.

They were overwhelmed by the magnetism of their magical night, which seemed endless, as they gazed on the inviting bed, which crowned the room with elegance. It was covered by a beautiful damask comforter in soft shades of pink, with white satin sheets, delicately and artistically embroidered.

Diana noticed a beautiful, long-stemmed red rose on a pillow, which gave the ambiance a romantic touch. A lovely parchment envelope accompanied it addressed with golden letters to "My Zamindarin."

Diana was touched by the tender offering and immediately took possession of the elegant letter, which filled her with a sense of joy.

"Thank you, dear Zamindar?" She said with a bright smile on her face as she eagerly prepared to break the seal.

"Please, my love, do not open it just yet," he answered as he gently touched her hand."

"I asked Emma to place it on your pillow as a small surprise and an additional token of my love."

"I look forward to the special surprise," Diana answered, "and as a benevolent omen to the beginning of our wonderful life together."

Diana was thrilled by the surrounding, enhanced by the moon's shimmering light that filtered through the windows with a silvery glow.

She retrieved the red rose and inhaled with joy the beautiful aroma that radiated from the bloom. Then without further reticence, she disappeared into the connecting dressing room of the lavish bedroom suite.

Left alone, the Zamindar entered his dressing area where a tub filled with warm, scented water had been prepared for his comfort by the efficient Emma.

After the relaxing interlude, Ramakanta, dressed in an elegant silk housecoat, gazed with admiration and satisfaction at the beautiful and peaceful surroundings. Like a magical dream, there was the fulfillment of a perfect wedding night's celebration. He now paced the room a bit impatiently as he waited for his bride to reappear.

Finally, Diana made her entrance, and she was a vision to behold in a white lace nightgown, topped by a matching housecoat that draped elegantly to the floor. The ensemble complimented her tall and shapely figure, which appeared through the fabric's delicate transparencies.

She looked almost ethereal in the soft light of the room, with her cascading hair resting on her shoulders and shimmering in the moonlight, as she approached one of the stately windows.

There was an enticing glow on her face, and the exciting emotion didn't escape the Zamindar's vigilant eyes. He was immediately by her side and placed his loving arm firmly about her waist.

"As I look at you in the moonlight, you are an enchanting vision," he whispered in her ear.

"I rejoice in all our blessings and the amazing gift of happiness."

The Zamindar gently caressed her flowing hair and kissed her lips before saying.

"It is time for my little surprise, darling. I saved it for the end of this eventful and amazing day. The gift is a special poem I composed in honor of my bride on the blessed day of our wedding. Emma, on my request, placed it on your pillows, and I now wish to recite it to you…"

"Thank you, my love," interposed Diana with great emotions. "I know your priceless gift will be the crowning glory to this joyous and perfect day."

~ My Zamindarin ~

As you emerge with the splendor and loveliness of the rising Venus from the magical brush of the master Sandro Botticelli. With the allure and glory of your form drawn in classic sensuality. You project an eternal cycle of life at the altar of my fantasy.

Allow me to initiate my nocturnal odyssey in the silken abode of cascading jasmine fragrance of your waist-long tresses, framing in beauty the outlines of your sensual femininity, in the seductiveness of your swan-neck and the smooth contour of your lovely shape.

The virgin undercurrent, which flows pristine like a crystalline shower but will soon become riveting and overpowering like the force of a monsoon, I will gladly succumb to the earthy scent of the pristine soil of your essence. Let me linger in ecstasy at the undercurrent of your virginal lake that flows through your body with endless desire.

As spring sets in and unleashes a plethora of scents, from gardens and wildflowers, nectar oozes out of the unfolding petals of your rosy lips.

I bend my knees in loving reverence to the splendor of your anatomy. I plant burning kisses as warm as summer on your silky skin as I enter my world of desire through the seductiveness of your personal firmament.

The Zamindar's Bride

I kiss you passionately, my Zamindarin, an eternal prisoner of the elusive spring and helplessly entrapped by the magnetism and softness of your lips. I plant burning kisses upon your cool, soft skin and spread with un-refrained desire a blanket of my passion upon you, eternally.

§§§

CHAPTER TEN

THE COLORS OF INDIA

The fateful day of Ramakanta and Diana's trip to India finally arrived and proved to be emotionally painful for the young bride. Diana had to face the difficult task of saying good-bye to her country and all the people she loved.

Aunt Amelie was visibly distraught as she escorted the couple to the pier accompanied by Prince Louis. He was also at hand to bid the Zamindar and Diana good-bye.

For days Lady Amelie had been haunted by unexplained fears that some danger might be lurking in the path of her beloved niece, who was moving to a faraway land and a very different culture.

"I will visit you soon," she finally said, as she embraced the young woman with a brave smile, as burning tears flowed down her face.

"Please take care, my dear Diana. I pray the good Lord to keep you safe in all the steps of your life."

Noticing the two women's difficulty in dealing with the stressful situation, the Prince intervened in his usual calm and positive way.

"There is no need for sadness since aunt Amelie and I will visit India very soon. It's only a temporary separation, and we will be together again."

He then held Diana's hand, attempting to dispel her concerns about leaving aunt Amelie alone.

"My dear, please don't worry about aunt Amelie. She will be fine since I considered her to be a valued member of my family."

"Thank you so much, dear Louis, for all your help and kindness…I will miss you almost as much as my beloved aunty," said Diana in tears.

With gallantry, the Prince handed a handkerchief as he embraced her warmly while saying.

"Be happy, my dearest little sister, go peacefully with God's blessings and my very best wishes."

"Thank you, my dear friend," said the Zamindar, deeply moved by the Prince's kindness and generosity. He had remained discreetly apart, allowing Diana to say a proper good-bye to all the people she loved, as he continued.

"I hope Louis that you will honor us soon, with a visit to my country, in the company of dear aunt Amelie. You will both be very welcomed guests in my estate."

"It will be my great pleasure to visit India, my friend, and I give my word that we will both visit very soon," answered the Prince.

By now, the intermittent sound of a horn signaled to all the passengers the vessel's imminent departure.

Without further ado, the couple climbed the many steps connecting the pier to the ship, and with the last wave good-bye, they quickly disappeared into the interior of the ocean liner.

The Zamindar's Bride

They later stood together on the deck as the vessel began to sail away from the Italian shores, slowly but deliberately distancing Diana's beloved country.

The beautiful sloping green hills were becoming progressively smaller on the horizon, as a gentle mist covered the landscape in a mighty veil, giving it the appearance of a mirage or a lovely dream.

The Zamindar could feel the overwhelming emotion Diana was experiencing in that cruel moment of separation as her beloved country slowly disappeared in the distance.

"How are you feeling, my darling?" He whispered with concern.

"I see so much sadness in your eyes, although it's understandable under the circumstances..."

"Forgive me, dearest," answered Diana while attempting to smile.

"I do not wish to spoil even a moment that we spend together. It is just that I..."

"Please tell me what is troubling you, my love?" Insisted the Zamindar," I feel your body trembling in my arms, and I don't understand the reason for such sudden fear. Are you feeling well?

"No need to worry, I am fine," answered Diana while caressing his face with love.

"I have difficulty in explaining it since it's a mystery to me as well...Just now, and without warning, I was suddenly overwhelmed by a sense of doom...It felt as if the icy hand of death had touched my shoulder with an ominous warning..."

"The hands of death?" Interrupted, the Zamindar shocked and disturbed by her words since he believed in the power of premonition and respected its meaning.

However, he was unwilling to frighten her and suggested that it was due to departing from her homeland.

"There is nothing to be concerned about, my love. Please don't dwell on it. I am certain that those disturbing feelings are due to the excitement and anxiety of the many changes that are about to take place in your life, and nothing more."

"I am sure you are right, Rami," answered Diana, attempting bravely to put a smile on her face, "but at the time, it seemed so real and ominous as if death or a deadly peril awaits me..."

"No danger is waiting for you, my love," interjected the Zamindar, "because you are safe as long as we are together, I pledge my life to that end."

"Forgive me, my dear Zamindar, I do not wish to worry you," answered Diana with a renewed sense of optimism.

"Perhaps it's because I am suddenly afraid that this great happiness may not last because it's too perfect and wonderful..."

In response, the Zamindar lifted her chin and kissed her lips with great passion, holding her close in the loving entrapment of his arms.

Diana smiled, and the disturbing sadness disappeared as she snuggled close to the Zamindar, finding joy and comfort in his arms.

"I love you, my darling," he whispered, "thank you for coming into my life. I value the sacrifice you are making, and I only wish to take your pain away and make it my own..."

Diana silenced him by placing a finger on his lips as she smiled through her tears. She then rested her head on his chest while whispering.

"My country is where you are, dearest. I look forward to seeing beautiful India, meeting your people, and sharing my life with you..."

The Zamindar interrupted her words with a loving kiss, and at least for the moment, in each other arms, there was contentment and optimism for the future, without the ominous fear of possible danger.

Finally, after many difficult and challenging days in the high sea because of stormy weather, India's arrival was imminent.

Diana was very interested in her new adoptive country. She asked many questions about the geography of the land and the location of the port of entry.

"We will arrive in Calcutta, my darling. The historical city is located on the eastern bank of the Hooghly River, a distributor of the sacred River Ganga, and located on the Bay of Bengal's western side," answered the Zamindar.

"I have heard of Calcutta, Rami, which is a large and populous city in India, but I know very little else about it," said Diana as she stared in the distance, attempting to see if the land was becoming visible in the far horizon."

The Zamindar's Bride

The Zamindar was delighted about his wife's interest in learning about his country and tried to answer her questions in the best way possible.

"How is the political climate right now?" she asked, "since India is presently under British occupation."

"There is trouble brewing dearest since Indian people resent English presence on our soil." Answered the Zamindar, "however, the Bengal Presidency administrative headquarters are located in Calcutta, also the governing power, and the economic, cultural and educational hub of the British Raj…The Governor-General of Bengal is concurrently the Viceroy of India."

Ramakanta paused for a brief moment, appearing a bit serious before continuing.

"Darling, you are aware that the British occupation was instrumental to my family's power and fortune, including the important title of Choudhury…However, I agree with my people's rightful demand for independence, and they will always have my support."

Diana was impressed by her husband's patriotism as she continued asking with increased interest.

"You resent the British presence in India, even though they have been generous to you and your family?"

"Of course, I appreciate all the wealth and considerable power that I have," answered the Zamindar. "But foremost, I am an Indian man, and any personal gain must take second place to what is just and fair for all the people."

A shadow of sadness flashed upon his face as he continued the fascinating recount of the wealth and power of the Choudhury dynasty under the British regime."

Dearest, there are many pitfalls connected with my country's invasion by a foreign power, even for Zamindars. One sad example is the *Sunset law*, created during the British occupation by Lord Cornwallis, and is generally regarded as one of the most draconian laws ever. It stipulates that the Zamindars shall deposit their revenues to the British government before sunset of a given day, without exception. The smallest infraction in taxes' payment will face harsh measures. Their land will be confiscated without the possibility of pardon or any period of grace."

"You mean that your power is hanging by a thread?" She finally said with surprise, "even considering your efforts to improve and modernize the cultivation of the fertile lands, for a more prosperous life for all the people involved?"

"Yes, dearest," answered the Zamindar, "unfortunately this is the law today, unfair and disappointing as it is...Of course, my family, through generations, has amassed great wealth. Even without the title and the land, there is no fear of poverty. However, it's a different story for all the people who cultivate the land. With all probability, they could become victims of the exploitation of the new people in charge."

"That is truly unscrupulous," said Diana, frustrated by the unfairness of the circumstances."

"Don't be upset, my darling," said the Zamindar, "life is unfair at times, and we all know it...Although significant changes are taking place, and I have faith that soon again, my country will belong to the Indian people."

They both smiled with a renewed sense of optimism for India and in their future life together.

AN EVENTFUL ARRIVAL

Diana's first glance at her new adoptive country was the bustling port of Kolkata, with a large and tumultuous crowd. She had never witnessed such a massive gathering of people in one place before, as she looked on with wonder at the picturesque scene. The young bride marveled at the exotic view and felt a sense of joy in the lively surroundings since they seemed welcoming to her.

She was fascinated by the lovely Indian ladies in their beautiful sarees, gracing the scene with garments in bright shades of the rainbow.

The fascination was mutual since Diana soon became the center of attention in the crowded scene. Men and women alike stared with curiosity at the beautiful western woman who walked with such graceful flair by the Zamindar.

She looked lovely in a lavender gown with a tight corset that showcased so well her slender waist and tall, shapely figure. A matching parasol topped the elegant ensemble.

She was a bit overwhelmed by all the attention and attempted a friendly smile as she moved closer to the Zamindar, who protectively held her by the waist.

They were soon respectfully guided to a waiting carriage, and Diana was relieved to find shelter from all the unsettling attention, which was unwelcomed by her shy nature.

The Zamindar smiled as he held her close to him, noticing the tint of crimson that brightened her cheeks.

"You are blushing, my darling," he said as he caressed her face with a loving touch.

"Please tell me about your first impression of India since you seem a bit overwhelmed by the surroundings?"

"Calcutta at first glance looks exciting and colorful," answered Diana, "it seems like a very welcoming and friendly place...However, I am a bit surprised by all the attention I am receiving since I am shy by nature."

"They are staring because you are so beautiful, my love," answered the Zamindar with a smile.

"But, there is no cause for concern since I am always vigilant and protective by your side."

"I am not concerned, dearest," said Diana while glancing with interest at the crowd.

Adriana Girolami

"The place seems so full of life. I am pleased to be in my adopted home. But where are we going now?"

"We are taking a carriage ride to the train station on our way to Cuttack," answered the Zamindar, "which is the next leg of our journey, and a large city in the eastern state of Orissa on the Bay of Bengal."

Ramakanta then unfolded a small map finely engraved and pointed to it while saying to Diana.

"Look darling, in this area is located the twin city of Bhubaneswar, which is close to Cuttack and stands near the ruins of Sisupalgarh, the ancient capital of the former province of Kalinga, renamed as Orissa…The historic areas in and around Bhubaneswar go back to the 7th century BC. It is a confluence of Hindu, Buddhist, and Jain heritage boasting of some of the finest Kalingan temples…"

"It sounds so interesting, dearest," interposed Diana, "a beautiful and exotic new world opening before me."

"I will help you explore it," said the Zamindar, "and someday we will visit Bhubaneswar, which is home to hundreds of temples dating back many centuries. I know you will find it exciting and

224

interesting because of your great love for history and archeology."

"Please tell me more, dearest, of the fascinating history of Orissa and Cuttack. Since it will be my newly adopted home, I like to learn as much as possible about this unique land and its people.

The Zamindar had a vast knowledge of his state's distinguished history and was proud to share it with his bride.

"The earliest history of Cuttack goes back to the Keshari dynasty, while present-day Cuttack was established as a military cantonment by king Nrupa of the Keshari dynasty in 989. However, there are several historical suggestions that Cuttack became the capital of a kingdom founded by Raja Anangabhimadeva III of the Ganga Dynasty in 1211."

Diana listened with fascination at the historical accounting as the Zamindar continued.

"We take pride in our land, whether in a historical text or even through word-of-mouth…As the Ganga rule ended, Orissa came under the Suryavamsi Gajapati Dynasty during the years 1434 to 1541, in which time, Cuttack continued to be the capital of Orissa. However, after Raja Mukunda

Deva's death, the last Hindu king of Orissa, Cuttack, first came under Muslim rule and later under the Mughals. They made Cuttack the seat of the new Orissa Subah, an Imperial top-level province, under Shah Jahan..."

"The evolution of your country," interposed Diana, "is similar to the history of Italy, which suffered invasions of many people from different lands."

"Yes, dearest, the history of the world is in some way always connected," answered the Zamindar.

"Many people have walked on this land, but somehow India always remained proud and strong...We Indians value our great history and our splendid cultural and spiritual heritage," added the Zamindar with dignity and pride.

"You have so many sacred places in India," said Diana, "the religious aspects seem to be very much part of your society...I know that the world-renowned Ganges River is considered sacred by the people."

The Zamindar smiled, pleased by her thirst for knowledge, as he answered.

"Yes, my love, the Ganga River is considered sacred and honored by our people. The Hindu religion traditions are vital to the majority of Indians and the center of our lives. For thousands of years, we have been worshiping our many idols with reverence and devotion. Little changes have occurred, despite the countless generations and the passing of time."

The young woman remained silent, overtaken by a strange feeling. She focused on her life's path, which had changed so drastically since the Zamindar's appearance. The possibility that they might have been married before in several lifetimes still lingered and continued to be a conflict since it contrasted sharply with her beliefs as a Christian.

"I think of having slighted my beliefs," she said with sadness, "although, I have accepted the difference in our religions…But an uneasy feeling came over me when you mentioned the worshiping of idols since idolatry is considered a mortal sin in my religion. It felt that in some way, I betrayed all that I believed and respected."

"No, my darling, you must not have those negative feelings," the Zamindar insisted.

"Idols depict images to those who crave to see metaphors of their gods …I only believe in the abstract of a Supreme Being, despite how it's portrayed…For me, it's a matter of faith that we are all the children of God, regardless of the name we choose to give it. This premise brings people together, rather than encourage dissent and hatred."

Diana was pleased by the answer and said.

"You are right, dearest. God wishes for all the people to live in harmony. I don't believe he favors any special groups since we are all his creation and his children."

The young bride continued with a happier sound in her voice.

"I think it's now time to move on and embrace my present life with joy. I look forward to learning as much as possible about my beautiful adoptive country."

The Zamindar was pleased as he pointed to the train station that was fast approaching.

"We will now travel to Cuttack, dearest. The Millennium City and Silver City due to their history of 1000 years and famous silver filigree. If you wish, you might be able to purchase some of the beautiful jewelry manufactured there and sent it as gifts to your family and friends."

"It sounds so wonderful, Rami," said Diana with excitement in her voice, "I feel happy while discovering the many facets of this great land and the historical beauty of India."

The Millennium City

At their eventful arrival in Cuttack, Diana began shopping with enthusiasm and the helpful guidance of the Zamindar.

They entered the old, an essential part of the city centered on a strip of land between the Kathajodi River and the Mahanadi River, bounded on the southeast by the famous Old Jagannath Road.

As she entered on her exciting discovery journey, Diana soon learned that the typical Indian bazaars are the best sensory guides to its diversity. The sense of organized chaos was an enthralling and overwhelming experience for the young woman—the kind of shopping where every purchase is unique and always has an exciting story to tell.

She marveled at the exquisite silverwork executed by talented artisans and purchased many beautiful jewelry pieces for family and friends with great appreciation for the artistry.

Suddenly her eyes were drawn by a splendid silver tea set, shimmered in the sunlight behind a glass enclosure.

The silver set appeared to be in the classical European styling, with delicate and intricate engravings very reminiscent of the exquisite Florentine craft.

Diana was intrigued by it, and she moved closer to have a better look and was stunned to discover that the beautiful set was manufactured in Florence, Italy.

The shop's owner, noticing the distinguished guest's interest, quickly approached Diana and explained that he had purchased the tea set on a trip to Italy.

Being an expert in silver manufacturing, he was very impressed by the Florentine styling and artistry. He was now proud to display the silver tea set in one of his many stores.

Diana was stunned by the happy coincidence of having found the beautiful Italian tea set on her first shopping spree in India. She then asked the shop owner if the tea set was for sale because she wished to purchase it.

The man answered that it was not for sale, but he would gladly make an exception since she was interested in it. Diana was thrilled by the answer and said to Rami with excitement in her voice.

"I believe that the silver tea set will make an appropriate gift for your mother. I wish to give her a souvenir from my country and an expression of my affection for her. Unfortunately, in Italy, I had no time to purchase an appropriate gift. Do you think she will like it?"

The Zamindar, who was busy talking with the shop owner, approached Diana and said approvingly.

"It is quite beautiful, my darling, and very expensive too, according to the price just quoted. It's a thoughtful and generous gift that anyone would appreciate, including my mother."

At that exciting moment, Diana failed to notice her husband's lack of enthusiasm since her optimistic nature always guided her. She hoped to develop a relationship with her very traditional mother-in-law since she knew how important it was to her husband. After all, she was the one who had given birth to the man she loved, considering that fact she had a deep sense of respect and affection for Laxmi Devi.

Diana thought that the best course of action would be to try and make her understand how much she loved her son and her willingness to respect and learn about her culture.

Unfortunately, regardless of her good intentions, the Zamindar had given little hope to any possibility of compromise on the part of Laxmi Devi. But she thought that the challenging situation was important enough to give it a try.

At that point, they had decided to spend a few extra days in Cuttack before their final destination to the Zamindar's estate in Kendrapara. He asked the shop owner to have the silver tea set delivered to his mother, with a special note of greeting from his bride, hoping that the sign of affection and respect would somehow break the ice before their arrival.

The journey to Kendrapara proved exciting and full of surprises for the new Zamandarin. As the excursion progressed they finally, reached the Mahanadi river bank.

The Zamindar's Bride

Diana was thrilled by the sight of a beautifully decorated boat waiting for them in the tranquil waters of the mighty river. It seemed so romantic to her, as if she was living in a fairy tale.

The elegant vessel was a particular sign of respect for the Zamindar and his bride and used in bringing the distinguished couple to the other side of the river.

Ramakanta was elated by the special homecoming after his eventful journey to Europe, especially Italy's memorable vacation.

Before stepping onto the boat, Diana's eyes were suddenly drawn to an old sailor, surrounded by a small group of people by the riverbank. The man spoke with great emphasis, and the young woman was fascinated by the scene.

Unfortunately, she could not understand the language the man was speaking and asked.

"Rami, can you tell me what the man is saying? I would like to know?"

The Zamindar was pleased to see her interest in his country, as he answered.

"He is a maritime trader explaining trade relationships through the years, focusing on the golden age of Kalinga's hoary past."

"That sounds so interesting, Rami. Could you please translate it for me? I like to hear what he has to say."

The Zamindar consented with a smile and began the English translation, which was their form of communication.

"The man explains that the saga of maritime exploration and trade is part of Orissa's folklore and festivals, held with great nostalgia by the people. It began at the end of the second century BC when Kalingan mariners, through studies, learned to utilize the monsoon winds and ocean currents, which were present during mid-November. Their ships would use the north-eastern monsoon winds' power, combined with the ocean currents, to sail across the Indian Ocean and Sumatra's northern tip. They also ventured in the Straits of Malacca towards Palembang, Borneo, Vietnam, Bali, and Java. After finishing their trade activities, most ships would use the counter-current with the early South-West monsoon winds to bring them back home…"

"They were very ingenious, interposed Diana in finding a way to use nature in such a positive way."

That is true, said the Zamindar while guiding

Diana aboard the decorated boat as he continued the narration.

"You see, darling, one of their most important Indian export used to be our cotton textiles whose incomparable beauty remains popular even today."

"I know, dearest," I have noticed the unparalleled beauty of the fabrics of India," answered Diana, "the talent and creativity of the people are also well known."

"There are many different talents that my people are very proud of," answered the Zamindar. "During excavations in South East Asia, various semiprecious stones, different types of metals for trade and commerce were discovered. By the first century, the Kalingan merchants traded with Mediterranean countries, including the Romans, Greeks, and Arabs. Also, the valuable maritime trade helped the economic development and cultural assimilation of the whole region."

"The Indian maritime traders were also trading with the Romans?" Asked Diana with excitement and surprise, "I think it's a wonderful coincidence that a connection with our countries existed so long ago."

"Yes, my love, and now we are together in the present, which is all that matters..."

The Zamindar paused and smiled while saying.

"This time, you will enjoy together the festival of *Bali Jatra*, which remains the largest trade festival in India, and the name means a voyage to Bali. People came in masses to Cuttack and purchased large varieties of imported goods. Bali Jatra continues till today as a favorite festival that honors this ancient tradition."

"Thank you, dearest, for all the pertinent information that truly fascinates me. Although, I will have to absorb it a little at the time," said Diana, a bit overwhelmed by all the fascinating pieces of information.

They finally reached the opposite bank of the river on the way to her new home. Diana marveled at the beauty of the pastoral surrounding and the lively and picturesque streets filled with people, happy to welcome their beloved Zamindar back home.

Diana was proud and impressed by her husband's connection to the people. It was apparent he was respected as a kind and benevolent ruler.

However, most surprising was the friendly

welcome she received from the good people of Kendrapara, who greeted her with warmth and joy.

Their display of affection deeply moved the young woman as petals of flowers and dry rice were thrown in grand profusion in the path of their carriage.

However, there was a sense of reverence toward them, which sharply delineated the caste system of the Indian society and the social difference between the peasantry and the aristocrats, which proved a bit disturbing to Diana.

Discrimination also existed in the western world, with separation and bigotry based on social status. But it was more apparent here, by the humble demeanor of some of the people, which made no eye contact and lowered their heads with great respect, as their carriage approached them.

Diana was grateful and tried to connect with them as she waived happily with a bright smile on her face and very appreciative of all the friendly people that made her feel so welcome in her new adoptive country.

The Zamindar, who had been very concerned about the reception she might receive, was greatly relieved in seeing Diana's joy and excitement on their entrance in Kendrapara.

He loved her spontaneity and warmth, lacking the usual snobbery of people born to wealth and privilege. She exuded a friendly aura that always made individuals feel comfortable and welcomed in her presence.

Ramakanta smiled with approval as she gathered some of the petals of flowers from the carriage floor and held them close to her heart.

"Are you happy, my darling?" he said lovingly, "welcome to our home, and I hope your walk through life will always be joyous and enhanced by the scent and beauty of flowers."

"How poetic," she gushed while snuggling closer to him. But in that romantic moment, she suddenly noticed a quick contraction of his body in response to her overt display of affection.

She understood that her husband was now back in his world, and his demeanor as the Zamindar was more dignified than the free spirit she met during his vacation in Europe.

Diana immediately regained a more proper posture, befitting the occasion, while saying with an understanding smile.

"Please forgive me, dearest. It is not my intention to diminish the dignity expected in front of your people."

"Our people," answered the Zamindar.

"My reaction was just a force of habit and tradition because, in reality, I am the happiest when you are close to me, my love... Please forgive me."

"There is nothing to forgive. We have the same etiquette back home in Italy. Even if, at times, I find it a bit annoying. It was just that I was overwhelmed by the beauty of the moment and felt truly happy."

"This is my dearest wish," answered the Zamindar," for you to be happy and welcomed in my country as you have been today, among the affection of our people."

Diana paused and looked deeply into his eyes as she asked.

"Do you think your mother will welcome me?"

"Hopefully, my love," answered the Zamindar with a more subdued tone of voice as he lowered his eyes toward the ground.

The magical interlude and joyous entrance in Kendrapara seemed spoiled in that moment of uncertainty. The rest of the carriage ride toward the Zamindar's estate was less cheerful, while an uncomfortable silence had suddenly taken over. They were about to face their biggest obstacle since their marriage, and an uneasy feeling overwhelmed them.

Diana had great respect for her family and culture. However, in contrast to that repressive time in history, she received great latitude to choose the course of her destiny.

The young woman had the greatest love and respect for her parents and gratefulness for the gift of freedom to retain her individuality.

She understood that it was very different for the Zamindar, raised to believe that the family and Hindu religion were central to his world. Obedience was paramount, and the will of the family always took precedence over independent thinking.

By marrying a woman of a different culture, he had broken a sacred tradition, and Diana feared that the repercussion would be harsh as far as his mother was concerned. Her rejection and disapproval would undoubtedly cause him great sorrow.

Noticing her uneasiness, Rami held her hand tightly as they approached his beautiful estate on the bank of the mighty Mahanadi River.

By now, it was getting close to sunset, and the golden rays of the sun were giving way to the impending shadows of darkness while a cool, refreshing breeze was present in the air.

Diana was overwhelmed by the lovely sight. It was even more appealing than she had expected.

A sense of tranquility was infused in the environment, which gave the young bride a feeling of peace as they finally arrived at the Zamindar's palace's front entrance.

Staff members of the estate were present, standing respectfully in line, ready to welcome the Zamindar and his bride back home.

Ramakanta immediately noticed that his mother was missing from the welcoming comity since it was customary for Laxmi Devi to be at hand to greet all the important guests to the estate.

"Where is my mother?" he asked with an imperious tone in his voice to one of the attending guards. The obvious displeasure was written all over the Zamindar's face, and the guard appeared intimidated by it, as he answered with polite deference.

"Her Ladyship is waiting for your arrival in the vestibule because there is a cool breeze in the air, and she found it uncomfortable out here… She begs your indulgence for the inconvenience."

Diana, who had been standing discreetly apart, touched his hand gently, and with a comforting sound, she said.

"It is a bit breezy, dearest. It would have been unwise for your mother to stand here and perhaps catch a chill. It will be pleasant to meet her in the vestibule.

His wife's classy and positive demeanor diminished Ramakanta's anger. Her presence was for him a great source of joy, mitigating his displeasure.

He gazed at her with love and admiration since she was more stunning than ever in a blue satin gown with Venetian lace inlays around her décolletage and sleeves. The ever-present, matching parasol completed the elegant attire, enhanced by her innate grace and sense of style.

The Zamindar looked equally smart and handsome with a Jacquard Sherwani jacket and white pants. A turban restrained his unruly hair, and he looked every inch the aristocratic leader of the people as he guided his bride toward the stately doors and accessed the interior of the palace.

.

§§§

CHAPTER ELEVEN

THE SILVER TEA SET

It was the end of the day. The incoming sunset was diffusing the last vestige of light in preparation for nightfall.

The bucolic scene of greenery and open spaces, which had given Diana a feeling of joy and hope, was now lessened as anxiety emerged in the incumbent rising of darkness.

The apparent cold and unfriendly welcome from her mother-in-law didn't diminish Diana's optimism at the first sign of trouble. However, the short walk to the entrance seemed a lot longer since, according to the protocol, she had to walk by her husband's side without holding on to his arm, which would have helped the stressful moment.

On her entrance to the palace, she experienced a sense of awe at the beauty of the vestibule. She marveled at the delicate mosaics, which decorated the space with exotic and intricate designs. The entire area was faithful to the grand Indian style, with graceful archways, high ceilings, and ornamental structure, which must have satisfied for generations the refined taste of the aristocratic dwellers.

There was a solemn feeling of peace in the area, although at the moment, there was no one in sight to welcome the newlyweds. The young woman felt uneasy about entering the unfamiliar surroundings, coupled with the unpleasant feeling of being openly rejected in her new home.

Diana glanced at her husband, who smiled in a sign of encouragement. She quickly regained her cheerful demeanor and smiled back at the Zamindar, attracted by a beautifully detailed statue of an Idol with the head of an elephant.

She was fascinated by the Deity's whimsical appearance since she had never seen anything like it before. The statue appeared benevolent and friendly, as a smile brightened her face at the perception that at least the Indian Deity had made her feel welcome in her new home.

Noticing Diana's interest, the Zamindar gave his bride some general information about the elephant-headed God.

"His name is Ganesha, who is exceptionally beloved among the Hindu pantheon of gods, worshiped as the Lord of good fortune who provides prosperity and success. He is also the remover of obstacles of both material and spiritual kinds.

Diana smiled at the sound of those words while saying with a tinge of sadness in her voice.

"I suppose that with those exceptional attributes, he is the perfect God for us since we can certainly use some obstacles removers."

Ramakanta concurred with his bride, filled with frustration at the apparent rejection she received from his mother. He hoped that the unconditional love he had for her could offset the excessive rudeness from Laxmi Devi.

He continued with the elephant-headed God's description since it distracted Diana from her absurd and uncomfortable position.

"Ganesha is widely revered by almost all castes and in all parts of India. He is a patron of the arts, sciences, and the destroyer of vanity, arrogance, and hurdles…"

The Zamindar suddenly stopped speaking as two women suddenly made their entrance in the vestibule. The elder of the two, who appeared to be in charge, advanced a few steps toward them, then paused as her companion followed her lead.

At that point, they made no effort to welcome the bridal couple. Instead, the women remained motionless, apparently waiting for the Zamindar and his bride to approach them.

Diana looked with interest at the elder of the two women, who appeared to be the lady of the house by her patrician and dignified demeanor. However, a cold and unfriendly aura radiated from her.

None-the-less, her innate sense of style was impressive since she wore a splendid silk saree accented by precious jewels, which adorned her neck with aristocratic affluence and sparkled in the many lights of the vestibule.

The young woman understood that she must have been Laxmi Devi, the Dowager Zamindarin, and Ramakanta's mother.

Diana's heart skipped a beat at sight, dreading the uncomfortable meeting with her mother-in-law, whose demeanor appeared to be openly unfriendly.

To his dismay, the Zamindar recognized Aamani standing by his mother's side. She was the young woman selected by the stars and his family to become his bride.

A feeling of resentment overwhelmed him in witnessing his mother's deliberate abuse of power, and the cruel and open insult to his wife, besides the incredible breach of etiquette and respect toward him, as the Zamindar.

Regardless of his displeasure, he felt helpless to express his feelings at the moment, in deference to Diana since the young woman was oblivious of Aamani's true identity and his ruthless mother's scheming.

The Zamindar knew his mother to be an expert in palace protocol and was shocked by her disrespectful behavior toward his bride because of her staunch belief in proper etiquette.

He escorted Diana toward his mother and her companion with considerable self-control while bowing coldly to Laxmi Devi. He deliberately ignored Aamani, whose presence he considered offensive and intrusive.

He managed to suppress the harsh tone in his voice as he introduced his bride to her reluctant mother-in-law.

The young woman was still unaware of the full measure of rejection, and a friendly smile was on her face.

"Mother, it's my distinct pleasure to introduce to you my wife Diana, the former Countess De' Gautier, and now my beloved Zamindarin."

The honorable Laxmi Devi remained silent for a few moments as she stared at Diana with great intensity and then greeted the new bride with icy politeness.

"Welcome, my lady. I have received many reports of your loveliness. However, by seeing you in person, I believe that they were truly understated. It speaks clearly of my son's susceptibility to the allure of feminine beauty."

It was apparent to Diana that the compliment was, in reality, an accusation of having little to offer except for her physical attributes to capture the attention of her son.

She chose to ignore it with her usual class and instead answered politely to the unusual greeting.

"I thank you, my lady, for your kind words of praise and your gracious welcome."

A sardonic smile appeared on Laxmi Devi's face in response to the classy answer. She then moved toward her companion and said with a deliberate sound in her voice,"

"Please allow me to introduce to you my dearest daughter Aamani, who is a true blessing and a great source of joy in my life."

Diana remained silent for a moment, surprised by the introduction since her husband never mentioned that he had a sister.

Noticing her surprise by the uncomfortable silence, Laxmi Devi quickly clarified her words,

"Aamani is my recently adopted daughter…but because of the love I have for her, she is dear to me as my very own child."

"I am very pleased to meet my husband's sister," answered Diana graciously, extending her hand in greeting with a smile on her face.

Aamani answered with a polite bow but remained silent. She was intimidated and fully aware of the Zamindar's great displeasure of her presence in the palace.

The young woman appeared to be a pawn in a ruthless, psychological game of control and was powerless to do anything about it.

Ramakanta glared at his mother, unable to reconcile with her outrageous manipulations. Her irrational disdain toward Diana was almost a form of paranoia that had no possible religious derivation since Hinduism teaches love and not hate.

Laxmi Devi seemed oblivious to her son's displeasure and deliberately ignored him as she continued to talk to Diana with haughtiness.

"My lady, I wish to express my appreciation for the lovely gift of the Italian crafted, silver tea set. Although I am grateful for your generosity, I have always made a rule of using merchandise made by local artisans to help the business of our people, instead of using creations by silversmiths from foreign lands."

Laxmi Devi looked for an adverse reaction to her patronizing words, while Diana remained silent as she continued.

"Besides my lady, there are far too many tea sets at the estate, and I thought best to give it to my dear daughter Aamani since I am certain she will have better use for it."

"Mother!" exclaimed the Zamindar, unable to control his anger in response to his mother's unwarranted rudeness toward his wife.

Diana did not immediately react to the apparent rebuff and attempted instead to deflate the escalating situation. She was aware that Laxmi Devi purposely created dissent and decided not to allow her manipulations to control the situation.

She gently touched her husband's arm to diminish his distress as she addressed Laxmi Devi with her usual class and dignity.

I appreciate your effort to help your people, my lady, especially your talented local artisans. I am sure they are grateful for your support. I am also pleased that Lady Aamani will receive the silver tea set. I hope she will enjoy it as a symbol of friendship and affection between my country and yours."

"I thank you, my lady, said Aamani, impressed by her words, "I am most grateful for the special gift... I hope one day soon, to share with you a cup of tea with the silver set, in friendship."

"It will be my pleasure," said Diana, grateful to Aamani for her apparent friendliness.

Not knowing her true identity, Diana was glad to have met Rami's adoptive sister and hoped that she could become a friend to compensate for Laxmi Devi's blatant rejection of her.

The Zamindar was disturbed by the strange development and his wife's friendly overture toward Aamani. Since he wanted the young woman removed immediately from the palace before Diana found out who she was.

He felt it was of the greatest urgency to talk to his mother and assert himself as the person in charge and the only one with the power to decide who was allowed to live in the palace.

He signaled to a couple of attendees to come forward while saying with warmth to Diana.

"You must be tired from our long journey, my darling. It would be best if you go to our rooms where you will be able to make yourself comfortable. I will remain here a little while longer and speak to my mother in private, but I will join you as soon as possible."

"Yes, dearest, I will follow your advice," answered Diana, relieved by the suggestion and eager to have some privacy.

Without further ado, she quickly said good-bye to Laxmi Devi and Aamani, then escorted by the attendees, she disappeared through the imposing doorway.

The Dowager stood tall and defiant in front of her son, then immediately dismissed Aamani with a gesture of her hand.

The young woman appeared relieved by the command since it removed her from the embarrassing situation. She bowed politely and, with a speedy stride, left the vestibule.

Laxmi Devi's apparent affection toward the young woman centered on her need for control. Since the Dowager's unrelenting desire for Aamani to become the new Zamandarin was mostly based on the assumption that the girl was obedient, timid by nature, and easily manipulated.

However, unknown to the Dowager, Aamani was more ambitious than anyone would suspect. She carefully hid a willful and unyielding nature behind a demure veneer of shyness.

There was a great, secret passion for Ramakanta and the unrelenting dream of becoming the new Zamandarin. However, her reserved demeanor made it impossible to imagine that so much fire burned within her.

Laxmi Devi was the only hope left to archive her aims of power as the chosen companion to the man she so desperately desired.

Aamani held on to the possibility that Ramakanta and Diana's marriage would soon collapse because of all the unrelenting pressure induced by Laxmi Devi. She would then take her rightful place by the Zamindar's side as his bride.

However, so far, she had been bitterly disappointed by Diana's eventful appearance in the palace since she was more beautiful than expected, besides being intelligent and kind.

But what was most hurtful to the young woman was the love Ramakanta had for his wife and the great passion they shared, which was evident for all to see.

The jealousy Aamani experienced in witnessing their happiness was a cruel and devastating emotion. A burning poison, which gnawed at her without mercy, although her despair was invisible to anyone else.

Laxmi Devi was also oblivious to Aamani's ambitions, as she walked with some reluctance with her son toward her rooms. Knowing how angry he was and how difficult their conversation was going to be.

But despite her concerns, and even if a bit overwhelmed by it, she was determined to have her way despite the Zamindar's position of power and the great love he had for his wife.

As they finally entered the Dowager's rooms, Ramakanta dismissed with an imperious gesture of the hand the many handmaidens in attendance while addressing her with a harsh sound in his voice.

"Maa, why did you behaved with such disrespect toward my beloved bride? Diana is an honorable, kind person who entered our society with respect and an open heart?"

The Zamindar's Bride

Laxmi Devi glared at her son before answering. The rage within her was apparent as she spoke almost in a hissing sound.

"I would never disrespect your bride, my son if she had been a legitimate spouse...The western wedding ceremony you engaged in is considered invalid in Hinduism and not accepted as a true marriage."

The Zamindar took a deep breath before attempting to speak with his highly judgmental mother.

"Maa, because I love you, it would please me if you accept my marriage to Diana. Who is a special person that anyone would be proud to call a daughter-in-law."

At that point, his voice became darker as he moved closer to his mother.

"But I would like to make it clear that your acceptance is not a requisite since it's *my* prerogative to marry the person of my choice. I am the Zamindar, and according to our laws, the only one who is in charge here..."

"You are unworthy of such title," interrupted Laxmi Devi with defiance.

"You should be aware that it's a sacrilege to turn your back on your religion and traditions of the family. However, rest assured that you will suffer the consequences for such irresponsible behavior."

The Zamindar shook his head in disbelief as he answered.

"Maa, are you threatening me with celestial retribution? I would like you to know that I believe in a God of love and not of vengeance."

The Zamindar moved closer to his mother with determination while continuing.

"I am shocked by your behavior, which I am trying to overlook, because of my devotion to you as my mother…However, I will not allow anyone to disrespect my bride, who will always come first in my eyes."

Laxmi Devi appeared impervious to her son's words, almost disinterested, as he continued with some impatience in his voice.

"I am legally married to Diana, and our union is valid according to the norms of the civilized world. We are also planning a Hindu wedding ceremony in deference to my religious belief. At that time, I will introduce my bride as the new Zamindarin to the people, which should be to everyone's satisfaction."

Laxmi Devi appeared unmoved by his words. She stood erect and proud as she answered her son with regal haughtiness.

"Aamani is the only one I will ever accept as a daughter-in-law and worthy to stand by your side as the Zamindarin...She is part of your heritage, unlike the lovely Countess De' Gautier who offers very little, except for her physical appeal."

"Your rejection is tainted with prejudice, Maa since you know absolutely nothing about my bride." Answered the Zamindar seething with contempt at his mother's insulting words toward the woman he loved.

"There is so much more to Diana than her beauty. She is knowledgeable, kind, and very generous. She left her country with courage, willing to face an unknown culture because of her love for me..."

"Love," interposed Laxmi Devi with anger and contempt in her voice.

"You have learned nothing from your heritage and teachings if you think that love is necessary for a marriage. It can be even disruptive, like your infatuation for the western woman that you insist on calling your bride."

"The Zamindar had reached the end of his tolerance toward the barrage of insults against his wife. He was furious now and allowed his rage to run unrestraint as he answered his mother without the usual respect.

"*Love*, yes, mother *love*, which is necessary for happiness. The *Love* you reject because you never experienced it in your life, the *Love* you craved and never received from my father. The *Love* I know now you never had for me, or you would rejoice in my happiness instead of trying to destroy it."

The Zamindar paused to ease the disdain that overwhelmed him as he stared coldly at his mother before continuing.

"But what I believe is most important, Maa, is the *love* you never had for yourself...in your cold and unhappy life."

Laxmi Devi seemed to lose her footing in response to her son's cruel words that pierced her protective veneer like the lethal blade of a dagger. She staggered as if she was suddenly dizzy and unable to keep her balance. The Zamindar placed his arms about her to prevent a possible fall.

"Maa, I regret my harshness. I didn't mean to hurt you, but you pushed me too far," said the

Zamindar as he helped his mother toward a nearby divan.

"Ramakanta was now deeply concerned for his mother's welfare and quickly offered her a glass of water to calm her distress.

The Dowager held the glass with her trembling hands and took a deep gulp of the refreshing liquid.

However, her distress seemed mitigated by her son's more accommodating words in the face of her possible illness. In her manipulative mind, she thought it best to continue playing the wounded victim to gain more control, capitalizing on her son's concern for her welfare.

The Zamindar was not oblivious to his mother's manipulative games but decided not to push her too far, fearing that the stress of the situation might cause her real harm.

After a few minutes in which she seemed to have recovered, Laxmi Devi attempted to call her servants to get ready for bed and abruptly end the conversation.

"I am not ready to go, Maa because there has been no resolution to the problem," said Ramakanta with determination.

"I hope that you have recovered well enough to understand that Aamani cannot remain in the palace under any circumstances...Tomorrow, early in the morning, she will receive a safe escort back home."

Laxmi Devi was shocked by her son's unexpected behavior. Feigning illnesses always worked in the past, but he seemed less receptive now. She was angered and disappointed, as she stood up suddenly, without any signs of dizziness.

However, her inner turmoil was evident by the loud sound of her voice since the Dowager was always soft-spoken and well-mannered, even in her most challenging moments. It was apparent that her son's stubborn resolve had pushed her to the limit.

"Aamani will remain in the palace," she insisted angrily, "the foreign woman is the only one who should return home!"

"I decide who remains in the palace, and no one else, including you, can override my wishes," said Ramakanta, tired of his mother's manipulations.

"Very well," answered the Dowager, barely able to control her rage, "if you will remove Aamani from the palace since you have the power as the

Zamindar. I will join her and *never* return to the palace again."

She then pointed an accusatory finger toward her son as she continued with contempt in her voice.

"You have turned your back to your family and your heritage, and now I am turning my back to you...because, as of now, I no longer have a son, and you no longer have a mother."

Ramakanta was now sadly aware of his mother's destructive behavior, which was worse than he had anticipated. She was unable to compromise, even if it could lead to her destruction. That is, to punish and control her disobedient son.

"Please, Maa, be reasonable. You know that you belong in the palace where you are cared for and protected," said the Zamindar, frustrated by her stubbornness. Nonetheless, he attempted one more time to reason with the difficult woman.

"Diana is my wife and the new Zamandarin. You can't expect Aamani to live in the palace because of what she represents. Her very presence is most disrespectful to her, and if she knew the truth, my bride will not tolerate it and will quickly return to her native country."

Then the Zamindar said with determination in his voice as he moved closer to his mother.

"I will follow her if she returns to Europe since she is the woman I love, and I will not live without her…Because of your manipulations, I will leave my country permanently. Is that what you wish for Maa?"

A devious look flashed in the Dowager's eyes as she answered.

"The foreign woman will never know Aamani's true identity if she is allowed to live in the palace. You have my word of honor, my son. Besides, you know that I am held in great esteem by the people. If I leave the palace, rumors will spread that it was the will of your foreign wife to removed me, and she will be blamed and hated for it…"

"That is a lie, and you know it!" Exclaimed the Zamindar, appalled by his mother's despicable behavior.

"It's not a lie, only a rumor," answered Laxmi Devi with sarcasm, "however, since there will be no denial on my part, it will become a reality since silence consents…"

"Stop it, Maa," the Zamindar said with disdain," as he moved abruptly away from her while saying.

"My people will never believe that I have forced you out of the home you shared with my father."

"Perhaps you are right since you are beloved by the people," said the Dowager with determination as she stared deeply into his eyes.

"But there will be a fanatical few who will believe it and place blame on the foreign woman who corrupted you with her beauty and turned you against your mother…That is how it will be if Aamani is not allowed to live in the palace."

A cruel smile highlighted Laxmi Devi's face as she felt victorious over her son. At least for the moment, she had regained control, while a sense of dread overwhelmed the Zamindar.

He was aware that his beloved Padma could be in grave danger if some fanatics believed that she was responsible for removing the revered Dowager from the palace.

He felt suddenly helpless and entrapped by Laxmi Devi's manipulations, and at least for the moment, he was unable to find a suitable solution.

The thought of lying to his wife was disturbing. But he decided it would be prudent to let Aamani remain in the palace until he could find a proper solution to the alarming situation.

He was suddenly very concerned for his wife's safety and blamed his naivete in believing that he would have been able to handle the situation with greater ease.

Without further delay, since there was very little he could do now, and appalled by his mother's behavior, the Zamindar walked out of Laxmi Devi's room feeling defeated, at least for the moment.

A smile brightened the Dowager's face. She was happy now and apparently in control again.

§§§

CHAPTER TWELVE

THE GODDESS TOUCH

Life in India, at least for the moment, seemed full of promise for Ramakanta and Diana. Despite the difficulties encountered in confronting the openly hostile dowager.

Laxmi Devi chose to remain distant and uncommunicative for days in the privacy of her rooms. Aamani was also missing. A situation welcomed by the Zamindar, deeply disturbed by her intrusive presence in the palace.

The peaceful interim gave him the golden opportunity to introduce his splendid and exotic world to his bride.

Diana was happy during that blissful time while getting acquainted with the exciting world opening before her.

The new bride learned to appreciate and care for the many people who tended the estate and the farmers who worked tirelessly on the Zamindar's great land's expansions. They appeared warm and friendly toward their new Zamindarin, even though she was a western woman from a very different culture.

The couple rejoiced at the privacy they had been afforded and treasured each intimate, passionate moment they shared, which continued to burn brighter than ever, as they reveled in the ecstasy of being in each other's arms during the long, sultry, Indian nights.

Since their idyllic marriage, Diana went to sleep each night in her husband's arms. She felt peaceful and safe, surrounded by the overwhelming power of his love, and grateful for the blessing of having met the perfect man of her destiny.

They had much in common, on an intellectual level, and shared the fascination of becoming one with nature during their many hours on horseback.

Diana scouted with glee the endless acres of the Zamindar's estate, relishing in the beauty of her new adoptive home.

She felt so alive there while inhaling the scent of flowers and reveling in the lush greenery that spread far and wide as far as the eye could see.

It was a feeling of being at home again, and a sense of familiarity and peace surrounded her.

There was a special allure to the open-air orchards that burst with bright colors and sweet aromas. Natural ponds enhance the place's beauty with therapeutic herbs that infused the area with a sense of serenity, conducive to sit and meditate.

The site possessed a truly cathartic atmosphere that was infectious. The Zamindar explained that the gardens are often a natural refuge and sanctuary for birds and other wildlife guided by the principle that everything in the universe is sacred. That is, including plants and trees, held in exceptionally high regard.

On that eventful day, the couple was interested in exploration. Diana had expressed the desire to travel far, toward the end of the estate, which seemed more mysterious and intriguing.

The place appeared more natural and less manicured than the rest of the property, filled with overgrown shrubberies and large, stately trees.

Diana's focal point was to reach that remote place as she eagerly gazed toward the far horizon.

There was a feeling of restlessness and urgency that overwhelmed her.

Driven by an irresistible force to venture further, she increased her stallion's speed and distanced herself from her husband, who was traveling at a more leisurely pace.

She soon entered a wide pathway flanked by many Hindu deities. The statues partly shielded by the lush vegetation retained the unique styling and splendor of Indian art and appeared to be relics of past eras because of time ravages.

Although the surroundings were more natural and less pristine, they seemed welcoming and familiar to the young woman, who spurred her stallion on, attracted by the irresistible lure of the place.

While moving forward in the pathway, her mood seemed to change suddenly, as if she had entered a time and space far removed from reality.

It was a pleasant, relaxing feeling, and she reveled in the breezes that caressed her face and disturbed the perfection of her long, flowing hair.

She gazed forward in an almost hypnotic trance, marveling at the beauty of the lush, emerald greenery that was opening before her so majestic and mysterious.

Diana was mesmerized by the landscape and many ponds, which were visual in the distance and glistened like sparkling diamonds in the sun's reflected light.

The Zamindar, who had been temporarily left behind by her sense of urgency, spurred his horse to a faster gallop. He soon flanked his runaway bride, wondering why she was in such a hurry.

But at that point, Diana seemed almost oblivious of his presence and continued to explore with great care the surroundings, apparently searching for something.

"What are you looking for, my darling," he finally asked, openly curious about her unusual behavior.

Diana remained silent for a few minutes as she continued to look around the area with some concern before saying.

"Rami, I am looking for the statue of the Goddess Kali, but I don't seem to find it anywhere...I hope it's still in the estate since she was my favorite among the other statues of deities."

The Zamindar remained silent and confused by her answer

Diana pulled back the reins of her horse, bringing it back to a slower pace. She seemed openly saddened and displeased as she continued speaking.

"You must know Rami that I always had a strange fascination for the Goddess Kali....I remember that her statue was very imposing and made of granite. It was beautifully sculpted, although the idol was rather frightening, with a dark sort of beauty..."

"You remember the statue of Kali being here?" interrupted the Zamindar stunned and fascinated by Diana's description.

"Of course I remember it, dearest," answered Diana, apparently oblivious of her husband's amazement, as she continued speaking with a deliberate sound.

"The statue depicted the fierce Kali, with the red tongue protruding from her mouth, a garland of skulls around her neck, and a decapitated head in one of her many hands...She also stood triumphantly over the sleeping image of Lord Shiva."

At that point, Diana paused as she looked around, a bit confused and visibly disappointed as she continued.

"I don't see the statue in the usual place. I looked forward to seeing Kali every time I galloped on horseback through the area. Why was I not informed that she was removed since she was so important to me?"

The Zamindar was becoming concerned and wondered what was happening to Diana's state of mind since the unusual dialogue appeared connected to another entity from a different time and place in history.

He had always hoped that she would reconcile with the possibility of past lives and reincarnation. But he was now disturbed by her unusual questions of places and objects she couldn't possibly have seen in her lifetime.

The young woman now validated his firmly held beliefs that they had known each other in past lives.

It overwhelmed him to hear his bride address issues with the estate, which she couldn't have had any knowledge of, because they occurred at a time far removed from the present. He was naturally concerned about her well-being.

"You remember the statue being here, my darling?" he finally asked while moving his steed closer to her.

"I am also under the impression from your words that you have a feeling of veneration and deference toward the Goddess, even though she is not part of your religious belief?"

"Not deference, Rami, or any religious beliefs," answered Diana with a deliberate sound in her voice.

"It's only a fascination with her artistic image and an attraction I can't explain...I used to make sketches of Kali ever since I was a child. She seemed strangely familiar..."

Diana paused and inhaled deeply before continuing.

Her unusual, dark beauty fascinated me. I also know that Kali is the Hindu Goddess of death and is often associated with sexuality and violence. Although there is a benevolent side to her as well since she is also considered a symbol of motherly-love..."

"You are truly interested in her," interposed the Zamindar, surprised, "and have some basic knowledge concerning the Goddess, which I find very interesting,"

"Dearest, I have always been interested in Indian culture and the myths connected with your Gods."

Answered Diana as she gently touched his arm while asking.

"Why is Kali's tongue red and protruding in many of her images? What is the religious significance behind it?"

"Her red tongue distinguishes her from all other Gods of the Hindu pantheon of Deities," answered the Zamindar.

"Ritualistically in Kali's temple, her tongue is smeared with the blood of sacrificial animals as a reminder that Mother Nature is giving life as well as taking it away."

"She looks so frightening and intimidating," insisted Diana, "but always in a captivating sort of way…Her bloodthirsty appearance can be interpreted as evil and violent."

"No, my darling," answered the Zamindar.

"The Goddess is misunderstood because of her frightening images. Kali Ma is the most loving of all the Hindu goddesses, regarded by her devotees as protector and Mother of the universe. The blood-red tongue of Kali is unfurled in her role as the ultimate deliverer, a weapon to be feared and a reminder that nature ultimately consumes all life."

Diana was silent for a few moments, fascinated by the mythology of the Goddess. She then asked, a bit confused.

"Dearest, I would like to know where the statue of Kali is now? I believe that it used to be here, lined up with all the other deities. That is if I remember it correctly. There was an open-air temple with many deities. The Goddess occupied a lofty and enviable position among them, on a pedestal with a stone canopy where Vedic hymns were engraved."

The Zamindar's Bride

The Zamindar was astounded by his wife's graphic recollections and the possibility that she relived memories of a past life. He decided it would be best to let her speak since he wanted to know the depth of her remembrance of that bygone era. He then pointed his finger toward a large pond visible in the distance and said.

"No need for concern, darling, Kali's statue it's considered a revered and historical relic on the estate…However, it was moved a long time ago in the vicinity of that large pond and placed on a pedestal by the wishes of one of my ancestors."

Diana looked on with some apprehension since the statue of Kali was not visible from her vantage point due to the overflowing vegetation in the area.

However, she was pleased by the picturesque and beautiful landscape, which made an excellent backdrop for the statue. She then said with excitement in her voice.

"I am so glad they moved the statue there. It's a much better location for it. The treasured idol deserved an honored place. I am certain that I would have chosen that spot myself,"

"Perhaps you did choose that special spot, my love," said the Zamindar, "perhaps you did."

Diana was deeply disturbed by Ramakanta's words. A feeling of confusion overwhelmed her. Despite her concerns, she felt compelled to spur her steed into a fast gallop, moving toward the direction suggested by her husband in the vicinity of the large pond.

There was a sense of agitation to find the elusive statue that seemed unreachable, encircled by the lush vegetation, which protected the idol as an emerald shield.

Finally, as she drew closer to the area, she saw the statue's outline partially hidden by the overflowing vegetation.

It had become imperative for Diana to see the Goddess at close range and make sure that it was like the detailed image imprinted in her mind and memory.

She was deeply conflicted at that point, although she wished to finally have closure, even if it would validate her doubts about reincarnation, which had haunted her ever since her connection with the Zamindar.

Although the perception of an eternal life disturbed her deeply, she could not ignore her recollection of the estate, which she appeared to remember with exceptional clarity.

Kali's image was imprinted with great details in the recesses of her mind, and she could not dismiss the possibility of having seen her before. Nonetheless, she stubbornly held out to some residual doubts.

Perhaps the statue was not as she remembered. In that case, she could dismiss the situation as a series of strange coincidences and faulty memories, combined with her fertile imagination.

The young bride desperately wanted to put all her fears to rest and think about her happy marriage as a beautiful gift from God and nothing more.

By now, she had reached her destination and was in very close proximity to the large pond. The statue's outline was slowly emerging from the greenery's stranglehold and was by now visible on the imposing pedestal.

Her heart skipped a beat at the sight since the statue was identical to the image she so clearly remembered.

She was suddenly overwhelmed by great emotions as she dismounted her horse with athletic prowess and approached the mysterious deity with a determined stride.

The idol appeared so familiar to her and almost welcoming, despite her frightening appearance. She suddenly felt a sense of calm in front of the deity.

Her hands caressed the cool stone with affection as if she was reconnecting with a dear and valued friend.

The statue was, as she remembered, and exceptionally well preserved because of its granite structure. However, she had suffered from neglect, abandoned to the elements' ravages, and the profusion of greenery's that protectively embraced her.

A flood of memories suddenly surfaced in her mind. She recollected many details, about the statue, especially about a Kris dagger that Kali held in one of her many hands.

She remembered her fascination with the kris, which is known for its distinctive wavy blade, a striking weapon originating from Indonesia, and considered a spiritual object, which possesses magical powers.

There was now a clear recollection about the origin of the statue, which had been a present given to the Zamindar by some distinguished people, escaping Indonesia's repressive regime of the time.

They had requested asylum, and the statue of Kali was a goodwill gesture.

The memories of the historical occurrence were so distinct that Diana could not dismiss them as a fruit of her overactive imagination, and a sense of anxiety overwhelmed her again.

By now, the Zamindar was standing directly behind his bride. Although he could not see her face, her emotions were apparent by the slight tremor in her shoulders and the soft sounds of sobs.

"My love, you are crying," he said, as he placed his arms protectively about her.

"What is making you so sad, my darling? Please tell me?"

Diana moved closer to him, openly frightened and looking for refuge in his embrace, as she said softly, almost in a whisper.

"It's very confusing because the Deity is so familiar...Please tell me Rami, was the statue of Kali imported from Indonesia?"

The Zamindar remained silent for a moment as a smile brightened his face, overwhelmed by the stunning statement. There was certainty now that she was his Padma, the beloved wife lost in the dust of time, but by some miracle found again in the present life.

"Yes, my darling, you are correct," he answered, as he looked with reverence at the idol.

"The statue of Kali was a gesture of gratitude by Indonesia's Balinese aristocrats, who were escaping from political conflicts and the repressive Dutch regime of the time...The precious gift originated from the temple of the Goddess in Bali and was transported here, with great effort and devotion by the patriots."

The Zamindar surveyed the statue from every angle. He then pointed to some writing sculpted on the body of the deity. The message was not visible because of a greenish layer of mold, which appeared throughout the effigy. With a bit of effort and using some large leaves, he cleared the script embedded in the stone.

At that point, the Zamindar translated the pertinent message, which recalled the occasion and the origin of Indonesia's gift. He also added with some hesitance.

"Dearest, the date of the Goddess' arrival was over a hundred and fifty years ago."

"The statue arrived over a hundred and fifty years ago?" Repeated Diana as she recoiled from the statue filled with dread.

"How can that be possible? Since I have such a clear recollection of her arrival as if it was today. Rami, please, believe me, I know I was there for the occasion, next to the Zamindar, who looked very much like you..."

Diana paused and smiled as she gently caressed the idol with affection while the memory flashed before her eyes.

"It was a wonderful day of rejoicing and reverence from all the people at the arrival of the sacred statue...The Goddess Kali was on a chariot decorated with a profusion of beautiful flowers. A crowd of devotees welcomed Kali to her new home, followed by a religious procession in honor of the idol throughout the estate."

Diana became suddenly silent and placed her hand on her forehead, which by now seemed to be burning like fire.

"Am I going mad?" She whispered, "how could I possibly have been there since it was so long ago and not in this lifetime?"

The Zamindar gently caressed her hair with love, understanding her distress and difficulty embracing the possibility of reincarnation since it was unsettling to go against her firmly held religious beliefs.

He was now sure of her rebirth since no one present at the estate was aware of the statue's history and her origin from Indonesia, except his mother.

The Zamindar's memory was also vague on the historical occasion since he visited the statue as a child and never again.

The details of the grand event were given to him by his grandfather, according to family traditions, regarding the preservation of the Choudhuri dynasty's historical landmarks for posterity.

However, there were still many questions that seemed unclear about the statue to the Zamindar.

He was aware that the idol had been removed from its original place by his ancestor's wish. But no one knew the real reason why the statue had a place of honor over other important Hindu Deities.

By now, Ramakanta firmly believed that it must have been the Zamindarin who wished for the statue to have a place of honor.

What made the situation more mysterious was the apparent abandonment of Kali's statue for over a century, despite being such a valuable, historical relic on the property. Diana was openly curious about it and asked the Zamindar.

"Why was the statue allowed to languish amid overgrown vegetation, despite being of great historical value to the estate?"

The Zamindar was silent at first since he realized that he avoided the area for a long time, with no apparent explanation. Gardners manicured the estate's grounds, but the statue seemed to have been condemned into oblivion.

"I don't know," he finally answered, "until today I never thought about it...I realize now that for some reason, I was avoiding the place without being aware of it."

A feeling of anxiety overwhelmed him as he remembered Diana's sudden fear of death aboard the ship on their way to India. Was it in some way connected to Kali and that time in history?

He wondered why unlike Diana, he had no memories of the grand occasion concerning the statue of Kali. She had such a detailed recollection of it and even remembered his presence there since the Zamindar supposedly looked very much like him.

Did something tragic occur during that time, which was so painful that he wished to erase it from his memory forever? Was he reminded by the idol of an immeasurable loss, and therefore condemned it to oblivion?

Despite all the unanswered questions, there was only one reality for the Zamindar. The love he had for Diana, which was deep and all-encompassing. He held her close in his arms in that particular moment, almost fearing that he might lose her again in the inexplicable path forged to them by destiny.

His mind wandered and questioned what could have happened to them in former lifetimes?

"Did past failings needed to be rectified to find the perfect union that had eluded them in the eternal cycle of life?

"My love, please, never leave me," he said as he held Diana tightly in his arms."

"I will never leave you, dearest," Diana answered with a smile, "you should know by now that even the eternal cycle of time cannot separate us,"

Ramakanta was more invested in the present than dwelling in the past shadows in that sobering moment. It was a new dawn, and he was eager to conquer it with his bride by his side. He looked into Diana's face and noticed that emotional tears continued to flow from her eyes.

He removed a handkerchief from his pocket and dried her tears while saying.

"No more sadness, my darling, this is a moment to rejoice since there are no more doubts that we have finally found each other due to the generosity of a merciful God."

Diana smiled through her tears and caressed his face with warmth while saying.

"I admit fearing the unknown because of the mystery of our existence, which might transcend even the finality of death…"

"You must not be afraid, my Padma." interrupted the Zamindar passionately, "apparently we have been allowed to live again since our connection might have been badly interrupted through some failings. We must make amends, now, to possibly validate our existence…"

"You truly believe it?" Interposed Diana, but I question why we are so favored?"

"No need to question the workings of God," answered Ramakanta, "the same way it's impossible to define the infinity of the universe...We have limited minds and must defer to this superior, benevolent power, regardless of the name we choose to give it."

"You are right, dearest," answered Diana, much relieved.

"We must be grateful for all our blessings and the greatest gift of our life and our love."

The Zamindar held her in a tight embrace, filled with passion and love. He then said joyfully.

In honor of this memorable day, I promise to you, my darling Padma, to deliver the Statue of Kali from the ravages of nature and bring it back to its original splendor for all our people to admire and see."

Diana reached for his hand with a bright smile, and they walked together toward their horses with a renewed sense of hope. They soon spurred the steeds to a fast gallop on their way back home.

§§§

CHAPTER THIRTEEN

THE BEAUTIFUL SAREE

The following day, Ramakanta and Diana received a surprising invitation from Laxmi Devi to join the Dowager in her rooms.

At first glance, the lady appeared to be in an excellent mood and behaved amiably toward the couple. She then said to the Zamindar with some urgency in her voice.

"I hope you have not forgotten my son that next Sunday you are scheduled to holds a *durbar*, the usual ruler's court's run-on of the feudal states, which will take place in the palace. It's the occasion when friends, relations, and field workers will offer their greetings and pay their respect to you, the Zamindar.

"Of course I remember, Maa," Ramakanta said, pleasantly surprised by her cheerful mood.

"Since it falls on the Full Moon day," continued Laxmi Devi, "our traditional yearly festival in honor of Lord Krishna, we will celebrate it in the gardens of our estate, where you will receive high officials of the state of Orissa."

With a disarming smile and her usual aristocratic bearing, the Dowager walked toward Diana and said.

"My dear, this is the perfect occasion to introduce the new Zamindarin according to the age-old traditions of our dynasty. I will host a special luncheon in your honor, followed by a reception on a grand scale, with more than 3,000 people attending from all walks of life,"

"My lady, I am humbled by the honor, and thank you for your consideration," answered Diana, surprised by the offer but still skeptical of the unexpected friendliness from Laxmi Devi.

"I assure you that it will be a memorable day on a grand scale worthy of the Zamindar."

"I look forward to the splendid occasion," said Diana with appreciation, "it will be an honor to meet the people in my beautiful adopted country."

"Yes, my dear," answered Laxmi Devi, "I am also happy to relate that I have a special surprise for you. Since the celebration is in your honor, your entry should be the focal point of the day as the new Zamindarin, and in that regard, you will be riding a palanquin…"

"I will be riding a palanquin?" interposed Diana feeling suddenly, uneasy with the suggestion, "may I ask what a palanquin is? Coming from the west, I am not familiar with the terminology."

"The word *palanquin* derives from the Sanskrit," answered Laxmi Devi as she moved closer to Diana.

"It's a covered litter, my dear, with a long history in India, which goes as far back as the Ramayana era."

"That is very interesting, and I thank you for the valuable information," answered Diana, a bit apprehensive while facing for the first time the cultural difference with her adoptive country.

"No need to worry," insisted Laxmi Devi with a warm smile while noticing with a bit of satisfaction Diana's anxious demeanor.

"You will be very comfortable on the litter as you make a grand entry safely carried by four men."

Diana was unhappy with the suggestion, especially about being carried by four men. It depicted self-importance and a tinge of slavery, which disturbed her and went against her modesty and respect toward people.

She moved closer to her husband, hoping for support, not wanting to be disrespectful toward her mother-in-law, who at least in appearance seemed friendly and accommodating.

The Zamindar understanding his wife's displeasure, addressed his mother with a polite but firm sound in his voice.

"Maa, why must Diana ride the palanquin? It might prove disturbing and even embarrassing to her. I am certain she would favor walking among the people on her own, which is part of her friendly personality."

"But my son," insisted Laxmi Devi with her usual determination.

"The palanquin has been part of our family's tradition and history for generations. Besides, your bride is now the Zamindarin and must be open to experiences that are part of our culture and traditions."

Noticing that the conversation was becoming a bit challenging, Diana decided to interject her opinion, not wanting to arouse her mother-in-law's susceptible nature while retaining some control over the situation.

"My lady, I appreciate the honor and offer to ride a palanquin. Although I respect your traditions, I would prefer to walk among the people in my usual way. Besides, my gowns would be unsuitable for the confinement of a litter and uncomfortable."

"We are in total agreement on this point," interposed Laxmi Devi with a touch of sarcasm as she assessed Diana's beautiful gown and the fullness of her flowing skirt.

"Your western attire would not be appropriate for the litter or even for the occasion."

A cold and disagreeable look flashed in the Dowager's eyes as she moved slightly away from

Diana and suddenly clapped her hands in the direction of the door.

In immediate response to the sharp sound, a young servant girl rushed into the room, carrying a splendid silk saree in her arms. The garment was encrusted with precious stones that sparkled while reflecting the many lights.

Laxmi Devi proudly caressed the fabric's smooth silkiness with her palm while saying with friendliness

"My dear, this will be the proper attire for you to wear for the occasion, as the new Zamindarin. It will be comfortable and light as you ride the palanquin. Sarees are great outfits that every Indian lady wears proudly. Even those who aspire to become one of us despite being born in different cultures or ethnicity…"

Diana was stunned by Laxmi Devi's patronizing behavior, which suggested she aspired to become an Indian lady while ignoring the fact that she was born a proud, western woman.

She finally understood the reason for the Dowager's unexpected friendliness, which appeared to be a ploy to manipulate and assert control over her.

However, Diana thought it best not to show anger and disrespect while retaining her sense of dignity and control of the situation.

She walked toward the servant girl and looked with admiration at the splendid saree and smiled. She then turned toward the Dowager and spoke with a respectful but firm sound in her voice.

"It is a most beautiful gift, my lady, and I am thankful for your generosity…I will be honored to wear it for the Vedic celebration of our marriage, following the religious tradition of the occasion."

Diana paused for a moment and looked at the Zamindar before continuing.

"I will wear the saree in the same spirit of compromise of my husband, who wore western attire in honor and deference to our Christian wedding."

Diana then stood tall and determinate as she continued.

"As a western woman, I will meet the people as I truly am, sarees are beautiful, but they are not part of my identity or culture. I came here to embrace my new adopted country and all the Indian people with respect for their traditions. However, in return, I hope to be accepted for who I truly am and not a manufactured interpretation of an Indian woman…"

Diana paused for a moment with a look of pride before continuing.

"I chose to leave my beloved country, family, and friends in deference of my husband's need to remain the Zamindar and leader of the people. All this I did gladly for the sake of our love. However, I will never betray the legacy of my beloved parents, to become someone other than who I truly am."

Silence followed Diana's words since Laxmi Devi's great displeasure was always expressed by silence. An aura of coldness permeated the room now, and her anger was almost palpable. The Dowager was aware that her attempt to gain control was lost, at least for the moment.

Diana was, in her estimation, far worse than expected. She dared to intrude into the sanctity of her family and culture by becoming the new Zamindarin. Still, her independent nature appeared problematic since it was apparent she would be unable to control her in any way, and the idea was intolerable to her.

The Zamindar broke the silence as he affectionately placed his arm around his wife's waist in a sign of support, noticing her uneasiness in facing the situation. He addressed his mother with respect but also firmness.

"We thank you, Maa, for the generous offer to host Diana's introduction to the people as the new Zamindarin...However, my bride is very proud of her heritage. As the scion of a distinguished family line, she holds the title of Countess De' Gautier and is the sole heir to a vast and beautiful estate in Italy..."

"I understand, my son, no need to discuss it further," interrupted Laxmi Devi with a sharp sound in her voice.

"I will honor my word and host the luncheon in the Zamindarin's honor, as promised..."

The Dowager paused and stood still in the middle of the room. There was a proud and defiant look in her eyes while shielding her wounded pride behind the veneer of her aristocratic bearing.

Ramakanta and Diana understood that it was best to leave at once and avoid causing further embarrassment with their defiance.

They bowed politely and left the room, followed by the servant girl carrying the beautiful saree.

Honoring the Zamindarin

As promised, the celebration to introduce the new Zamindarin was a grand occasion. The palace and the surrounding gardens shimmered in traditional Indian style, with brightly colored lanterns hanging from trees and a profusion of flowers throughout the ambiance.

A lavish display of food was served buffet style to the thousands of people in attendance from all walks of life. Diana had seldom seen so many fragrant flowers in a myriad of colors in one place before.

Local musicians were on hand to fill the atmosphere with vibrant, exotic music that enhanced the festive occasion's many folds. Lovely dancing girls moved with rhythm to the music's beat, gyrating gracefully in traditional Indian costumes, performing the rich, ancient folklore of Orissa.

However, the day's highlight was the eagerly awaited appearance of the new Zamindarin, as she made her grand entrance by her husband's side.

The Zamindar's Bride

The young woman looked stunning in a blue silk taffeta gown tightly fitted at the waist, with puffy, short sleeves, which beautifully framed her décolletage. The classy attire was enhanced by a single jewel, the exquisite sapphire pendant that glistened in the lights and rested on her graceful neck. Diana's long, flowing tresses styled for the occasion in an elegant up-do with Jasmine flowers entwined in her hair. As a unique, romantic touch, the Zamindar personally placed the flowers since he favored Jasmine's delicate beauty and loved its intoxicating scent.

Diana was excited and happy with the warm welcome she received from the people. Whispers of admiration rose like a crescendo in the air at her sight. However, the great curiosity exhibited by the guests was a bit overwhelming for her shy nature.

But Diana understood the interest she inspired, as the mysterious western woman from a faraway land, which had captured the heart of their Zamindar.

Throughout the festivities, she remained the center of attention as she walked among the guests with her usual grace and style.

Representatives of the province of Orissa were in attendance at the celebration for the new Zamindarin. She also met many tenants who behaved toward her with great humility and deference, although, to be fair, they participated in the festivity as everyone else.

The difference in culture became more apparent to the young woman and caused her some difficulty because of her nature's fairness. Although she was born an aristocrat with great privileges in her opulent world, she always respected all the people regardless of rank and social status, valuing real character in favor of exalted positions.

However, regardless of her independent nature, Diana made sure to respect traditions. She ensured that all attending guests felt comfortable in her presence, as she safeguarded the required etiquette expected of her as the new Zamindarin.

The only sour note to the perfect day of celebration was her mother-in-law since Laxmi Devi's eyes followed her every move, which was a bit unsettling under the circumstances.

The Dowager had chosen to remain apart from the Zamindar and Diana while observing the scene from afar and judging, perhaps too harshly, her daughter-in-law's first contact with the people.

Aamani was also present in the glittering scene. Standing silently by Laxmi Devi's side, with her petite frame elegantly attired in a shimmering, silk, orange saree, studded with semi-precious stones.

Pearls were entwined in her lengthy, raven hair, while an impressive gold necklace with matching earrings completed the ensemble.

She appeared lovely that evening, with her bronzed complexion contrasting so well with the saree's vivid color, while her bright eyes emphasized the perfection of her oval face. As always, she was submissive to the Dowager but dignified in her aristocratic bearing.

Although everyone was oblivious, she was in great pain, considering her sense of defeat, That is, in facing the festivities celebrated in honor of her rival, the new Zamindarin.

The situation was made worse for the unfortunate girl by the apparent love the Zamindar had for his bride as he walked proudly by Diana's side, seemingly happier than Aamani had ever seen before.

Unaware of the unhappy situation and thinking that she was Ramakanta's adopted sister, Diana was warm and friendly toward her, making it even more challenging for Aamani to dislike her.

Unfortunately, there was a dark side to the girl since she had a perception of failure compared to the Zamindar's beautiful bride, which created a deep sense of jealousy. She deemed Diana unduly fortunate and unfairly gifted by nature and destiny.

However, no one during the festivities was aware of the lovely Indian girl who felt helpless and forgotten. At the same time, Ramakanta and Diana looked deep into each other's eyes with happiness and love.

There was nothing fair about it, and Aamani felt like the victim, while the lovely foreigner, who dared to enter her world and take everything rightfully hers, was victorious.

She closed her eyes as a sense of dread overwhelmed her. She felt so alone, forgotten, and invisible.

Suddenly, she recoiled toward the back wall feeling unsteady on her feet. She wished to disappear and avoid the agony of participating in a celebration that only caused her unbearable pain.

Unfortunately, no one seemed to notice the girl's distress. The oblivion included Laxmi Devi, who was too busy spying on her daughter-in-law, hoping for some significant mistake that could cause some dissent in the marriage.

Strangely enough, it was Diana who finally noticed that there was something wrong with Aamani, as the young woman appeared almost hidden in the dark shadows of the room.

Worried by her strange behavior, she excused herself from her husband and quickly joined Aamani in her secluded space.

"Why are you here by yourself, dear Aamani?" She asked with concern in her voice, "Ramakanta and I are delighted that you have joined us on this special day, and we hope that you will share in our happiness."

She then moved closer to the girl and gently touched her shoulder while saying.

You look so beautiful, Aamani. You belong out there among the people and enhance with your lovely presence this wonderful celebration."

Aamani regained her usual demeanor at the unexpected intrusion of Diana. It was frustrating for her to see how nice she was, making it harder to despise her rival, which would have given her some satisfaction.

She put her hands together and bowed politely in greeting while attempting to smile. She then said softly.

"Thank you, my lady, for your concern. I am enjoying the celebration, but I felt a sudden headache coming on, and I looked for a dark corner to help relieve the pain,"

"I am so sorry you are not feeling well, dear Aamani. Perhaps you should return to your rooms, and take care of yourself, which is most important right now. Ramakanta and I will understand…"

"No, my lady," interposed Aamani, "I am feeling much better now, and I don't wish to miss the celebration."

"Then come with me," said Diana happily, and with friendliness, took Aamani's hand while saying.   "Let us join the guests and the festivities. Your presence will be a most welcomed addition."

Aamani removed her hands from Diana's almost abruptly, but she very quickly regained her self-control while saying with a soft but deliberate sound in her voice."

"You are the center of the attention, my lady. No one will notice anyone else but you. Because you are so beautiful, and your gown is stunning with the silky fabric shimmering in the light."

"Thank you for your nice words Aamani. I am also glad you like my gown. I know that is different from the exquisite sarees you Indian ladies wear with such style. But it reflects who I truly am since wearing a saree would feel like a costume because it's not part of my culture."

"I understand, my lady, no need to explain," answered Aamani with a smile, "perhaps I would feel the same in western clothes…"

At that point, Aamani paused and stared with admiration at the sapphire pendent, which decorated her neck and sparkled brilliantly in the lights, then asked.

"My lady, your blue sapphire pendant it's so beautiful and compliments your gown to perfection. Was it manufactured in Italy?"

"Yes, Aamani, this is a jewel with special significance for me since it was a gift from Ramakanta on the occasion of our engagement. In many ways, it represents the love we have for one another, which was strong enough to bring me across the ocean and away from my beloved country."

Diana caressed the jewel lightly with a smile on her face, remembering with fondness the happy celebration of her engagement to the man she loved.   In that particular moment, she was oblivious to her surroundings and missed the look of hatred and jealousy in Aamani's eyes

§§§

CHAPTER FOURTEEN

THE "HOLI" DAY

It was the dawn of a new day, and the rising sun was dispersing with its power the shadows and darkness of night.

As an early riser, Diana was impatiently looking forward to enjoying the excitement and challenges of a new day while getting ready to take her morning bath.

Eagerly she stepped into the scented waters of her bathtub, which welcomed her with a warm embrace. She felt happy on that auspicious day and grateful for the people's acceptance in the exotic world she loved more each day.

The young bride delighted in the rose petals floating in the water, placed there by the thoughtfulness of the room's attendees.

The Zamindar was still sleeping when she got up. Lovingly she blew him a kiss but refrained from touching him for fear of disturbing his peaceful rest.

After the pleasant interlude, Diana rose unwillingly from the soapy waters and wrapped her lovely body in a soft pink towel, placed nearby for her convenience.

A joyous feeling overwhelmed her as she stretched her arms toward the ceiling, feeling free and unusually relaxed.

It was exceptionally liberating for the young woman to have her body unrestrained from the cumbersome Victorian corsets, as she pirouetted happily with the grace of a ballerina, relishing those moments of true freedom.

She then hastily dressed in a silk housecoat, whose delicate fabric adhered to her body like a second skin and allowed her sensual curves to show through.

With a bit of flirtatious playfulness, she glanced in a mirror but was startled by the reflection of the Zamindar's smiling face, looking with love and admiration in his eyes.

Diana felt a little shy in confronting his intense, passionate stare and instinctively wrapped her housecoat tighter around her body, while with a tone of mild reprimand, she asked.

Dearest, how long have you been standing there? I was under the impression that you were sleeping since I took great care not to disturb you."

The Zamindar answered with a smile as he moved closer to his bride.

"I am always disturbed when you are not in my arms, my love...I have been admiring you with discretion for a few long moments because you are so beautiful, and I desire you so much."

Diana lowered her eyes in shyness while a crimson glow suddenly appeared on her face.

"You are blushing, my darling. I can see it clearly on your face," said the Zamindar as he gently lifted her well-shaped chin and gazed deeply into her eyes.

"You look even lovelier with that glow on your cheeks. Although, you must not feel shy or uneasy around me since I am your man, and I wish for you to be comfortable in my presence and my arms."

Before Diana had time to answer, the Zamindar slipped his left arm around her waist, drew her close, and kissed her passionately on the lips with all the emotional hunger of his heart.

For a few magical moments, they were oblivious to their surroundings, captured by the power of the sensual moment and the intense desire and joy they always experienced in each other's arms.

As the burning embrace slowly simmered down, Diana placed her head on his chest, nestling happily in his arms, captivated by the accelerated beating of his heart.

Suddenly she noticed that the Zamindar held his right hand in a clenched fist. Even during their moment of passion, she could feel slight pressure against her back because of it.

She now moved away as she pointed to his tightly clasped hand, with a bit of amusement and curiosity in her voice.

"What are you hiding, dearest, some deep dark secret? Please let me see what is shielded so carefully in your hand. Is it something for me?"

The Zamindar, equally amused, moved the clenched hand toward Diana in an enticing way.

"Of course it's for you, my darling, a special surprise on this special day. Would you like to see it now?"

"Yes, dearest, I want to see it," said Diana with excitement in her voice, as she attempted, playfully, and with some efforts to pry open his fist.

In response, Ramakanta recoiled slightly from her, opened his hand, and threw against the girl a fistful of colorful gulal. A rainbow of red dust rained upon the surprised Diana, staining her clean clothes, her hair and even caused some markings to her face.

"What are you doing?" she asked, shocked by the unusual behavior as she glanced with a bit of distress at her stained reflection in the mirror.

"Look at me, Rami, "she said with an affectionate chide in her voice, "I am stained all over now, and after taking a bath…"

The Zamindar interrupted her with a burst of naughty laughter as he held her tightly in his arms.

"Don't you know today we celebrate Holi, which is better known as the Festival of Colors? It's traditional to throw these multi-colored powders on one another. I thought it might be fun to surprise you. Am I forgiven for my transgression, or are you angry with me?"

Diana remained silent, feigning displeasure and wanting to get even with her husband for the unexpected trick he played upon her

Aware of her displeasure, since he had also stained her lovely housecoat, The Zamindar walked toward a table resting on a sidewall and retrieved a small silver dish filled with bright pink powder.

"Look, darling. *Abeer* is the traditional name given to the colored powders used for these typical Hindu rituals. You may now throw the powder against me and get your just revenge…"

"I have no desire to take revenge, my dearest," interposed Diana with a smile, "after all, it's a matter of tradition…I am only sorry that my beautiful housecoat is now soiled and ruined."

"Don't worry, dearest, answered the Zamindar, "I will gladly buy you a new one."

"There is no need to buy a new one," answered Diana with a smile…I like it this way. The staining seems to give it a unique decoration and design."

They both laughed as Diana took hold of the traditional pink powder and threw a fistful toward the Zamindar. She then moved closer and smeared the colorful hue on his face with gusto, savoring her revenge.

"You learn quickly, my darling," said the Zamindar, "I am sure this must be unusual and even strange to you. Still, it's an ancient ritual, and we enjoy it as a happy and wonderful celebration."

"It's not so strange, dearest," said Diana. The celebration is reminiscent of Mardi Gras, a holiday where people go a little mad with unusual costumes, parades and throw streams of colorful paper at one another. We all have fun, and just like Holi, Mardi Gras is a joyful celebration."

"Thank you, my darling, for joining in the fun. I am sure today will be a special and happy celebration for all of us."

"Tell me about Holi, said Diana, "I wish to learn about the tradition and try to make it my own."

The Zamindar was truly happy about his bride's interest in his culture and began the narration of the Festival of Holi.

"Dearest, Holi is one of the major celebrations in India, commemorated with enthusiasm and joy on the full moon day in the month of Phalgun, which is the month of March as per the Gregorian calendar. For many Hindus, the festivities of Holi mark the beginning of the New Year as well, and like in the western world. It's an occasion to renew our aspirations and rekindle relationships while ending past conflicts. It is also an excellent time to rid ourselves of emotional impurities from the past."

"This is very similar to our New Year resolutions and celebration," interjected Diana with wonder, "it's truly amazing to discover how similar people are regardless of different cultures. I am learning about it every day, and it's a source of great interest to me. Please tell me more about the celebration, Rami. I am fascinated by it."

"I am delighted to tell you in detail, my love," answered the Zamindar.

"Traditionally, in Orissa, Holi assumes the name of 'DOL Purnima.' Radha and Krishna's idols are worshiped in our family's temple and placed on traditional wooden *viman,* then taken from village to village in a procession and celebration with beating drums and metallic musical instruments. Devotees follow in droves while young women dance around singing traditional songs, as men keep spraying toward them colored powder called abeer. The devotees chant the name of the Lord in a typical musical chorus. This festival is an integral ritual in the famous temple of Lord Jagannath in Puri. Since Lord Jagannath is a reincarnation of Lord Krishna."

"You mean that the beautiful temple in Puri, whose images you showed to me recently, is the famed temple of Lord Jagannath?" asked Diana with curiosity.

"Yes, dearest, the temple of Lord Jagannath is an architectural marvel in my state and an important pilgrimage destination for our people," replied the Zamindar with pride and religious devotion.

"Lord Jagannath is also the reincarnation of Lord Vishnu, one of the Hindu trinity gods. He is the Preserver, whereas Brahma is the Creator and Shiva is the Destroyer. These three Gods compose the Trinity of Hinduism, better known as Trimurti. There are some similarities in the Christian faith with the Holi Trinity, which unifies the Father, Son, and the Holy-Spirit as three persons in one."

"That is true, dearest," answered Diana, "however, since, in Christianity, we believe in only one God, the Trinity is a metaphor of different aspects of the Lord and not defined as separate entities by religious scholars, besides the concept remains a mystery…However, no matter how depicted in Christianity, we all believe that the Trinity represents a God of mercy, love, and not of vengeance, as it sometimes described in the old testament…"

"That is very interesting, my darling," interposed the Zamindar," we have our beliefs and different rituals, but ultimately we share the same reverence and faith in God."

"Yes, we do, dearest," answered Diana. We should be united as a human family and respect different points of view. I now look forward to witnessing the rituals of Holi, especially the dance and music part of it," she insisted with excitement in her voice, "since I love the Indian folklore."

"I am certain you will enjoy the celebration, my love," answered the Zamindar, "perhaps it will be a bit crowded for you since you are not used to the many people that converge to all the festivities in my country."

"Yes, I am a bit intimidated by large crowds," answered Diana, but I appreciate their enthusiasm and joy of living."

The Zamindar was genuinely impressed and grateful for his bride's willingness to share the many complicated traditions that were part of the people's everyday lives.

"Tell me, Rami," Diana asked with a little concern, "is it traditional for the Zamindar to walk among the people on this special day, and will they be restrained and respectful toward him even during the celebration of Holi? Or will they indulge and throw colored water and powder on all of us."

The Zamindar interrupted with laughter as he answered in an apologetic tone.

"Sorry, my darling, but for today we are all the same with no privileged status. If they wish, they can indulge in targeting us without restraint with colored water and powder."

"There are no restrictions?" Diana said, suddenly alarmed, "I don't like to be all wet and covered with colors in the middle of the street."

Although, she continued with an understanding smile.

"Since it's a national holiday, beloved by the people, I will not be a spoiler and join the fun despite my reticence."

"Thank you, my darling," said the Zamindar as he held her tightly in his arms, "you will have nothing to worry about, I assure you, we will have a wonderful day, and a tub filled with warm, scented water will be waiting for our pleasure and comfort at our return to the palace…"

The Zamindar paused and smiled at that point, caressing Diana's face as he continued with passion in his voice.

"The scented waters will be available to both of us, my love. It will be the crowning moment of a special day."

Diana remained silent but moved closer in his arms, concurring with the sensual and pleasurable expectation.

"After, my darling bride," the Zamindar continued with a smile, "our talented chef will prepare special delicacies for the occasion, such as pethas and laddoos made of puffed rice and sesame seed. They are truly delicious. I am sure you will enjoy them. People in the villages prepare them for the celebration and share the delicacies with family and friends."

"It sounds wonderful, dearest. Sorry if I sounded a bit reticent. I look forward to sharing the Festival of Holi with you and our people," said Diana as she rearranged a rebellious strand of hair from his forehead."

"My mother will also join us, my darling," answered Ramakanta with a bit of apprehension in his voice, "it's traditional for the Zamindar and family to be together and intermingle with the people on this special celebration."

"She is most welcomed, of course, since it's traditional," answered Diana resigned to the inevitability of spending the day with her mother-in-law.

The Zamindar was greatly relieved by his bride's forgiving nature. He was happy that everything was going so well despite their many challenges. However, at this point, Diana asked the Zamindar a disturbing question.

"Will Aamani be joining us during the festivities? After all, she is a member of the family now and should partake in the outing."

The Zamindar remained silent for a moment, unable to hide his uneasiness and displeasure in discussing Aamani with Diana. His answer was forthcoming but tainted with curtness.

"I don't know if she will be joining us…I suppose we will have to ask my mother."

Diana noticed the change of mood in her husband as she mentioned the name of Aamani in connection with the family. She was disturbed by it, having witnessed her husband's unexplained coldness toward his adopted sister.

"Is there a problem with Aamani, dearest? I noticed that you are not very friendly toward her. Besides, you never previously mentioned that you had a sister."

The Zamindar was uncomfortable with the subject since he hated lying to his bride. Instead, he attempted to answer her truthfully while avoiding unnecessary details about who the young woman actually was.

"You must understand, my darling, that I didn't know I had an adopted sister during my vacation in Italy. My mother adopted her without my knowledge, which is the reason why I never mentioned her name to you."

But despite the reassuring words, Diana was still not persuaded since she had a strange feeling that something was not quite right between her husband and Aamani.

She answered the Zamindar with a bit of skepticism in her voice.

"I think the reason your mother adopted Aamani is that she thought to have lost her son when you married a foreign woman...But I fail to understand your coldness toward her, who has been so gracious and welcoming to me. Therefore unless there is some specific problem that you have not shared with me, I hope that for my sake, you will be a little friendlier toward her."

The Zamindar thought best not to challenge Diana and change the uncomfortable subject. He smiled and said with a hurried sound in his voice.

"I will make a greater effort toward Aamani, although she has been singularly privileged to live in the palace due to my consent...But now, darling, it's time to get ready since we have a wonderful and exciting day awaiting us."

Diana smiled and quickly disappeared into the dressing area, eager to get ready for the holiday.

The holiday's excitement was palpable as the Zamindar and his bride stepped into the great outdoors. Diana faced her adopted society's cultural challenge as she entered the festival, chaotic and exciting scene.

She dressed simply for the occasion and favored a Salwar suit instead of her usual western attire, which would prove uncomfortable and problematic under the circumstance. Her flowing hair was braided and less susceptible to staining from the colored water that rained steadily throughout the area.

Laxmi Devi and Aamani joined them, as expected for the family's traditional outing, but remained deliberately at a distance as they walked through the crowd.

The revelry was in full swing in the boisterous crowd during a day of unification. The people temporarily ignored the ever-present caste system, as individuals from all walks of life intermingled in an informal and friendly way.

The young woman remained very close to her husband, overwhelmed by the sea of humanity that surrounded her. The Zamindar squeezed her hand lovingly in a comforting way.

However, the festive mood was infectious and enticing, as people celebrated with gusto the return of spring and the triumph of good over evil.

Diana was enticed by the revelry as colored powder and water were tossed into the air, drenching everyone in a rainbow of splendid hues. However, it was getting pretty messy, and the young woman placed a scarf over her head to prevent further staining to her hair.

She was amazed to see Laxmi Devi's typically immaculate attire, all soaked and stained with colors. The sophisticated and aristocratic lady laughed heartily and eagerly joined the fun without her usual haughtiness, which was so much part of her persona.

The unusual experience was a revelation to Diana. She admired that side of her mother-in-law, who at least could have fun while obediently follow the Hindu traditions.

She gazed around with amazement, admiring the beauty and tradition within the prevailing chaos

"Look, Rami," she said joyfully, pointing to the impressive presence of elephants at the celebration. "They are so splendid and majestic. I truly admire the creativity in decorating the mighty beasts with beautiful and lyrical designs painted almost throughout their bodies with such detailed artistry.

The Zamindar smiled happily and with pride in sharing the celebration's beauty with his bride, who valued and respected his culture.

Hand in hand, they walked deeper into the heart of the festivities as lovely young girls converged in a circle and began to dance accompanied by the loud beat of drums to the delight of the multitude of spectators.

Religious chants rose into the air, whose sounds were unfamiliar to the new Zamindarin but richly appreciated, as she attempted to become a part of the festive scene.

"You see, my darling," said the Zamindar, eagerly explaining the evolvement of the festivities to his bride.

"For this occasion, neighbors, friends, and family rejoice and pay respect to the gods…Holi also helps bring people together. Since rich and poor celebrate as one, strangers become friends, while the spirit of kinship prevails. People exchange gifts and sweet treats, strengthening the bonds of friendship. Here cultural celebrations and religious beliefs are blended into a unifying composite of traditions."

"Goodwill among people and exchange of gifts…" interposed Diana wistfully, "I guess that is reminiscent of Christmas, which was always my favorite holiday back home in Italy…Such a magical time, I used to look forward to it every year."

Noticing his bride's sadness and her longing for cherished memories, the Zamindar held her close to him as he said lovingly.

"We will celebrate your Christmas, my love, I promise it, and it will be as wonderful and festive as you remember it."

Diana placed her head on his chest, smiling as she said.

"Dearest, I am enjoying the celebration of Holi and also being here with our people because I am always happy when I am with you."

They held each other tightly, filled with joy, impervious to any challenges that may come their way through the power of their love.

The couple's loving overture did not escape Aamani's vigilant eyes since she was obsessed with them and oblivious to anything else. Her jaw suddenly tightened as jealousy and despair overwhelmed her.

She abruptly turned her head away from the sight that caused her so much sorrow. She felt lost and alone amid so much joy and celebration.

However, as a consummate performer, her anguish was invisible to everyone else as she blended in the celebration with ease.

Finally, after many exciting hours, it was time for the Zamindar and family to return to the palace. There was a sense of relief for Diana. She looked forward to washing away the colorful powder's stains from her body while continuing the wonderful celebration in the relative quiet of the estate.

She had made a great effort to learn about her new culture and society since she loved expanding her horizon and embracing new experiences.

However, there were exceptions, which proved particularly challenging to her. She was unwilling to compromise her fundamental values, even if they could prove unpopular to the people and her mother-in-law.

One day, while returning to the palace after a religious outing in the Dowager's company, a woman suddenly walked toward them. She greeted everyone with politeness and then faced Laxmi Devi with reverence and respect. She then went down on her knees before her, bowing so low that only the top part of her head was visible. Her body's positioning appeared to be following some ritual as she placed her hands on the dowager's feet. She then waited in that unusual position until the dowager touched the top of her head gently.

"What is she doing?" Diana whispered, unsettled by the strange occurrence, "why is that woman prostrated on the floor before your mother?"

Understanding her surprise at a ritual unfamiliar to people in the west, the Zamindar explained the reasons behind the ancient custom.

"Touching the feet of elders is an age-old Indian tradition considered to be a mark of respect, my darling. It's practiced in almost all Hindu families. Since Indians believe that when a person bows down and touches their elders' feet, it diminishes their ego while respecting the experience, achievements, and wisdom of the person whose feet are touched. The older person then, in turn, blesses the person touching their feet."

Diana remained silent for a few moments before answering, looking with interest at the unusual scene, and finally said.

"I don't like to question the social conduct of people from other cultures, and although I agree with the respect and value of elders, I believe there are other ways to show your appreciation…"

"I know this ritual is strange to you, dearest," interposed the Zamindar, "but is important to our people as a treasured tradition. Because of my status as Zamindar, they perform this ritual upon me as a sign of respect. Although only men may touch my feet and only women will touch yours. I am sure that this lady will wish to perform this ritual upon you as their Zamindarin."

Diana recoiled, disturbed by those words, and said with a deliberate sound.

"No, Rami! I don't mean to be difficult, but I will not allow anyone to perform this ritual upon me. I hope you will understand that in my belief, no one should go down on their knees or prostrate themselves on the floor before another human, regardless of their social status. There are other ways to show respect, and we should only show such humility in front of God."

"Don't worry, darling," answered the Zamindar with understanding and warmth, "no one will force you to go against your strongly held beliefs."

"Thank you, dearest, for understanding my feelings since I don't wish to disrespect the lady's religious point of view, and I truly appreciate her kindness toward me."

Laxmi Devi, who was near enough to hear the conversation, walked closer to the Zamindar while saying with a bit of sarcasm and loud enough for Diana to hear.

"I warned you, Ramakanta, she will never be one of us…"

The Zamindar ignored her words and held his bride by the hand with warmth and love. They soon walked happily together toward their beautiful estate, which glistened in the twilight.

§§§

CHAPTER FIFTEEN

THE OLEANDER'S TOUCH

Diana's life in her golden palace was a journey in discovery. She was learning to love her new life and the exciting world opening before her, filled with challenges also joy, and satisfaction.

She was amazed by the relative ease of the transition, considering the usual difficulties of entering into a society so different from her own.

Of course, there had been the expected difficulties concerning her mother-in-law, but the great love she had for her husband made the integration considerably easier. She trusted him completely and felt happy and safe by his side. Besides, the Zamindar was always at hand and available, making sure that she never felt lonely and unhappy in the unfamiliar surroundings.

The most significant challenges she suffered were the separation from her beloved country and the people she loved. However, Aunt Amelie and Prince Louis were always available through the steady correspondence they kept concerning the family. Besides receiving news of her estate, which gave her a sense of peace.

Diana was ecstatic to learn that they planned a trip to India. The possibility of seeing her dear Aunt Amelie again, also Prince Louis, considered an adopted brother in many ways, made her joy complete.

Meanwhile, elaborate preparations were in progress for their Vedic wedding ceremony, although, at Diana's request, the marriage vows would be private and only attended by family members. However, the celebration was open to everyone else and meant to be shared with the people.

The Hindu marriage ritual was much more elaborate than Diana expected it since it required considerable study to understand the symbolism connected with the occasion.

She made the necessary effort to learn it because she knew how important it was to her husband and all the people concerned.

"In a couple of days, we will be *truly* married in comparison to most people!"

She announced happily to the Zamindar as they walked into the garden.

"Besides being married in a legal ceremony in Italy, we shared our vows in the Christian Church, and now we shall marry once again in the Hindu tradition…I suppose it will be impossible for us ever to be separated."

The young woman laughed in amusement while speaking those words.

"No, my love," said the Zamindar, "we will never be apart again. Even in jest, the possibility is very painful to me since there could never be any joy in my life without you."

Noticing his distress, Diana caressed him gently with a smile while saying.

"No need to worry dearest, the connection given to us by destiny can't ever be diminished or destroyed."

Ramakanta regained his usual sense of humor as he answered.

"Well, my darling, perhaps we should marry a few more times in different ceremonies, just to play it safe."

They both laughed as they warmly embraced, relishing the beauty of that particular moment, whose perfection they wished it could last forever.

During dinner that evening, Laxmi Devi announced her willingness to host a pre-wedding celebration in honor of the forthcoming nuptials. The occasion would include musical offerings and traditional folk dances reflecting eastern India's rich and artistic heritage.

Diana was delighted since she loved the Indian folklore and especially the dancing, whose beauty held a special allure for her.

She was also aware that Indians traditionally tossed elaborate feasts in connection with weddings. Considering the celebration was in honor of the Zamindar and Zamindarin, it would surely be an exceptional event with a greater degree of elegance and style.

Although Diana was a private person who favored smaller gatherings, she was fascinated by the Indian traditions and looked forward to the Hindu pre-wedding celebrations with all its glory and enthusiasm.

In honor of the special evening, Diana wore a splendid royal blue and silver saree instead of her usual western attire. Her hair was pushed back and parted to one side, allowing her beautiful diamond earrings to sparkle in the reflected lights. The ever-present sapphire pendant graced her neck and completed the ensemble.

Soon the festive sounds of music resonated in the hall. Boys and girls engaged in a variety of traditional dances, moving around the area to the rhythm of the music in celebration of the grand event. They also performed many Indian classical folk dances, which were traditionally held the night before the nuptial. They made an exception in this case since the wedding was to take place in a couple of days.

The Zamindar's Bride

Diana and Rami shared the wonderful celebration joyfully, and the Zamindar was elated to see his bride so happy and comfortable in his world. He looked into her eyes with infinite love and gently caressed her hair.

"Thank you, my darling," he said softly, "for choosing to live in my country and embrace my culture...I hope we will always be as happy as we are today."

Ramakanta and Diana held each other's hands in that romantic moment, and their look of love was more eloquent than a thousand words.

Soon they were joined by Laxmi Devi, who made a surprising declaration.

"It is my great pleasure to announce that my daughter Aamani has graciously consented to dance in honor of the celebration. She will perform Odissi, which is indigenous to Orissa and believed to be the oldest of our country's classical dances."

Diana was thrilled by the unexpected announcement since she had no suspicions of manipulation from her mother-in-law, especially in connection with Aamani, whom she considered a dear friend in her new country.

However, in the excitement of the moment, she was unaware of her husband's obvious displeasure with Aamani's participation in the pre-wedding festivities. At the same time, she said with enthusiasm to the dowager.

"This is such a wonderful surprise, and I am very grateful to Lady Aamani for the generous gift since I am certain she is an exceptional dancer and will give an outstanding performance…"

"Yes, my dear," interposed Laxmi Devi with a sarcastic smile, "Aamani is experienced in the art of classical Indian dancing, besides having a natural talent for it. Odissi is a particularly complex and expressive dance form, with over fifty mudras, which are symbolic hand gestures used in the performance."

"This is very exciting," said Diana as she moved closer to the Zamindar with increased enthusiasm."

"Aamani knows how much I love Indian folklore, especially the dancing, and it was so nice of her to surprise us with this wonderful gift."

The Zamindar smiled in response to his bride's excitement. But anger rose within him, in the face of his mother's manipulations, to the detriment of his bride, who was unaware and considered Aamani, a friend.

The power of the family structure was all-encompassing in Indian society. Even the title of Zamindar couldn't diminish it. Reverence and deference to the elders in marriage were sacred, and Laxmi Devi knew that she would win the court of public opinion.

Ramakanta realized how difficult it was to control his mother's manipulations. He should have stopped her from the beginning by being honest with Diana about Aamani's true identity. It was too late now to make changes since the damage was by now irreparable. He glared at the dowager with contempt, but the lady ignored him and continued the conversation with Diana.

"I am very pleased you approve of Aamani's gift, my dear. Dancing is one of the most revered Indian arts because it incorporates melody and drama. Thus the human body becomes a vehicle of worship while invoking through artistic gesture the divine approval."

At that point, Laxmi Devi excused herself and moved toward the middle of the room, facing the general audience. She then clapped her hands, signaling an order.

In immediate response to the command, the young dancers receded toward the exit as Lady Aamani made her grand entrance in the center hall.

She looked lovely as she bowed in greeting to the audience, dressed in a colorful red and purple Odissi costume decorated with gold details and semiprecious stones.

The attire was unusually sexy with an exposed middle, which reached down to her navel. The hairstyle was accented with sparkling jewels and golden accents, while kajal makeup heavily outlined her expressive dark eyes, and henna red colored her full lips.

An intense sensuality emanated from her as she commenced the dance steps in her bare feet, which were covered by meticulously and artistically drawn red designs.

With each intricate step of the choreography, the silvery sound of little bells decorating her shapely ankles resonated in conjunction with the drums' dramatic beats.

Aamani executed the dance with panache and grace, which was equal to the finest, trained professional dancer, and the delighted audience richly appreciated her effort.

Diana was elated by the splendid performance and congratulated the girl with sincerity and warmth.

"I am very grateful dear Aamani, for such a lovely gift and your beautiful tribute to the dance folklore of India. I thank you for sharing your great talent with us."

"It was my honor to perform for such a special occasion. I am grateful for the appreciation, my lady," answered Aamani with a subdued, almost gloomy sound in her voice.

Diana was a bit surprised by her apparent sadness and lack of enthusiasm. Still, she thought it was inappropriate to question it at the moment since it could have been due to the stress and difficulty of the performance.

"I just loved your dancing," insisted Diana, "and I would be so grateful if you could teach me a few simple steps before the Hindu marriage ceremony. I would love to surprise Ramakanta on our special day because I believe it will make him happy."

"It is an honor to teach you, and I am certain you will be a most adept pupil," answered Aamani politely.

"I will do my best," Diana said with a smile," in honor of becoming the Zamindar's bride according to Hindu traditions because it's doubtful that the people accepted our western marriage. But now, at long last, I will take my rightful place by my husband's side and become the new Zamindarin."

"Yes, you will, finally become the new and true Zamindarin, beloved by your husband and all the people," said Aamani almost in a whisper as a look of anguish flashed in her eyes. She then suddenly stumbled as if she had lost her balance.

Diana immediately helped her while noticing her somber, depressed mood and asked with concern.

"What is the problem, Aamani? Don't you feel well?"

"I am fine, my lady, no need to worry. I am just overwhelmed by the stress of appearing in front of so many people."

"I can understand it," said Diana with a sympathetic smile, "I don't think I would have been able to do it since I am shy by nature. However, I am very grateful to you for the wonderful gift and amazing performance."

Aamani's smile couldn't overshadow the sadness in her eyes. She thanked Diana and excused herself politely before leaving the glittering hall, in such a sharp contrast to the grand entrance she made just a short time before.

In the early afternoon of the following day, the Zamindar received in his private office the unexpected visit from Dinesh Maharathy, the palace's head gardener.

The elderly gentleman had been in service to the family for decades. He was known for his loyalty, dedication, and creative ability in preserving the stunning and manicured beauty of the sprawling gardens in the estate.

"Good afternoon Dinesh," the Zamindar asked, a bit perplexed by the unexpected visit. "Is there a problem looming in your perfect, bucolic world?"

"Forgive me, my Lord, for the intrusion," answered Dinesh in a somber tone, which sharply contrasted with the Zamindar's cheerful greeting, as he respectfully placed his hands together and bowed to Ramakanta.

"I know you are busy, but I thought it was important to make you aware of a recent and disturbing situation, which I believe merits your attention…"

"What disturbing situation?" Interposed the Zamindar, slightly distracted as he rearranged some papers on his desk. He then continued, apparently ignoring Dinesh's serious demeanor.

"What is the problem, my friend? Are we expecting a drought or a looming monsoon at the estate?"

"No, my Lord," answered Dinesh with a deliberate sound, perhaps a bit miffed at not being taken seriously by the Zamindar.

"The problem has nothing to do with the caretaking of the gardens or the weather…It concerns Lady Aamani."

The Zamindar's friendly and casual demeanor changed immediately in response to his words. He became suddenly alarmed and moved closer to the gardener with renewed interest in the conversation as he asked with urgency in his voice.

"What is the problem regarding Lady Aamani? It must be serious if you deemed it important enough for my attention?"

"Yes, my Lord, it is important enough, or I wouldn't have disturbed you...The situation with the lady occurred earlier in the day, actually just a short time ago," answered Dinesh, a bit flustered by the sudden urgency displayed by the Zamindar, as he cleared his throat before answering.

"Today, while working in the vicinity of the greenhouse, I heard some strange noises coming from there and noticed that someone had broken in and was rummaging the place. As you know, this is the area where we store our most precious and delicate flowers, also a large variety of chemicals and pesticides. Because of it, the greenhouse is a restricted area, and only a few are permitted access."

Dinesh paused to gather his thoughts as the Zamindar held on to his every word.

"I was disturbed by the situation and immediately decided to investigate and confront the intruder. However, as I entered the area, I was stunned to see that the trespasser was none-other than Lady Aamani, who appeared startled by my presence, and attempted unsuccessfully to hide behind some large potted plants."

The gardener took a deep breath at this point before continuing, as the Zamindar appeared anxious and disturbed by his words.

"The lady seemed nervous and quite distressed by my presence, as she attempted unsuccessfully to hide from view a bottle that she had taken from our greenhouse collection of pesticides. I noticed at first glance the skull and crossbones on the label, and I knew it was a potent poison, which contains arsenic, a restricted chemical."

Dinesh paused as the Zamindar asked with alarm in his voice.

"Did Lady Aamani explain the reason for her presence there?"

"I did ask her for the reason of needing such dangerous chemical," answered Dinesh, "but she did not answer and appeared increasingly upset, almost in a state of panic…"

Dinesh paused and shook his head, disturbed by the recollection, before continuing.

"At that point, my Lord, because of her lack of cooperation, I attempted to remove the bottle from her hands, but she pushed me away since I was blocking the exit door. I lost my balance in the process while she ran away, still clutching the bottle before I had the chance to take it away from her."

The Zamindar was stunned and deeply disturbed by the unsettling occurrence. Alarmed, he immediately rang a bell, summoning one of his guards, and asked with urgency in his voice.

"Where is lady Aamani? Is she with my mother?"

"No, my Lord," answered the guard, "Lady Aamani is not with her ladyship, who is presently busy attending to the wedding preparations."

"Then where is Lady Aamani? Have you seen her?" Asked the Zamindar with a sharp sound in his voice.

"Sorry, my Lord," answered the guard, "I have not seen her today, but if you wish, I will do the necessary search and try to locate her as soon as possible."

The Zamindar signaled consent as the guard began to leave the study with haste. He then suddenly stopped and said as if he had just remembered.

"My Lord, I believe that lady Aamani must be back in her rooms by now. According to the palace scheduling, she is playing host to the Zamindarin for afternoon tea."

A cold shiver went down the spine of the Zamindar at the sound of those words. Sheer terror overwhelmed him with a sense of dread that his beloved Padma was in imminent danger.

With panic rising, he shouted an unusual order to the guard.

"I command you to sound the alarm right now!"

"The alarm? For what reason, my Lord?" asked the guard, stunned by the sudden order.

"Don't waste time with unnecessary questions," said the Zamindar sharply. "Sound the alarm, now!"

In response to the command, the lugubrious resonance of gongs spread in the palace.

Many guards appeared throughout the area in reaction to the alarm as an unsettling sense of anxiety mounted among the palace dwellers.

Time was fleeting, terrified, and fearing the worst in a desperate attempt to save the life of his beloved bride. Without giving any explanations, he started running with the speed of a gazelle through the endless maze of corridors toward lady Aamani's rooms. Unfortunately, they were at the far end of the palace.

He began shouting the name of Diana on top of his lungs, apparently trying to create as much noise and disruption possible, hoping desperately to stop a looming tragedy from taking place.

Although he was running swiftly and very light on his feet, the Zamindar felt as if he lived in an altered state of reality because of his panic and anguish. It seemed to him that the world was standing still and he was helplessly frozen in a time warp and unable to move, as little pearls of cold sweat appeared on his forehead while he moaned with despair

"Diana, my love, my life...Please God, let me arrive in time."

§§§

CHAPTER SIXTEEN

THE RISING DAWN

The alarm's ominous sound suddenly disrupted the Zamindar's palace peace and harmony. No one knew where the danger was coming from and how to protect themselves. Therefore, panic ensued.

Many guards followed the Zamindar, while others began to patrol the estate without knowing who the enemy was or the reason for the disruption.

It was impossible to garner any information from the Zamindar, whose panic and distress was evident to everyone, although the mystery remained on the reason why.

Like everyone else, Laxmi Devi rushed out of her rooms in response to the commotion but could not receive any explanations or answers to her lingering questions. She then shouted with anger in her voice.

"What is going on around here, and why is the alarm on in the palace? Will someone answer me, or has everyone gone mad!"

With rising frustration in receiving no answers to the reason for the panic, the Dowager finally, and with reluctance, decided to join the guards who were following the Zamindar in the directions of Aamani's rooms.

Meanwhile, Ramakanta's nightmarish journey took only a few precious minutes since Aamani's residence in the palace was at a relative distance from his office. But it seemed like an eternity since Diana's premonition of danger and death flashed in his mind and contributed to his sense of panic and despair.

Finally, still breathless, he arrived at his destination and could now see the beautifully sculpted doors to Aamani's rooms, which were just a few steps away.

However, as he approached them, he suddenly stopped, overwhelmed by a sense of terror that almost paralyzed him, fearing what he might find on the inside.

Finally, without further delays, he pushed with determination the bronze handles, and the mighty doors gave way without resistance as he erupted aggressively into the room.

Because of his state of panic, it took the Zamindar a few seconds more to find some clarity in the dimly lit area. The fear was so intense that he had difficulty catching his breath because of the violent beating of his heart.

Mercifully, as clarity suddenly prevailed, with indescribable relief, he was immediately rewarded by the sight of Diana sitting comfortably by a nearby table.

Aamani was standing by her side after apparently having poured tea in two cups. She still held in her hand the beautiful silver teapot, which initially had been a gift from Diana to her mother-in-law

Both women seemed startled by the unexpected aggressiveness of his presence. Aamani, in reaction, immediately released the silver vessel on top of the table. She then grabbed one of the teacups and held it firmly in her hands as she slowly moved toward the rear of the room.

The Zamindar ignored her for the moment, seemingly in a state of euphoria after the terrible fright he endured. He rushed toward Diana and lifted her body off the chair, leaving her breathless from the tight embrace. He then asked with concern in his voice.

"Padma, my love, my life, are you all right?"

Diana was stunned and shocked by her husband's panicked behavior while struggling to catch her breath from the loving stranglehold he had on her.

"Of course, I am all right, dearest," she finally said with trepidation in her voice as she attempted to calm him down by gently caressing his face.

"What is the problem, Rami? Why are you so distressed? I can still see the fear in your eyes..."

She paused for a moment, trying to understand all the disruption that was taking place in the palace and the reason that caused her husband such anguish.

"Rami, there must be a valid reason for your eruption into Aamani's rooms in such an aggressive manner...I don't understand why you are so distressed. Please tell me, dearest, what is the problem I have the right to know?"

Diana then pointed to the silver teapot on the table, surrounded by various desserts, prominently displayed in elegant trays as she continued.

"Just a few minutes ago, we were startled by the sound of the alarm as we were preparing to enjoy our afternoon tea and biscuits.

Aamani graciously offered them in honor of our forthcoming wedding, but the ominous sound of the alarm disrupted the celebration, and we still don't know the reason why?"

The Zamindar remained silent, unable to answer the question at that moment, although finally, convinced that his bride was unharmed. He now focused his attention on Aamani.

There was a look of terror in the young woman's eyes as she retreaded further in the room while holding tightly in her grasp the fatal teacup.

She appeared to be in a state of panic, feeling entrapped and exposed, in rooms that had suddenly become a military compound in response to the alarm. A multitude of palace guards had dutifully invaded the area to protect the Zamindar from possible danger.

Laxmi Devi had also entered the rooms, concerned about the disruption in the palace. She wondered the reasons why the Zamindar and the guards had invaded Aamani's rooms. She looked around with curiosity, trying to understand what hidden danger was lurking in a peaceful environment that had mysteriously created so much panic.

The Dowager attempted to question her son, but he ignored her and waived her firmly away with a motion of his hand. He then continued to focus his attention on Aamani.

Terror was visible on her face as she continued to recoil toward the back wall, almost wanting to disappear in the shadows of the room.

Ramakanta was concerned that the precarious situation appeared aggravated by the palace guards' ominous presence, who frightened Aamani. He also looked on with real concern at the teacup, which she held so tightly in her hands, as a possible, desperate way to escape the entrapment of the situation.

The Zamindar moved slowly toward her in an attempt to diminish her distress since, at that moment, she was quite unstable and vulnerable. With a friendly tone, Ramakanta addressed her soothingly.

"Please don't be afraid, Aamani, I promise that no harm will come to you, and there will be no dire consequences for any actions you might have taken because, thankfully, no injuries have occurred…"

He paused for a moment while slowly moving toward the girl as he continued speaking.

"Please, come voluntarily with us without fears of reprisal…In this regard, I give you my word of honor as the Zamindar.

The young woman continued to remain silent, but there was a look of clarity in her eyes for a moment. She looked around, glaring at the fearsome guards who had invaded her domain, but her fear and panic seemed slightly diminished in response to the Zamindar's words.

That was until her eyes met Laxmi Devi's disapproving gaze. The Dowager's disdain was plain to see as she glared at Aamani with anger and contempt.

The domineering woman was furious that her usually obedient pupil brought such negative attention upon herself and disruption within the palace. However, she was still in the dark about the reasons why.

The apparent rejection of the powerful lady proved devastating to the young woman. She felt lost without her protection and friendship. In her delusion, she thought no one other than Laxmi Devi ever valued her, and she now felt alone and hopeless.

In her twisted mind, there was only one way to escape the entrapment of a world that had ignored her and made her feel invisible. It was time to be noticed by showing her determination, courage, and resolve.

Without warning, before anyone could do anything to stop her, she brought the fatal teacup to her lips, and without hesitation, drank the liquid with a fast gulp.

"No, Aamani, nooo!" shouted the Zamindar as he attempted desperately to reach and stop her.

But it was too late now. The tragic young woman stood silent and defiant, almost triumphant In her madness. She thought everyone finally noticed and appreciated how special, impressive, and courageous she was.

Sadly that euphoric moment was short-lived since within seconds, in front of the shocked audience, with a bloodcurdling scream, she fell to the floor with her body twisting in agonizing pain.

Diana, who had been standing silently by, was shocked by the unexpected turn of events. Overwhelmed and horrified, she quickly approached the girl, trying desperately to find a way to help her.

The Zamindar attempted to induce her to regurgitate the poisoned brew by compressing her middle with considerable force.

But no help was humanly possible or available at that time, as the cold hand of death was triumphant and taking greedy possession of the tragic girl.

The agonizing pain she suffered was gut-wrenching and terrifying to see as a slimy greenish foam began oozing out of her mouth, twisted in torturous pain.

Although suddenly, like the burning of a candle whose light shines brightest in the end, Aamani's convulsive contortions stopped, and a deadly silence permeated the room as everyone looked on in shock and horror.

She seemed almost peaceful as she stared at the Zamindar who was leaning toward her, overwhelmed with dread at the pitiful sight.

Aamani attempted to lift her body with some effort as she moved closer to the object of her obsession. Then suddenly, without warning, she grabbed his hand with unusual strength and whispered passionately.

"I love you, my Zamindar, I love you forever..."

But the sound of those words died in her throat as another ferocious attack of agonizing pain ensued, more violent than before. Piercing screams erupted from her mouth, followed by a choking, gurgling sound that brought chills to everyone's spine, until there was only a deathly silence, as her body lay lifeless on the floor. But her hand remained in death, tightly clenched around the Zamindar's wrist.

A stunned silence followed the horror of the moment, as they all looked bewildered and unable to comprehend the tragedy that had just taken place.

Ramakanta began to take control of the tragic situation. He extricated his wrist from Aamani's death grip and returned quickly on his feet.

He immediately went toward Diana and gently lifted her from the floor since she was on her knees leaning over the young woman's body, overwhelmed by grief and shock.

He held her in a loving, protective embrace while attempting to calm her anxiety and despair.

"Why did she do it Rami, why?" Diana repeated desperately, "Aamani was so young, so lovely."

Ramakanta remained silent while continuing to hold her tightly in his arms. He had difficulty reconciling with the unspeakable tragedy that had just taken place in his home and his life.

Because of the terrible shock, Diana was unable to understand, at least for the moment, the full scope of the tragic situation. She was heartbroken because of Aamani's suicide. Her concern was all for her since the girl was someone dear, and she believed to have been her friend.

However, after the initial shock, clarity finally set in as she glanced at the silver teapot resting on the table and glistening in the many lights of the room.

The vessel looked beautiful and inviting while still holding the poisoned brew in its middle that killed Aamani.

Sadly, she gazed at the artistically crafted container from her native Italy, purchased as a token of friendship, while now it was only a symbol of death.

Diana lowered her head, overwhelmed by the pain of loss. But her mind was now clear, and she was finally able to discern the cruel reality without the confusion of deep emotions.

Her eyes immediately focused on the second teacup still resting on the table. The deadly cup she was about to drink in celebration. That is, if not disrupted by the fortuitous alarm and the unexpected appearance of her husband.

She held her breath, gazing in horror at the cup Aamani drank from, which had caused such an agonizing death. The venomous goblet that now laid fragmented on the floor next to the young woman's corpse.

At that moment, there were no more pretenses to obscure the grim reality. The poisoned tea was also meant for her since Aamani, whom she thought to be her friend, wanted her to die for unknown reasons.

A cold shiver went through her body at the terrifying thought. She now recalled the girl's passionate words of love, spoken to her husband in her native language of Oriya, before her death.

Romantic expressions she was familiar with since the Zamindar had mentioned them to her so many times before.

The devastating reality was much too painful, and Diana backed away almost abruptly from the Zamindar's loving embrace, beset by a sense of dread. He still attempted to hold her in his arms, wanting desperately to comfort her distress in that terrible, revealing moment.

The young woman was not receptive since her feelings of trust had been challenged or perhaps shattered.

It was now clear to Diana that her husband had saved her life because, for some unknown reason, he knew that Aamani wanted to kill her and had been successful in preventing it.

It was painful to think that he had not been honest with her since the grim reality was impossible to ignore.

At this point, she only wanted to know why the young woman chose to die and attempted to murder her in the process.

"Rami, please tell me who was Aamani?" she asked with an uncompromising sound.

"I have always been suspicious that there was something strange about your attitude toward her. I even asked you the reason why but never received a proper answer. However, now I must know the truth, and without any further delays."

"I promise to tell you all you wish to know as soon as possible, my darling," answered the Zamindar, as he glanced at the crowded room, "but with more privacy, and not in this place of death."

Diana was not very amenable to the reasonable suggestion. She had been too deeply wounded, not only by escaping a terrifying death but because of the perceived notion of betrayal, from the person she loved and trusted most in the world.

"No, Rami, I want to know the truth *now*, since I believe we belong here because we are very much part of this tragedy…"

She stopped and looked around emotionally drained, noticing the multitude of guards who had invaded Aamani's rooms. The onlookers included the palace workers who had crowded the entrance doors, openly curious about the unfolding events.

"I think there is very little to hide at this point," she continued with a somber tone. The people's limited knowledge of the English language might give a little protection to our privacy. However, right now, it makes little difference to me considering the circumstances…"

Diana paused and inhaled deeply to control the pain that overwhelmed her. She then continued with her innate dignity and determination.

"Before she died, Aamani said that she loved you, there was passion in her words, and it was *not* the love of a sister…"

Diana closed her eyes as bitter tears flowed down her face. She had been terribly hurt by the tragic events and felt lost and alone, almost a stranger in the new world she had learned to love so deeply. But like a mirage, it was disappearing before her eyes, in that tragic moment of death and betrayal.

The Zamindar was distraught because of his failings toward his bride, the woman he loved above all others. It was terrifying to realize the danger he had inadvertently exposed her life in the useless attempt to appease his mother's cruel manipulations.

He knew it was too late now, but it was essential to tell the absolute truth concerning Aamani. He wanted to be as honest as possible and regain some measure of trust in the invisible divide that now existed between them.

"Aamani was the girl I was supposed to marry," he finally said, "she had been chosen with a chart by the stars to become the future Zamindarin when we were still children," he paused with a painful sigh before continuing.

"I never realized she had such strong feelings toward me since our union was arranged, and in many ways, we were like strangers..."

The Zamindar closed his eyes beset by emotions before continuing.

"Weeks before the actual wedding, I knew I couldn't go through with it because I was not in love with her. She was to me like a little sister and nothing more…"

He now glanced at the girl's body before continuing with great sorrow.

"I knew that she would be disappointed in not becoming the Zamindarin because it's such an important title among our people. However, she had many suitors and came from a distinguished family. I expected her to marry someone else and find happiness in that union."

Ramakanta moved closer to Diana while continuing with determination.

"Please try to understand, my darling, that I followed my heart and the will of destiny. It was a powerful lure that guided me to a faraway land to find you, the girl of my dreams and the love of my life."

Ramakanta now remained silent and deeply concerned about her response to his true feelings of remorse.

Diana answered, but there was disappointment and sorrow in her voice. She felt betrayed and not receptive to any explanations. She shook her head in disbelief while saying.

"Aamani was the girl you were supposed to marry…The one chosen by your family according to traditions?"

The young woman was unable to control her disappointment while speaking.

"You knew the truth but allowed your mother's meddling to continue and kept it from me. While Aamani lived in the palace under false pretenses."

There was a bitter sound in Diana's voice as she continued.

"Neither Aamani nor I have been treated with respect, under the circumstances. She was a tool for creating friction in our marriage, and I was lied to…"

The young woman stood tall and proud before continuing with a more determined sound in her voice.

"You should have trusted me with the truth. I knew how deeply marriage and family connection are ingrained in the Indian society, far more than to people in the west. I expected rejection and dissent by my presence here. But I hoped to face it with you by my side and with the strength of our love."

Diana glanced briefly at Laxmi Devi before continuing.

"I know the reason for this cruel deception, deliberately created as a wedge between us to destroy our marriage. In this case, the ploy has been highly successful."

Diana became silent for the moment, unable to shield the pain that overwhelmed her in the tragic surroundings, while the Zamindar addressed her with great emotions.

"Can you forgive me, my love, for my failures in not understanding your courage in facing the adversity of the situation? This tragic deception has proven me unworthy to be your husband and even the Zamindar."

Ramakanta glared at his mother as he held Diana's hands while continuing.

"Please believe, my darling, that I was not aware of Aamani's love for me and a mindset capable of committing suicide and even murder. She was always very respectful and reserved, making it impossible to understand her true nature and the destructive fire that burned within her…"

"I have no desire to cast blame," interrupted Diana in a somber tone, "I know you love me and never meant to cause me pain or harm. You saved my life, for which I will be forever grateful. But something inside of me is broken right now. I feel lost, terribly alone, and overwhelmed with sorrow…"

Her voice broke suddenly, filled with emotions. She then pointed toward Aamani's pitiful remains while saying.

"There is no question she must have been mentally unstable. But, bringing her into the palace without any regard for her feelings was irresponsible at best. She witnessed our love and happiness, which disrupted the delicate balance of her mind, and I believe it prompted this tragedy."

Diana closed her eyes for a moment, trying to gather her thoughts before continuing.

"To Aamani, I was this foreign woman who usurped everything she felt entitled to…I am sure that she must have hated me because of it and decided that I deserved to die.

Diana slowly walked toward Aamani's body, then respectfully went down on her knees and crossed herself devoutly.

She was shocked and overwhelmed by the awful metamorphosis upon her face, which a short while before had been so fresh and lovely.

With respect, her trembling hands closed her eyes, which in life had been so luminous and bright but now dull and static in death. She also rearranged her disheveled hair around her face to give some dignity to her poor remains.

Then Diana remained silent and in prayer for a few seconds more before whispering with heartbreak.

"Goodbye, Aamani, may you rest in peace, in God's merciful arms…I forgive you!"

The young woman stood now, attempting to retain a sense of dignity in the crowded room while burning tears flowed down her face. She turned toward the Zamindar for a brief moment, with all the pain of that terrible day etched upon her lovely face. Then without further hesitation, she ran out of the tragic area.

The Zamindar immediately followed Diana, ignoring all who were present, including his mother. No orders were given since his priority was to help and comfort his deeply wounded bride.

His heart was in turmoil, as a feeling of dread and loneliness prevailed because an emotional barrier now existed between them, and he feared that he might not be able to remove it.

Laxmi Devi, ignored by her son, and left alone without the usual, deference in front of the large audience, struggled to contain her anger and disdain.

She felt no compassion for the dead girl, only contempt. She blamed Aamani's weak character and lack of dignity for all the disruption in the palace and the humiliation she had to endure because of it.

The young woman had proven to be a failure and a great disappointment to the lady. Therefore unworthy of her favoritism for the title of Zamindarin.

Filled with anger and nursing her bruised ego, she pointed to Aamani's pitiful remains with disdain and commanded the guards in a sharp and deliberate tone.

"Take her away!

§§§

CHAPTER SEVENTEEN

FOREVER IN MY DREAMS

For the first time since their marriage, Diana slept alone, without her husband's loving arms about her. The tragic circumstances had created an invisible barrier between them, and it seemed impossible at least for the moment to penetrate it or destroy it.

The young woman seemed to have regressed into a world of our own. She was overwhelmed by grief, and a sense of loss, whose magnitude she never experienced before in her young life.

The Zamindar's Bride

All her dreams of a happy and bright future in the beautiful exotic world she had hoped to conquer with her love had suddenly disappeared like dust in the wind. She was left only with the depths of her despair, in surroundings that suddenly seemed remote and unfamiliar to her.

That night Diana sought comfort in the plush softness of her lonely bed. She wrapped the covers tightly about her to quell the fears that beset her usual calm and optimistic nature.

The sensation of loneliness was pervasive in the surroundings of the splendid palace. A place she had hoped to find welcoming as her new home and to live happily by her husband's side.

Unable to find solace to her despair, a torrent of burning tears clouded her vision and flowed unhindered onto her pillow, drenching the delicate silk fabric to the core.

She felt helpless to control her emotions, and a sense of panic overwhelmed her as if all the bright lights of her life had suddenly dimmed and turned into gloom. After a long while and out of sheer exhaustion, Diana fell into a deep, troubled sleep.

The Zamindar, who was also present in the room, sat dejected in a dark corner, almost obscured from sight. He felt powerless at that moment to comfort her despair and remained instead at a discrete distance, overwhelmed by a sense of remorse and sorrow.

He dwelled on the danger he had unintentionally caused her and his inability to bring some comfort to his bride. There was a sense of loss and disconnect from his beloved Padma, which at the moment seemed so very distant, almost unreachable to him.

Ramakanta knew how devastating the day had been for Diana, especially in the awareness of having escaped a terrifying death. There was nothing he could do at that moment to bring her peace since she wanted to be left alone to cope with her sorrow.

After a while, he finally decided to let her rest in the expectation that she would forgive some of the failures he had embraced as a responsible person. He held on to the hope that somehow she would retain her sense of faith in the future of their marriage. However, it was a tall order, considering the magnitude of the tragedy and the turbulence that had disrupted their lives.

He walked with a soft stride toward the bed for fear of waking her, almost holding his breath. He then decided for her comfort to remove the tear-soaked pillow and exchange it for a fresh and dry one.

The Zamindar gently lifted her body and held her close for a brief moment as he placed the new, soft pillow under her head. He caressed her face with infinite love and marveled at how peaceful she looked in her deep slumber.

Diana had found solace in the oblivion of sleep, the only refuge available to stifle her fears and the grim reality of that terrible day.

He planted a soft, gentle kiss on her lips while whispering with great emotions.

"Sleep well, my love, my life, and may the sunshine of a new day bring you peace as you first awaken."

He then stood still, disheartened, as he stared at her loveliness for a few minutes more before walking swiftly toward the exit door.

However, the Zamindar did not notice in that moment of parting that her eyes were now wide open, and an overwhelming look of sorrow followed him as he walked out of the room.

The Zamindar, in deference to her distress, chose to remain close to her, although in an adjacent bedroom. He feared disrupting her sleep or forcing his presence upon her since she favored the blessing of solitude.

The night was long and filled with restlessness for Ramakanta as he attempted to sleep. There was a painful feeling of loneliness without the presence of his beloved bride. He needed to hold her in his arms as he did many times before. Suddenly, there was a sensation of emptiness that was very disruptive and painful to endure.

He tossed and turned, aching to find some solace in the blessing of sleep, as he attempted with little success to stop the disturbing, racing thoughts that haunted him without mercy.

For the first time, he felt a loss of control and the inability to bring back some order into his life.

Finally, as dawn was slowly breaking, he fell into a sound sleep out of sheer exhaustion, although disturbing images and gloomy, unsettling nightmares filled the blessed interlude.

Several hours later, he was awakened from the deep, unpleasant slumber by the sun's bright light. He was a little disoriented at first, but as his mind cleared, he became aware that it must have been late in the morning since the sun was by now high in the sky.

The Zamindar was usually an early riser, although strangely, on this eventful morning, his servants had failed to awaken him at the usual time and bring him his traditional cup of tea.

He looked around with sadness at the elegant but empty room, as the name of his beloved *Padma* immediately flashed into his mind.

With great haste, he jumped out of bed, retrieved his housecoat from a nearby chair, and without hesitation, entered the splendid rooms he had shared with his bride.

His heart skipped a beat as he noticed that the area and the bed were now empty. He walked around searching for Diana, hoping that she was dressing or taking her bath.

Unfortunately, she was not there, and the bed in the room appeared to be back in perfect order. However, the silken pillow placed under her head the night before was now a disturbing sight since his bride's sapphire pendant now rested there by a handwritten note.

Although there was no trace of Diana, Jasmine's scent from her hair was still alive on the silken fabric.

With his heart in turmoil, he grabbed the delicate parchment, which appeared to have been stained by tears. He read the few phrases written by his bride that unfortunately confirmed his worst fears.

My love,
Something is broken inside of me,
and I must find a way to mend it.
I will come back to you only if
I can be whole again and regain
the peace of mind that seems
to be lost at this time.
Destiny brought us together
and I hope that it will show us
the way back to each other again.
Remember Rami. I love you eternally.
Padma

The Zamindar's Bride

The Zamindar closed his eyes as he held the note close to his heart. He then gently caressed the sapphire pendant, which had been his engagement present to Diana, and she had often called it the symbol of their love.

Despair was all that remained of their ideal marriage. The painful, grim reality of an unwanted separation filled the Zamindar with desolation and loneliness.

He quickly summoned the palace head guard and asked with trepidation.

"Where is the Zamindarin? Is she still in the palace, or has she left by now?"

There was a look of sorrow in the guard's eyes as he immediately answered the probing and disturbing question.

"Yes, My Lord, she is gone...The Zamindarin requested a carriage earlier this morning and left the palace with a few personal belongings over an hour ago. She made a further request that you should not be disturbed from your sleep and allowed to awaken at your leisure."

The Zamindar remained silent and dignified, not revealing to the guard his inner turmoil and the despair that overwhelmed him. After a brief pause, the man continued with some apprehension in his voice.

"We followed the orders of the Zamindarin, my Lord, out of respect, we dared not challenge her request…"

"You did well," interposed the Zamindar with a positive and dignified sound in his voice, understanding the guard's concern.

"My wife has always been free to travel as she wished. I approve that you gave her the proper respect."

He paused, took a deep breath, and rearranged the belt of his housecoat before continuing as he attempted to control the anxiety in his voice.

"Where did she go? Do you have an itinerary of her travels?"

"Yes, my Lord," answered the guard, "She wanted to be taken to the train station and travel to Calcutta, where she is planning to board a ship on the way back to her native Italy."

A deep sigh erupted from his chest at the sound of those words. The pain the Zamindar experienced was plain to see, and he didn't care at that point about appearances or his dignity. He then asked with an imperious sound.

"Was a proper escort provided to the Zamindarin for her safety until she boards the ship?"

"Yes, my Lord, rest assure that all precautions have been taken and provided for the Zamindarin to ensure her safety until she leaves the Indian soil."

The Zamindar, at that point, dismissed the guard with a gesture of his hand. He felt nothing at that moment. He was numb from the shock of having lost, at least for the moment, the woman he loved.

What made the situation worse was the reminder that it was the day they were supposed to be married in the Vedic ceremony, which was to be a festive occasion to be shared with his people.

Diana had made great efforts to learn the elaborate ceremony, to honor his heritage with love and enthusiasm. But now, all was lost in the Zamindar's eyes, and there was an emptiness that no one else could fill as if life had suddenly lost its colors.

He thought about following her in an attempt to convince his wife to remain by his side. But he dismissed the idea in deference to her wishes and the great love he had for her.

Ramakanta dared not ask for more since she had given up so much when she came to India as his bride. He understood that after the devastating occurrences, she needed the comfort of her country of origin. To be in familiar places and find the peace of mind that was missing for the moment.

The Zamindar wished that his Padma would return on her own volition, without undue pressure, and have once more faith in their marriage, or it would have no value at all.

He walked toward his office and sat desponded by his desk, trying to gather his thoughts and calm his anxiety. Suddenly, the lovely image of Diana appeared before his eyes, reminding him of the cruel reality.

A deep sigh erupted from his chest as he finally experienced the pain of loss, which was acute and devastating.

"Padma, my love," he whispered, "please come back to me. I will wait for you forever, in this life and beyond if necessary."

He felt alone and needed to express his feelings the only way he knew how in his poetic soul.

The Zamindar's Bride

He grabbed a pen and began to compose a message to his beloved bride, and he felt a sense of comfort as he wrote.

* My Padma *
The love for you, my Zamindarin, pervaded the vastness of my world, my sky, my dreams in a helpless moment.
Imagine me now, a solitary and ostracized barren cell lost in a limitless sandy habit where my virgin dreams were sprouted.

But now, I am being tossed by the seasonal onslaught of blinding winds and sweeping shadows under a looming and barren sky.

I felt the primordial thirst in my parched throat, of lost dreams and endless desires, during my lingering, lonely nights, in the solitary confinement of my soul.

I wait on a forlorn hope of a pregnant cloud and pining for the chaotic drops of a torrential monsoon to restore the verdant splendor of our love.

******

A month passed from that faithful day when his beloved bride walked out of his life and returned to her native country. For the Zamindar, his very existence seemed to have lost meaning. Now each day seemed pretty much like the next. However, he continued to work diligently, with his usual sense of responsibility and consideration for his estate and the people's welfare.

But he never felt more lonely or unhappy in his entire life. He had written to his friend, Prince Louis, with the plea of looking after his wife's welfare since he could not care for or protect her at present.

His friend answered quickly and encouraged him not to worry since Diana was safe and back in her estate in Italy. However, she had requested family and friends to respect her privacy and give her a little time alone.

The Zamindar's Bride

The Zamindar's missed his bride so much, and his desire for her was more intense each passing day, especially during the endless, lonely nights.

He hoped and prayed that she would return to him soon, and on her own volition. But the pain of loss increased each passing day since no one could replace Diana in his heart or fill the void in his life.

During the difficult time, Ramakanta had no contact with his mother. She didn't receive the usual invitations, which in the past used to be commonplace between them.

However, Laxmi Devi refused to be ignored, regardless of the existing protocol, which always deferred to the Zamindar's wishes.

Since no invitation from her son appeared to be forthcoming, she suddenly, and without warning, appeared in his office. She demanded his attention, with complete disregard for the Zamindar's great displeasure to her aggressiveness.

He stood up from his chair and bowed politely in greeting. There was a stern look on his face as he addressed his mother with a sharp sound in his voice.

"I am busy now, Maa. It's an inopportune time for a visit. I will let you know when I have more free time available."

Laxmi Devi ignored the apparent dismissal as she continued to venture into the room while saying.

"It is apparent, my son, that lately, you have no free time, as far as I am concerned. Therefore, I have taken my prerogative as your mother to request your attention since no invitation on your part seemed forthcoming."

The Zamindar began looking through some papers on his desk as he answered with a dismissive tone in his voice.

"Perhaps it's better this way, Maa. Besides, we have very little to say to each other at this time…"

"Why?" interposed Laxmi Devi as her temper began to rise, "it is because you blame me for all the disturbances that have occurred in the palace?"

"Disturbances, is that how you describe the recent tragedy?" Asked the Zamindar as he stared at her with anger and frustration. But he quickly regained his usual self-control as he continued."

"Besides, Maa, you are taking far too much credit in this situation since the blame belongs to me. You should know that as the Zamindar, decisions are made *only* with my permission and consent."

Laxmi Devi retreated from her son, seemingly intimidated by his angry stance.

But her indomitable spirit quickly prevailed, as she answered him with a much sweeter and condescending sound in her voice.

"I regret that you are displeased, my son. I can only say that whatever advice I gave was meant for your benefit. Although I have always deferred to you as the Zamindar, I have been your best advisor and lavished upon you the benefits of my life's experiences."

Ramakanta struggled to retain his usual, stoic demeanor in response to his mother's words. But because of the sense of devotion ingrained into him since he was a child, he felt compelled to treat her with the usual respect. He decided it would be best to end the conversation as soon as possible since her very presence caused him great distress.

"I suggest that you leave now, Maa. I regret if I sound dismissive, but I have a special meeting to attend, which cannot be postponed. We will continue the conversation at a more opportune time."

But the dowager would not be so easily dismissed, as she continued to address the Zamindar with a pleading but determined sound in her voice.

"Please, my son. I only request that you give me a few more minutes. I promise to be brief, although I have much to say at this time. Besides, we have a great deal in common now, which should bring us closer together at this moment in time, for I believe that we have now achieved a common purpose."

The Zamindar had difficulty containing his disdain at the outrageous, almost delusional words of his mother and addressed her with a cold and sarcastic tone."

"What could we possibly have in common, Mother, other than a misguided manipulation at my beloved bride's expense? By your deliberate interferences, you have destroyed my marriage and the most beautiful part of my life.

A look of anger flashed on the dowager's face as she continued.

"I only blame myself for having lavished my favor and protection upon a foolish girl whose lack of dignity caused me great humiliation. Besides the unforgivable disruption to the estate…"

The dowager suddenly paused and pointed an accusatory finger toward Ramakanta before continuing.

"You are equally at fault, my son, because of your naiveté in placing your beliefs in the loyalty and love of a foreign woman, who at the first sign of trouble abandoned you and quickly ran back to her native country."

At that point, the dowager paused and took a deep breath, seemingly filled with righteous indignation and unaware of her son's look of shock and anger in response to her outrageous words.

She now continued with an almost triumphant sound in her voice.

"Don't you understand, my son, that you are finally free? There are no demands now placed upon you. It is a great opportunity to choose wisely, according to your desires and discretion. I am certain that among our native girls from the best and most illustrious families, you will be able to choose a new and perfect bride, someone who will fulfill your passion and desires and be worthy of the title of Zamindarin."

There was a great silence in response to her words as the Zamindar attempted to stifle the uncontrollable rage rising within him. But, he had been pushed too far and was no longer willing to endure her hateful rhetoric. He moved abruptly away from Laxmi Devi, finding her very presence intolerable.

Suddenly, all the repressed anger toward her endless manipulations surfaced. It was a painful awakening to finally see her clearly without the impediment of emotions and misplaced loyalties that had been ingrained in Ramakanta throughout his life.

He spoke to her dispassionately and truthfully, like never before.

"Mother, you believe that the tragedy, which just took place in our home, is a great opportunity for my future? There is only hatred and contempt for my beloved bride in those words. Diana, with considerable courage, entered a foreign land and a different culture. She did it because of her great love for me and nearly met a terrifying death as a reward…"

Ramakanta paused at this point and closed his eyes, overwhelmed by the haunting memory. He continued to speak, but his voice was soft, hardly audible as if he was talking to himself.

"Thankfully, my bride was spared by the mercy of God. despite my failings to place her above all others and protect her from danger."

The Zamindar appeared determined as he glared at his mother, who was intimidated by his uncompromising demeanor and accusatory tone,

"Diana is my Zamindarin, the true love of my life, and no one else will *ever* take her place by my side or in my heart...I pray that God will forgive my failings and show me the way to bring her back to me."

Laxmi Devi attempted to regain some control over the conversation, but it was too late now, and her son was unwilling to listen to anything she had to say. He silenced her with an imperious gesture of the hand as he continued the conversation with passion and determination.

"There is no question of your irrational loathing toward my bride, for reasons that are behind comprehension and even against our faith, which teaches love and not hate."

The Zamindar moved closer as he continued undeterred the dialogue.

"However, I find appalling and surprising your true feelings for Aamani. Whom I thought you loved as a daughter since you knew her as a child. It was shocking to see the manner you manipulated this unstable girl in ways that her fragile mind was unable to withstand…"

The Zamindar paused and looked deeply into his mother's eyes as he continued.

"Aamani was expandable since she committed the unforgivable sin of failure, and there was no remorse for causing her tragic death…even if indirectly."

"Stop it, Ramakanta!" exclaimed Laxmi Devi filled with dread and rage as she boldly moved toward him.

"How dare you judge me so harshly? I am your mother, and you owe me respect. Besides, there is no truth in what you are saying. I lavished upon Aamani many favors and my protection because I truly cared for her…"

"Caring Maa? You don't know the meaning of the word," interrupted the Zamindar with a deliberate sound, unmoved by her protestations.

He walked toward his mother, who remained silent, seemingly shocked by the harshness of his words. He then addressed her with a softer but still uncompromising sound.

"I am sorry, Maa, it's not my intention to hurt you, but unfortunately, it reflects the reality and magnitude of the tragic situation...Perhaps you are not aware of it because of an innate coldness that appears to be part of your nature."

Laxmi Devi moved abruptly from him at the sound of those hurtful words while murmuring.

"How can a son be so ungrateful and cause his mother so much pain?"

The Zamindar stood silent before her in response to her despair. He then addressed Laxmi Devi with a gentler sound in his voice.

"Please, Maa, try to understand that these issues are impossible to ignore, and although it was never my intention to hurt you, our relationship might never be the same because of it."

The dowager turned away from him and covered her face with her hands. By now, uncontrollable sobs shook her graceful and delicate body, and she appeared frail and helpless.

The Zamindar remained pensive as racing

thought crowded his mind. He realized it was impossible to reason with his mother, who seemed incapable of accepting blame or expressing love toward anyone. She lived in her world of manipulations and delusions, desperately needing control over her golden surroundings. Perhaps, it was a way to manage the fears that possibly haunted her throughout her life.

Ramakanta had unconditional love for his mother and an unwavering sense of responsibility toward her. However, he was sadly aware that she could hurt him without feeling the slightest remorse. It was a reality he had to accept, which only increased his overwhelming sense of loneliness in that crucial moment in his life.

"You better go now Maa, it's best if you get some rest." He finally said as he gently but firmly guided her toward the exit door.

"But when will I see you again?" asked Laxmi Devi, filled with anxiety, "you have been so angry with me lately, and I fear that I am losing you, my son."

A shadow of sadness flashed on the Zamindar's face before answering. He had become resigned to the inevitability that he was truly alone and unloved, at least as far as his mother was concerned. She had no concept of how cruel her manipulation had been since she was incapable of taking responsibility for the consequences of her actions.

He placed his arm around her shoulder and slowly walked her out of the door while saying.

"Please go now, Maa, but rest assured that you will never lose me as your son. Or be deprived of your position of honor, as long as I remain the Zamindar."

Laxmi Devi smiled broadly at the sound of those words, she now stood proud, erect, and after the traditional parting, she walked in the long corridor with a fast stride.

Finally, alone, the Zamindar returned inside his study and approached the elegant desk, which was a treasured heirloom belonging to his distinguished family for generations.

He opened the center drawer and retrieved a small velvet box, exquisitely detailed with silver accents. He held the precious package in his hands for a few seconds before opening it and gazing wistfully at the splendid sapphire pendant resting in its middle—The gem, which was referred to so many times by Diana as the symbol of their love.

Ramakanta was beset with sorrow as he gently caressed the precious jewel. He closed his eyes and envisioned his beloved bride wearing it around her graceful neck, more beautiful and alluring than ever.

A painful sigh rose to his lips as he held the pendant close to his heart.

"Please come back to me, Padma, my love, my life. I miss you so."

§§§

CHAPTER EIGHTEEN

TOUCHED BY KARMA

In the beginning, Rami and Padma met through their dreams. For them, it was the ultimate reality in life since it became the catalyst that finally brought them together from faraway places on Earth

Was Morpheus, the Greek God of dreams, instrumental in their surprising connection? Or was a benign higher power who had blessed their endless love.

For the Zamindar, it was a fascinating mystery that had taken over every aspect of his life. He was now at an impasse and overwhelmed with sorrow by the tragic turn of events.

There was only one certainty that mattered and prevailed in his life, the great love he had for Padma and the desperate need to be reunited with her to regain the joy of living.

The matter of trust was also an overpowering issue since he knew that unwillingly he had failed the woman he loved. However, at this point, nothing else seemed to matter in comparison to his sense of loss, which was all-encompassing.

His mind traveled in many different directions, desperately trying to find answers to the many questions that burdened him.

Suddenly, a memory surfaced from the recesses of his mind in connection to his beloved grandfather, Choudhury Nishamani Das. A man of considerable wisdom and knowledge who had been instrumental in imparting values and information to the young Ramakanta.

The Zamindar recalled how his grandfather, during the early stages of his life, related to him many instances of the Choudhury dynasty's history in great detail.

It was the customary way to narrate by *word-of-mouth* the relevant information to family members. That is to keep the essential milestones of their history alive for posterity and honoring their distinguished family line.

He now recalled one of the many stories told by his grandfather, which at the time he paid little attention to since it had little relevance to a child, but somehow remained ingrained in his memory.

It was about a beautiful Princess who married one of his ancestors over a hundred years before and became his Zamindarin.

According to the account, she came from a faraway land and a different culture, although there was no mention of her country of origin.

Tragically, she suffered death by poisoning during the first year of their marriage. A disgruntle concubine perpetrated the murder. It is believed that the jealous woman was cast aside because of the great love the Zamindar had for his wife and enacted revenge.

The tragedy had significant repercussions and consequences. The Zamindar was devastated by his bride's death and never fully recovered or ever married again.

The murder of the beautiful Zamindarin seemed now ominously familiar and pertinent to Ramakanta. Unfortunately, his grandfather, the only person who could have shed more light on the subject, had been dead for years.

At this point, Diana's startling knowledge of the historical presence and significance of the Goddess Kali's statue on his estate couldn't be dismissed as a coincidence. It seemed she had been present at a different time in history and perhaps lived in a former lifetime.

"Could she possibly have been the tragic Zamindarin reborn?"

He wondered and recalled that she was introduced as Padma when the unsettling dreams about Diana began.

"Was Diana named Padma in a former lifetime?"

There were too many unanswered questions. Especially without written history to validate them, making it almost impossible to bring light to the mystery.

The Zamindar's Bride

The Zamindar pondered on the issue since it was essential for some resolution or closure. He felt that he was living in a time-warp and needed to find some order in his mental chaos.

Suddenly, a thought flashed through his mind about the Goddess Kali's statue since the precious relic was part of that turbulent time in history. Her image was the *only* tangible connection between Diana and the tragic Zamindarin, who had a great fascination for the historical statue.

With renewed interest, he now wondered about the fear of death that Diana experienced during their voyage to India.

Was Aamani's attempted murder the real reason for the premonition? Or perhaps, the latent memory of the violent death she suffered, as the tragic Princess in a former lifetime.

At this point, the Zamindar felt compelled to investigate, which gave him a renewed sense of purpose and mitigated the helplessness that overwhelmed him.

He believed that the Goddess's statue was the only available key to unlock the mystery of his love connection with Diana.

Filled with anxiety but also a sense of hope, he ran toward the stables and mounted his favorite horse, then spurred the splendid animal to a fast gallop in his sprawling estate. Soon after, he entered into the natural and verdant area that protectively surrounded the historic statue.

As he reached his destination, he quickly dismounted his horse and hastened with a deliberate stride toward the effigy.

Kali's fearsome image seemed almost benevolent to him, as the Zamindar bowed with respect in front of the Deity.

For a few minutes, he remained engaged in silent prayer. But, suddenly, he was overwhelmed by a sense of urgency and started investigating the splendid and artistic statue from every angle.

He had no idea what he was looking for, as his hands glided on the smooth granite surface with determination but also reverence. There was a strange certainty that important revelations were hidden within Kali Maa's image.

The unusual optimism lasted for quite a while as he inspected the statue meticulously, hoping that she would finally reveal her secrets.

But except for the historical dates scripted on its back, nothing new was discovered on the statue. Undaunted, the Zamindar continued the seemingly aimless inspection, with the stubborn belief that something of great importance *had* to be there.

Unfortunately, as time passed, he began to feel foolish, while frustration and disappointment set in, and grief suddenly resurfaced.

Anguish overwhelmed him as he placed his hands on the cool granite and asked in a pleading sound filled with deep emotions.

"Please help me, Kali Maa...I humbly and respectfully pray for you to show me the way. Have mercy on my despair and help me unlock the key to this mystery."

He remained silent and dejected since only the sound of the cool breezes answered his plea. He rested his head against the statue, hoping that the frigid stone would diminish the fire that raged within.

Finally, convinced that he could do nothing else, Ramakanta began walking away, still conflicted, with a slow and uncertain pace.

It was painful to give in to defeat, as the blessings of hope were inevitably fading away.

He was now standing next to Amir and gently patted the head of his horse, trying to find comfort in the faithful animal that he considered a valued friend.

Finally, he decided to get back on the saddle and face the disappointing trip back to the palace.

But strangely, the usually docile stallion abruptly backed away from his master. He lifted his powerful body on his hind legs as a loud neigh erupted from Amir's throat, breaking the surroundings' static silence.

Stunned by the horse's unusual behavior, the Zamindar attempted to grab the reins and regain control, but unfortunately, the animal remained uncooperative and continued to back away.

It seemed obvious at that point that his faithful stallion was refusing to leave for some unknown reason. Ramakanta felt entrapped in the relatively remote and isolated stretch of land. He looked around for signs of life while his eyes were drawn toward the Goddess Kali's statue.

Suddenly, it seemed almost like a revelation looking at the scene from that vantage point. A strange, riveting image flashed in his mind and appeared as he had entered another dimension and an altered state of reality.

He became the spectator while envisioning someone who looked exactly like him, galloping with great speed toward the area.

The man dismounted the animal and ran toward Kali's monument with great urgency. Although the scene was spellbinding, it felt unusual, as if it was a reality etched somewhere in time. Even the elegant Zamindar's attire seemed unfamiliar and appeared to belong in a different time of history.

As the vision suddenly disappeared, instead of confusion, it created a moment of clarity, and a look of recall flashed in his eyes as if he had remembered something of importance.

"Of course," he said with a surprising sound of recollection, "I know...it's hidden in the pedestal!"

He took a deep breath and stood erect, suddenly filled with determination as he walked briskly back toward the statue and placed his hands with great emotion on the granite base of the idol.

Before looking around the platform, he bowed his head and focused with great interest on the

Goddesse's right foot, which rested on the imposing pedestal.

There was almost a sense of euphoria and certainty as he immediately began to remove the deeply embedded debris near the semi shadowed area.

Ramakanta felt a compulsion to scrub with strength and determination in the selected space. He rubbed his hand mercilessly and incessantly against the granite until his fingers became raw from the impact on the rough surface.

Slowly, writings began emerging from the depths of the stone hidden from sight for over a century.

With his heart beating wildly from the excitement, the Zamindar increased his effort. He removed the remnants of the dust of time, which had been an impenetrable protective shield to the mysterious message.

Having completed the task, he lifted his bloodied hands and cleaned them with his handkerchief, then rubbed his eyes in an attempt to clear his vision. But before he had a chance to decipher the message, a sudden wind-shear deposited a few fallen leaves upon the cold stone, shielding once more the mysterious message from sight.

The Zamindar swiped away with an eager motion of his hand the unwanted foliage.

Almost miraculously, as the obstruction was removed, the embedded script was finally visible.

Ramakanta gasped at the sight as a painful recollection suddenly overwhelmed him.

The message was only a short phrase in his native language of Oriya, seemingly sculpted roughly within the hard granite surface.

"Padma, forever, my love." Were the simple words inscribed, as the Zamindar read them aloud almost breathlessly.

There was a dramatic change in his demeanor as he gently caressed with his palms the loving words. An agonizing memory that was shocking and heartbreaking at the same time inundated him with dread.

He knew of having written those words. He could even recognize his writing style, although they had been scribbled roughly. The agony of the tragic past came rushing in without mercy and overwhelmed him with the pain of loss.

Up to that point, only Diana appeared to have

had recollections of a former life, perhaps because it was too painful for the Zamindar to remember the sudden death of the woman he loved.

However, now he had asked Kali Maa, with courage, to erase the mystery, and the wish had been granted. It allowed the tragic past to rush in with the devastating power of a fierce monsoon.

All the pain of that tragic day of long ago became unfiltered and merciless. He remembered running toward the statue in despair after his beloved Padma's death because the agony of loss was so acute and devastating.

He then sculpted those passionate words with his sword. Humbly and with deference by the feet of the statue that had meant so much to his bride.

It had been a message of love, a pledge before the Goddess that he would wait forever, challenging the dust of time and the eternal cycle of life.

After his return to the palace, the unsettling feelings of loss were still all-encompassing for the Zamindar. He believed to have found irrefutable proof of a past life and the love he shared with

Padma. However, nothing had been resolved in his mind or his heart.

It was painful to acknowledge that although Diana appeared to have conquered the shadows of death. A renewed, deadly peril marred her miraculous return and once again nearly took her precious life.

The Zamindar was certain that dangerous intrigues fomenting in the palace during his former life had been directly responsible for Padma's death. There was a sense of responsibility for having failed his Zamindarin despite his great love for her.

It was a known fact that as part of his culture, concubines and harems were commonplace among the rich and powerful in India.

Because of the male-dominated society and the female population's inability to be self-reliant, many deemed it necessary to rely on their feminine-wiles to obtain favors, especially from Maharajas and Zamindars. That is to enjoy their protection, with a luxurious, affluent lifestyle

Competitiveness always flourished within a palace environment and created dissension among the women. Being chosen as a favorite by a

Adriana Girolami

Zamindar was a most coveted position, although difficult to obtain considering the plentiful and available competition. In extreme cases, even murder was perpetrated out of jealousy.

However, according to history, despite the many available concubines, the Zamindar fell in love with a western Princess. He asked for her hand in marriage, with the offer of becoming his Zamindarin.

Although the Princess was also in love with him, she refused to enter into a marriage, which might be shared with other women. Because of her Christian faith and independent nature.

The Zamindar had no difficulty in conceding to her request and immediately eliminated the harem from the palace out of the great love and respect he had for her.

Tragically, the necessary but fatal decision was the catalyst that precipitated the lovely Princess, premature death.

Now that she had miraculously returned, did he fail her once again? That is, by unwillingly allow the scheming in the palace to raise the specter of death yet again.

As those disturbing thoughts flashed through his mind, he cradled in his hands the sapphire pendant that Diana had called "the symbol of their love."

"Why did she leave it behind?" He wondered as the painful separation was still raw in his mind.

He knew that without her, it was impossible to regain the joy of living. There was a constant and desperate need to hold her in his arms, especially during the endless and lonely nights.

He was sure that he would not allow anyone to stand in their way if given another chance.

However, there was a silver lining in the note Diana left on the pillow before departing from the palace, which stated that she loved him eternally."

He caressed the beautiful pendant lovingly while saying with a determined sound.

"The pendant has no meaning without you, my Padma. It has to be with you and in your care to remain the symbol of our love…"

The Zamindar paused, overwhelmed by great emotions. He now believed that he should return the sapphire pendant as soon as possible to reconnect with his bride.

He felt a sense of hope and, without hesitation, began preparing for his return voyage to Italy.

He had no idea what to expect in that far away land, but there was comfort in the knowledge of being, at least, geographically closer to Diana.

The Zamindar was still uncertain about the best way to return the pendant to her. Nonetheless, a strong, positive feeling compelled him to go forward with the plan.

While preparing for the trip, he decided not to inform Prince Louis of his forthcoming travel to Italy for fear it might cause some uneasiness for his friend, under the circumstances.

In that regard, he secured hotel reservations rather than relying on the hospitality that the Prince would have offered.

Finally, after having made the proper prevision to care for his estate, he embarked once more on a faithful trip to Europe.

A poetic offering of love rose to his lips as he prepared to cross once again the majestic and treacherous waters that separated him from the woman he loved.

The Zamindar's Bride

* Oh my Bride *

Oh, my bride, from an alien, distant land, I dare for you this lonely voyage on the hostile seas.
As I sail on a long, unknown quest, challenging the fury of a brewing tempest.

Oh, My Bride, you are the damsel of my lonely soul, hidden within my solitary heart.
As I embark on a fearsome journey within the turbulent waters of an inhospitable ocean.

Oh, my bride, you are my love, my life. Test not my passion and loyalty as I color your secret dreams With the hues I have stolen from the rainbow of an Indian sky.
All for you ... all for you.

******

A faithful return

The voyage back to Europe was unusually long and lonely. There were concerns in Ramakanta's mind because of so many unknown factors. Although, a persistent sense of hope made it less painful and bearable.

As the ocean liner finally docked in Naples' port, there was a sense of excitement as the Zamindar stepped onto the pier and was safely once again on Italian soil.

He did not expect to meet anyone in the busy port. He hoped to mingle anonymously among the hundreds of people waiting impatiently for relatives and friends to disembark the ship.

Suddenly, he was surprised by the sight of his friend, Prince Louis, waving his hand from a distance, attempting to attract his attention.

The Prince appeared excited and happy as he walked toward him with a brisk stride and his usual friendly smile, as he said in greeting.

"Welcome back to Italy, dear Ramakanta. I am so glad to see you again."

The Zamindar remained silent and stunned at first. But after the friends warmly embraced in greeting, he asked with surprise in his voice.

"I am delighted to see you, dear Louis…But how did you know I was coming back to Italy since no announcements were made in that regard?"

The Prince interposed with a smile and a friendly pat on his shoulders as he answered.

"You forget, my friend, that you have acquired a celebrity status around here, your name was on the passenger's list, and it was released to the local papers."

The Zamindar felt suddenly uneasy in front of his loyal and hospitable friend while saying.

"I am sorry, Louis, for not letting you know about my visit…Please understand that it was a difficult decision for me to make under the circumstances."

"No explanation necessary," answered the Prince with his usual friendliness.

"I know how difficult the present situation must be for you…However, you are not alone and do not need a hotel filled with strangers. You are my friend, and as always, my palace is open to you, where you will find relaxation and complete privacy if you request it."

"Thank you, my friend," answered Zamindar, deeply moved by the generosity and kindness of the Prince.

He remained silent, overwhelmed with emotions as they walked side by side toward the waiting carriage. A thousand questions crowded his mind, but he felt uneasy and almost afraid to ask them. He finally said with some trepidation.

"How is my wife? Have you seen her lately? Is she well?"

The Prince appeared serious at that moment, and a bit of uneasiness transpired in his voice while answering.

"I suppose she is well enough, physically…I have only seen her once since she returned from India…"

"Does she know that I am here?" Interposed the Zamindar with some concern while stepping into the coach, followed by the Prince.

There was a small pause before the answer since it was apparent that the Prince was uncomfortable with the conversation.

"I doubt she knows that you are here since she favors to spend most of her time alone…At least I didn't tell her."

"I am sorry if you are uncomfortable with my questions, Louis," said the Zamindar, "but at this time, it's vital for me to know all I can about Diana…Did she tell you the reasons for leaving India?"

"I only wish I could be more helpful in answering your questions," said the Prince, "I know very little of what transpired in India...even aunt Amelie is pretty much in the dark about it."

"You mean that Diana did not confide about the reasons she left?" Asked the Zamindar, stunned and surprised by the answer."

"There was some mentioning about her difficulty with India's culture and the marriage's future. However, she loves you and said that you are not to be blamed for what happened."

The Zamindar was overwhelmed by the words as he whispered.

"My Padma still loves me..."

The Prince interposed with a sad tone of his voice.

"But I must tell you, Ramakanta, Diana seemed very distressed, and I dared not ask probing questions for fear of upsetting her further..."

The Prince paused briefly before continuing with concern.

"I have known her all my life, but I have never seen her quite like this. There was a look of sorrow in her eyes, which I found most disturbing since I couldn't help her. Unfortunately, right now, I see the same look of sadness in your eyes…"

"You mean that she is all alone, with no one to help or comfort her during this difficult time?" Interposed the Zamindar filled with despair at the thought of Diana's suffering.

The Prince touched his hand, trying to comfort his friend's distress while saying."

"Please don't worry Ramakanta, Diana knows that we are here any time she needs our help. Aunt Amelie agrees that it is best to let her deal with her sorrow the way she chooses. At least for a little while."

The Zamindar's seemed increasingly distressed by his words.

"I think it's unwise to let Diana deal with the situation, all alone…You don't know the real reasons she left, and what transpired in my palace, which is much worse than what she said to you…"

"You must remember my friend that Diana is a woman of faith," interposed the Prince with a comforting sound.

"Aunt Amelie told me that she often goes to the church of Saint Justin on her estate…The little church in which you celebrated your Christian wedding. She knows that Diana confides in Father Anthony, and at this time, he might be the only one who can help her."

The Zamindar was relieved by those words and appeared more relaxed as he spoke."

"Thank you, my friend, this news gives me some comfort...I know that Father Anthony is a special man of God and someone with great wisdom and caring. I truly believe that he will be of help to my dearest bride."

"I am glad this news gives you comfort, my friend," said the Prince.

"I believe now you should relax a little. Hopefully, tomorrow it will be a better day, and you will decide on what to do..."

"I already know what to do, dear Louis," interjected the Zamindar with a deliberate sound, "I will be traveling early in the morning toward Diana's estate and hopefully meet Father Anthony sometime during the day..."

The Zamindar paused, noticing the Prince's look of concern as he continued with a smile.

"Please rest assured, Louis, that I will not enter the church if Diana is there...I give you my word of honor that I will respect her privacy and not let her know that I am here until she is ready to see me again."

§§§

CHAPTER NINETEEN

THE LOTUS RISES

The Zamindar was an early riser, and the next morning without delay, he was on his way toward the church of Saint Justin, located on Diana's beautiful estate.

He borrowed one of the Prince's horses for the relatively long trip to the destination and chose to go alone. He was familiar with the area, remembering in detail the splendid surroundings and every wonderful moment he spent there with his bride.

Finally, galloping at a fast pace in the rural countryside, spurred on by the desire to reach his destination as soon as possible, he rejoiced at the sight of the lovely country church.

His heart skipped a beat since it brought back so many wonderful and unforgettable memories, which at that moment caused him only pain.

There was a sense of loneliness as he entered Diana's verdant and peaceful world, especially the holy place where they shared their vows of faith and love.

Strangely, it all seemed as if it happened a long time ago while he approached the entrance of the church with eagerness and trepidation.

The area seemed so peaceful in the picturesque surroundings with no signs of life. He looked around, and since no horses or carriages were present in the landscape, it gave some reassurance to the Zamindar that he would not be intruding on Diana's privacy.

He noticed a man busily working among the flowers and bushes, partly shielded by the greenery surrounding the holy place in great abundance.

He immediately recognized Father Anthony, the church pastor, who was now standing and looking around, a bit startled by the unexpected guest's sudden appearance.

The good Priest immediately hastened toward him in greeting as Ramakanta quickly dismounted his horse.

"Welcome, Your Highness, it's a great pleasure to see you again," said the Priest in a friendly manner.

"The pleasure is all mine, Father Anthony," answered the Zamindar feeling a bit comforted by the friendliness of the hospitable pastor. He then added with an apologetic tone.

"Please forgive this intrusion, reverend Father, since I was unable to let you know in advance about my visit...I hope this is not an inopportune time for you."

"Not at all, Your Highness. I am very pleased that you are here, only..." The good Priest paused and laughed as he displayed with a bit of reluctance the palms of his dirty hands while saying.

"I hope you will forgive my appearance because, as you can see, I am never truly happy unless I have God's good earth in my hands."

The Priest then motions the Zamindar to follow him while saying.

"Please, kindly join me in the sacristy of the church. It will afford me a little time to make myself more presentable and wash my hands. Afterward, we will be able to talk at leisure if you wish."

"Thank you, Father Anthony. I feel truly blessed to have your hospitality and your counsel," answered the Zamindar, grateful and relieved by the welcoming Priest, whose benign presence gave him a sense of hope and peace.

While the good pastor was busily removing some of the stain and dust from his labor in the garden, the Zamindar looked around with wonder at the modest sacristy, which appeared warm, comforting, and virtually spotless, with its whitewashed walls, decorated with religious images.

A simple and beautifully sculpted crucifix with a kneeling bench for devotional prayer was situated in a place of honor and decorated with fresh white flowers. An aroma of incense was present throughout the ambiance, giving it an extra flavor of spirituality and relaxation.

Soon after, the Priest joined him for a private conversation, with a comforting smile on his face to put his guest at ease, having noticed the Zamindar's distress, he finally said, with a soft and deliberate sound.

"My son, if there are any questions you wish to ask, please feel free to do so. I will be glad to answer, and hopefully be helpful, in some way…"

"Father Anthony," interposed the Zamindar, "I know that my bride Diana since her return to Italy, visits you often and confides in you. She is a person of true faith, and during this difficult time, I feel blessed that she can benefit from your wise counsel and help you can give her."

"The house of the Lord is always open to those that wish to enter and look for guidance," answered Father Anthony as he pointed to the image of Christ with reverence.

"However, there must be a willingness to find solutions through the counseling of a priest or directly from God without undue pressure. That is until a person is ready to receive it."

Father Anthony placed his hands together and closed his eyes in meditation and silent prayer before continuing.

"Your highness, I have been honored to receive Lady Diana's private thoughts about the recent occurrences in India. Unfortunately, I can do very little at this point unless she is more receptive and willing to be helped after the trauma she endured..."

"Did she tell you what happened and why she left India in such a hurry?" Interposed the Zamindar anxiously.

"Yes, my son, she confided in me in great detail," answered the Priest as he gently touched the Zamindar's shoulders.

"I can freely talk about it because she didn't share her thoughts in the secrecy of the holy confession."

Ramakanta closed his eyes, beset with remorse and regrets as he continued the conversation.

"Then, you know what happened and how my wife nearly lost her life because I failed to protect her..."

Father Anthony, a bit surprised, interrupted the Zamindar.

"Your bride's description of the tragic event is quite different from yours, my son...She casts no blame upon you and feels responsible for the tragedy that ensued while giving you credit for saving her life."

"Diana blames herself, but why?" Asked the Zamindar, stunned and distressed by his words.

"She was the innocent victim, and I was neglectful in not placing her above all others to prevent the tragedy."

Noticing the Zamindar's distress, Father Anthony offered him a cool glass of water and attempted to comfort him.

"Please, my son, listen with an open mind. I believe that both you and your bride are traumatized because of the magnitude of the tragedy. You see the situation emotionally rather than realistically."

The Priest paused at this point, appearing solemn and determined before continuing.

"We all understand that a precious life has been lost. However, you have done nothing to contribute to it. There was no malice involved and no wish from either one of you to cause her harm. You both cared for the poor girl and had no idea of how unstable she was."

The Priest moved a little closer as the Zamindar intently listened while he continued.

"Lady Diana, because of her kind and altruistic nature, suffers from the guilt of the survivor. She is endowed with your love and the possibility of a happy life, which makes her feel unduly fortunate at this time, while in her eyes, the tragic girl is only the recipient of death. There is irrational guilt connected to it. Your bride sees her as the victim and attributes no blame on the attempted act of murder perpetrated against her."

His words touched the Zamindar deeply, he stood up and walked a few steps across the room, trying to absorb what he had heard, and he finally said.

"There is much wisdom to what you say, Father Anthony, and I thank you...I never thought about the situation quite this way. I just felt guilty, while your enlightened words give me a sense of redemption and hope."

The good pastor nodded in consent, pleased by the Zamindar's receptive attitude. He remained silent, allowing him to understand the message he conveyed until Ramakanta addressed him once more with a bit of anxiety.

"Reverend Father, I would like to better understand my bride's frame of mind at this time...Because, when she left India so suddenly, I only witnessed her great sorrow without any insight into her private thoughts and the depth of her despair..."

"I wish I could be more helpful, my son, interposed the Priest sadly, "unfortunately, I can only relate that she is very depressed, which is expected in the circumstances. But as usual, Lady Diana remains strong, resilient, and appears to be in excellent health despite the difficulties encountered..."

The Priest paused at this point and appeared concerned as he continued.

"However, I must admit that I am troubled by a strange premonition that haunts her...It appears to be an overwhelming fear of a violent death, which she believes might be predestined, and waiting for her."

"Do you mean that my bride suffers from the fear of an impending doom?" Asked the Zamindar distraught by the Priest's words

"I suppose she does, and it's hard to explain the reason why," answered the Priest.

"At first, I thought that the premonition was due to her close call with death at the hands of the Indian girl. Although strangely, she seems to have forgotten that dangerous situation. However, the terror of a preordained, violent death remains, and she has difficulty in defining the reasons or the origin of the fear."

"Reverend Father," said the Zamindar with a respectful but deliberate sound.

"I would like to share some information, which might shed some light on my bride's distress...However, being from another faith, my beliefs are different from yours and might prove disturbing. In that regard, I request your kind permission to speak since I don't mean to be disrespectful in the presence of your Christ and your church."

"Please speak freely, Your Highness. I appreciate any help that might shed some light on the mystery of your bride's unusual fears."

"I thank you, reverend Father," answered the Zamindar as he moved closer to the Priest while speaking.

"I know that unlike the Hindu religion, the Christian dogma has a different view on the premise of reincarnation…"

The Zamindar paused for a moment before continuing with a more deliberate sound.

"Perhaps Father, it will be difficult for you to accept the possibility that my bride and I were married in previous lifetimes…"

The Zamindar paused as the Priest appeared engaged and receptive to the conversation as he continued.

"I know it's difficult to accept a principle that is different from our religious beliefs. However, both Diana and I remembered historical occurrences that are not part of this lifetime. She recalled in great detail the arrival of a statue of the Goddess Kali from Indonesia, which was an important historical occurrence that took place in my estate over a century ago…"

"Lady Diana conveyed these facts to me," interposed the pastor, "and they are issues of great interest that should be studied in depth. However, I don't see the connection with her present fears …"

"Perhaps the issue could be made clearer with a recent revelation I had with a past life, which occurred on my estate after my bride departed from India."

Said the Zamindar while taking a deep breath before continuing.

"When Diana suddenly departed from India, I recalled some pertinent information regarding the Choudhuri dynasty…It was about a lovely Princess from a distant land and different culture who married one of my ancestors and became his Zamindarin over a century ago. By the descriptions I was given, there is an amazing resemblance between the foreign Princess and Diana…"

Ramakanta paused, with sadness, before continuing.

"Tragically, in the first year of their marriage, the Zamindarin was assassinated and in all probabilities. She had been poisoned."

"You're ancestral Zamindarin was poisoned?" Said the Priest, shocked by the revelation.

"Yes, Father Anthony, and besides the historical information I received from my grandfather, I have discovered some irrefutable proof of the tragedy, which validates my conviction. It includes a written record on the pedestal of Goddess Kali's statue, on my estate…"

The Zamindar paused, visibly distressed, before continuing.

"I had a painful but clear recollection of having written those words on the statue's pedestal...It was a simple and loving tribute as the grieving spouse of the tragic Zamindarin."

Father Anthony remained silent but amazed by the revelation.

"You see, Reverend Father," continued the Zamindar with emphasis, "I believe that my bride is the tragic Zamindarin reborn. The terror she is experiencing now is the latent memory of the death she suffered in that former lifetime..."

"That is astounding," interrupted Father Anthony, as he pondered on the revelation.

"Even if it seems unbelievable, Reverend Father, I have told you the truth," continued the Zamindar, "however, I understand it can be difficult to accept it at face value, considering that your Christian beliefs contradict reincarnation."

"On the contrary, your highness, I do believe that you are telling me the truth about your experience." Said the Priest with a serious tone as he moved closer to the Zamindar.

"Perhaps you misunderstand our beliefs concerning reincarnation since religious historians have several interpretations concerning the subject...There are mysteries that great theologians and humble priests like me have explored to have a greater insight on the subject. In Christianity, we acknowledge the immortality of the human soul when the body is consumed by death, and we firmly believe in one life everlasting."

The Zamindar listened with great interest to the Priest as he continued.

"Some interpretations are accepted, or at least explored by some members of the clergy. They include unusual and unexplained situations, which might be perceived as some form of reincarnation. They are usually cases connected with violent death or as the result of murder..."

The pastor interrupted the conversation and appeared to remember something of importance.

"If I recall correctly," he finally said. "I have read some interesting articles about reincarnation, discussed in the Papal Curia. They created a great deal of controversy at the time, among the clergy..."

Father Anthony paused and walked toward a bible resting on a nearby table and looked through some of the pages while saying.

"There are also some interpretations on the subject that are considered controversial within the Holy Scriptures. They suggest that John the Baptist could have been a reincarnation of the Prophet Elijah..."

"Are you suggesting, Father Anthony, that you are open to the possibility of reincarnation in connection with my bride?" Interjected the Zamindar with excitement and curiosity.

"I am always open to new possibilities since there are many mysteries that our limited minds can never understand or explain...Perhaps, this could be considered a case of reincarnation," answered the Priest appearing a bit hesitant before continuing.

"There are Christian beliefs that disturbances exist within the soul of a murder victim, whose life had been suddenly and violently taken. The interruption of the spiritual essence, which had been expelled prematurely, leaves the soul in limbo, without the proper benediction."

Father Anthony devoutly crossed himself as he continued.

"It is accepted by some religious scholars that the essence of life is still powerful and vibrant within the spirit. Therefore since the body no longer exists, the soul's energy has the desire to continue through reincarnation, preferably within the same bloodline and the place where their previous life was interrupted…"

The Priest paused as a serious look appeared on his face before continuing.

"The most challenging possibility explored within Christian circles is about the tormented soul search for peace through benediction, to remove the stain of violence…The spirit might continue the search from birth to birth until it attains salvation, which ends the rebirth process."

There was a strange silence in the sacristy in response to the words of Father Anthony. The Zamindar had many questions but could not ask them, overwhelmed by great emotions as the good pastor continued speaking.

"Taking into consideration that Lady Diana might have lived in a previous life, which was interrupted by murder, it is conceivable that this might be a case of search for peace through reincarnation..."

The Priest paused and shook his head with a look of wonder before continuing.

"I have known her all her life, but I never remember seeing her so frightened. Besides, she also confided in me that during her travel toward India, she experienced for the first time terror and the fear of death..."

The pastor then added almost in a whisper.

"It might be plausible that by returning to the place where the violent act occurred, the hidden memory suddenly surfaced..."

"Yes, Father Anthony," interposed Ramakanta with great emotions.

"It makes sense now...I am convinced that you have unveiled the key to the mystery of our lives and the possible reason for my bride's torment."

The Zamindar moved closer to the Priest and, with reverence, touched his hand while saying.

"I believe you are a holy man, who is the chosen person to help my Zamindarin find peace...Perhaps it was ordained by a higher power that your blessing will give salvation to her soul."

"I wish I were so endowed my son since such power of healing is only in the hands of God," interjected the Priest with some apprehension.

"I only suggested a possibility of reincarnation because the facts that you have presented are quite compelling. However, regardless of my limited ability to help, I will be happy to bestow upon your bride God's blessings, with the hope that she will soon find joy and peace, which she richly deserves."

"Thank you, Reverend Father," said the Zamindar, deeply moved as he continued with great emotion.

"Conversationally, Father, it doesn't matter if you believe in reincarnation since when you dispense the blessings, it becomes a matter of faith…"

"You are right and very wise, my son," said the Priest, "miracles occur when we truly believe."

"Thank you, Father Anthony," said the Zamindar as he gently touched his hand with reverence.

"You have given me the blessings of hope, and I will be forever grateful."

The two-man remained silent in that particular moment, pondering on the mystery of the situation. The Zamindar was the first to break the uncomfortable quiet in the room.

"Father Anthony, if you don't mind, I have one more favor to ask of you…"

Ramakanta paused and quickly retrieved from his pocket an elegant velvet box. He handed the precious object to the Priest as he continued speaking with great emotions.

"Would you kindly bestow a special blessing to the engagement gift I gave my bride, and please would you return it to her."

The Priest smiled as he accepted the precious box while saying.

"I will bless it and return it to your bride, your highness…May I have the pleasure of seeing it?"

"Please do, reverend Father," answered the Zamindar, as the Priest opened the little box and smiled brightly at the sight of the splendid sapphire pendant.

"It's so beautiful, your highness, an exceptional gift." said father Anthony as he gently caressed the precious jewel."

"Thank you, Reverend Father," answered the Zamindar, "my bride called it the symbol of our love. Although, for some unknown reason, she left it behind when she returned to Italy."

"Perhaps she wanted you to bring it back to her," answered the Priest with an encouraging smile.

"You *really* think so?" Asked the Zamindar with renewed hope.

"I can't speak for Lady Diana, my son. It's only an assumption because I know she loves you."

Ramakanta felt uplifted by his words and moved closer as he gently caressed the little velvet box resting in the pastor's hands. He then said with great emotions.

"Father Anthony, when you will return the sapphire pendant to my Zamindarin, would you please tell her that I am waiting, and I love her forever."

"I will be glad to relate your message, my son, and return the precious pendant as soon as possible...I am certain that your bride will be delighted to have it in her possession, once again."

The conversation was now at an end. The Priest stood up in a sign of parting and began escorting the Zamindar out of the sacristy.

"Go in peace and with God's blessing, my son," He then added with an encouraging smile.

"Above all, have faith and don't be discouraged, since miracles occur when we truly believe…"

"I know reverend Father," interjected the Zamindar with a touch of sadness.

"I hope and pray that my beloved Zamindarin will soon come back to me."

Without further reticence, the Zamindar, after a respectful good-bye to the good pastor, mounted his horse and spurred it to a fast gallop. Father Anthony remained steadfast in front of the church and continued to wave his hand until the distinguished visitor disappeared in the distance.

WRITTEN IN THE STARS

A long and lonely week passed without any news from Diana. The sands of time slipped slowly through the hourglass and enhanced Ramakanta's feelings of helplessness.

To make matters worse, the scheduled return to India was disturbingly close, and Ramakanta couldn't ignore the many responsibilities that required his presence back home.

He was pensive as he peered through a window in the palace. When he was startled by a light touch of a hand on his shoulder, he turned and faced Prince Louis, looking at him with concern.

"Are you feeling well, Ramakanta…Why are you here all by yourself?" He asked.

"No need for concern, dear Louis," answered the Zamindar," I was just trying to clear my mind and do some thinking…"

"It will not be difficult to guess what subject you are thinking about," interjected the Prince, with a friendly smile.

"I know how difficult these few days have been for you while waiting and hoping, without the certainty of success…May I make a suggestion?"

"Please do, my friend. I will be grateful for any help you might give."

"Perhaps, it's unwise to continue wallowing in the entrapment of uncertainty that is causing you so much grief…I believe it would be best if you meet Diana as soon as possible. Tell her about your love and need for her. Also, ask about her feelings for you and what's in her heart."

The Zamindar shook his head in disagreement as he answered.

"My dear Louis, we have been friends for years and have much in common in so many ways. However, this time I fear that our different cultures come into play. You see, I believe that my meeting with Diana was fated and written in the stars. Perhaps, something tragic interrupted our perfect union, and the will of destiny was compromised due to some failings on my part."

The Zamindar paused as the Prince listened intently.

"I believe that if we are meant to be together, the feelings that we have for one another should be freely given, without being subjected to any undue pressure, or they will have no meaning at all…"

"Perhaps I understand your culture better than you think," interposed the Prince with a smile.

"You wish for your bride to come back to you on her own volition, to validate the great love you have for one another…"

"You understand me very well, Louis," interposed the Zamindar, "perhaps it's because in the East we have a greater reliance on the power of destiny and faith...When Diana is ready to come back to me, I will be there, waiting for her."

"I must admit, my friend, that because of you, I feel to have missed something truly exceptional in my life," interposed the Prince.

"Perhaps I am even a bit jealous of how fortunate you are to have known such a great passion and love...I sincerely hope that Diana will soon come back to you."

"Thank you, my friend," answered the Zamindar with appreciation, "however, love is universal whether we live in the east or the west."

"I guess we agree on that point," said the Prince as he moved toward the door with a more cheerful and positive attitude while saying.

"It's dinner time, my friend. We have a special Indian menu' this evening, in your honor, which I am sure you will enjoy...So, at least for the moment, let's think about the sumptuous meal and nothing else."

The Zamindar smiled and quickly followed him on the way to the exotic dinner.

The next morning the Zamindar was awakened by the bright light of the sun. It was a welcomed and cheerful sight for him since it rained the day before, and the sky was gloomy and covered with clouds.

The curtains in the stately windows of the room had been drawn back by the valet. At the same time, servants were attending to his breakfast, which had been elegantly displayed at a nearby table because he favored eating it in the privacy of his room.

After dressing in a silk housecoat, he lifted a cup from the table and took a few sips of his tea as he walked toward a window.

Ramakanta had been a guest in the rooms for days but avoided looking outside since there was a great view of the palace's manicured gardens. He recalled meeting Diana there in their first romantic meeting in the moonlight. It was a magical interlude whose memory at that moment caused him only pain.

But there was an unusual lure that morning to enter and explore the gardens' verdant splendor.

Without delays, he gulped down the rest of the tea and took a few bites of his buttered roll, indulging a bit in the rich selection of fruit preserves. He then dismissed the servants and prepared to take his morning bath before venturing into the great outdoors.

The splendid gardens looked quite different in the daylight, drenched in the bright rays of the sun. Dewdrops glistened like diamonds on the lush greenery, tended by the multitude of gardeners who were busily working on the scene.

Despite the loveliness of the surrounding, a stark reality prevailed that was disturbing to the Zamindar. The sense of loneliness, which was pervasive in the symmetrical beauty of the place. It felt as if he was walking into a verdant labyrinth of flora and trees.

He ventured forward, and in the distance, he was able to see the sensual statue of Venus, whose marble whiteness glistened in the sunlight and emerged victorious among the lush greenery.

There was an immediate attraction, and he walked with a faster stride toward it since the mythological depiction of passion was located in a more secluded area in the garden.

It seemed so peaceful there, more sheltered, without the usual intrusive presence of the palace guards. He remembered how in the moonlight, the statue of Venus reflected her voluptuous beauty in the dark, cool waters of the nearby lotus pond, which held such a great attraction to Diana.

The view was different during daylight, with the clear waters mirroring the cloudless sky, as a variety of lotus blossoms graced the surface of the pond with beauty.

Among the many aquatic plants, Ramakanta recognized the lovely *Nelumbo nucifera*, glistening in its whiteness. The flower is familiarly known as the Indian sacred lotus, while in the western world, it's referred to as a water lily.

The lotus blooms have been revered for millenniums for their mystical powers and are widely considered a symbol of rebirth.

The graceful plant rises from the waters' gloomy depths and opens its petals, turning into a beautiful flower at dawn.

The Zamindar was overwhelmed by their sight and attracted by the flora's stunning beauty, which felt to him pleasant and familiar. While approaching the edge of the pond, he reveled in the coolness of the water as he gently dipped his fingers in it. There was a sense of marvel at the circular images born out of his touch, which disrupted the liquid surface's stillness.

As the Zamindar remained transfixed by the glory of nature, a silvery voice suddenly broke the peaceful surroundings with a familiar sound, which said.

"It is written that *Padma* will rise at dawn from the murky, watery depths and bloom again in the warmth of the sunshine."

Ramakanta was breathless for a moment before turning toward the unexpected and beloved sound.

With indescribable joy, he saw Diana standing there with a bright smile on her lovely face.

She seemed like an apparition, embraced by the brilliance and glowing light of the sun. An exceptional beauty emanated from her, which almost ethereal in that unforgettable moment of true happiness that took his breath away.

There was a casual loveliness to the simple chiffon gown in shades of lavender she wore with innate elegance. It was gathered tightly around her waist, showcasing the curves and perfection of her figure. The long, flowing hair rested freely on her shoulders and framed her face with beauty, while a touch of crimson brightened her cheeks, depicting the excitement of the moment.

They both remained silent at that point, almost unable to move, overwhelmed by deep emotions that were difficult to define.

Diana was the first to break the magic spell while stepping closer to him with open arms, as she whispered with great emotion.

"I love you, my Zamindar…I love you forever."

The exultation Ramakanta felt in that magical moment was all-encompassing. Without hesitation, he ran into her arms and held her tightly in the loving entrapment of his embrace. For the first time after so much sorrow, he felt truly alive, joyous, and finally at peace.

They kissed with a burning passion, over and over again, seemingly unable to quench the thirst for each other. The feeling was overwhelming and dominated the love that erupted from within, unhindered like a flowing river.

"You came back to me, my love, my life," he whispered as he held her passionately in his arms.

"I never left you, dearest," she answered softly. You were always present in my heart and every single moment of my life…"

The Zamindar interrupted her with a kiss as he gently caressed her graceful neck and the sapphire pendant that once again decorated her décolletage with beauty. Noticing his attention to the jewel, Diana said with a smile.

"The symbol of our love is secure now, my Zamindar, and more perfect than before because of Father Anthony's benediction."

"I know my darling, he is a holy person and a true man of God," answered the Zamindar with deep appreciation," we have been fortunate in receiving his consul and blessings in our life."

He then cupped her face in his hands and looked deeply into her eyes with infinite love while saying.

"I see a special glow in your face that radiates with happiness, my beloved Zamindarin. I am grateful that because of God's mercy and blessings, we are together once again after so much sorrow."

Diana remained silent but rested her head on his chest, nestling happily in his arms.

"Tell me, my love," said the Zamindar softly as he caressed her lustrous hair.

"Where do we go from here, and what do we do from this point on?"

Diana looked lovingly in his eyes while saying.

"Any place will be perfect, dearest, as long as we are together."

They kissed and held each other tightly before walking hand in hand out of the garden, with a radiant smile on their faces.

"We have a lifetime together, my Zamindarin."

"No, my Zamindar…an eternity."

§§§§§

CHAPTER TITLES

Chapter one
The Elusive dream
Chapter two
The importance of tradition
Chapter three
Journey to destiny
Chapter four
A new world
Chapter five
A myth comes to life
Chapter six
A step into eternity
Chapter 7
Eternally yours
Chapter 8
Pledged to love
Chapter 9
A scent of Jasmine
Chapter 10
The Colors of India
Chapter 11
The Silver Tea Set
Chapter 12

OTHER NOVELS FROM
TIMBER CREEK PRESS
www.timbercreekpress.net

MILITARY ACTION/TECHNO
BLACK EAGLE FORCE: Eye of the Storm (Book #1)
by Buck Stienke and Ken Farmer
BLACK EAGLE FORCE: Sacred Mountain (Book #2) by Buck Stienke and Ken Farmer
RETURN of the STARFIGHTER (Book #3)
by Buck Stienke and Ken Farmer
BLACK EAGLE FORCE: BLOOD IVORY (Book #4)
by Buck Stienke and Ken Farmer with Doran Ingrham
BLACK EAGLE FORCE: FOURTH REICH (Book #5) by Buck Stienke and Ken Farmer
AURORA: INVASION (Book #6 in the BEF) by Ken Farmer & Buck Stienke
BLACK EAGLE FORCE: ISIS (Book #7) by Buck Stienke and Ken Farmer
BLOOD BROTHERS - Doran Ingrham, Buck Stienke and Ken Farmer
DARK SECRET - Doran Ingrham
NICARAGUAN HELL - Doran Ingrham
BLACKSTAR BOMBER by T.C. Miller

BLACKSTAR BAY by T.C. Miller
BLACKSTAR MOUNTAIN by T.C. Miller
BLACKSTAR ENIGMA by T.C. Miller

HISTORICAL FICTION WESTERN
THE NATIONS by Ken Farmer and Buck Stienke
HAUNTED FALLS by Ken Farmer and Buck Stienke
HELL HOLE by Ken Farmer
ACROSS the RED by Ken Farmer and Buck Stienke
BASS and the LADY by Ken Farmer and Buck Stienke
DEVIL'S CANYON by Buck Stienke
LADY LAW by Ken Farmer
BLUE WATER WOMAN by Ken Farmer
FLYNN by Ken Farmer
AURALI RED by Ken Farmer
COLDIRON by Ken Farmer
STEELDUST by Ken Farmer
BONE by Ken Farmer
BONE'S LAW by Ken Farmer
BONE & LORAINE by Ken Farmer
BONE'S GOLD by Ken Farmer
BONE'S ENIGMA by Ken Farmer
SILKE JUSTICE by Ken Farmer

454

SILKE'S QUEST by Ken Farmer
NO TIME to DIE by Buck Stienke
SILKE'S RIDE by Ken Farmer
ANGEL JUSTICE by Ken Farmer
SKINWALKER JUSTICE by Ken Farmer

SY/FY
LEGEND of AURORA by Ken Farmer & Buck Stienke
AURORA: INVASION (Book #6 in the BEF) by Ken Farmer & Buck Stienke

HISTORICAL FICTION ROMANCE
THE TEMPLAR TRILOGY
MYSTERIOUS TEMPLAR by Adriana Girolami
THE CRIMSON AMULET by Adriana Girolami
TEMPLAR'S REDEMPTION by Adriana Girolami

MYSTERY
BONE'S PARADOX by Buck Stienke
RECIPE for MURDER by Ken Farmer & Buck Stienke
SIN NO MORE by Ken Farmer & Buck Stienke
THE LOCK BOX by Terry D. Heflin
THREE CREEKS by Ken Farmer
RED HILL ROAD by Ken Farmer
THE POND by Ken Farmer

CIVIL WAR ESPIONAGE ROMANCE
SCARLET HEM by Terry D. Heflin
GOLDEN CIRCLE by Terry D. Heflin
THE AMETHEIST by Terry D. Heflin

Coming Soon
MYSTERY
FRIENDS by Ken Farmer

HISTORICAL FICTION WESTERN
McGRATH by T.C. Miller
DALIA MARRH by Ken Farmer

SY/FY
ANTAREAN DILEMMA by T.C. Miller

TIMBER CREEK PRESS

www.ingramcontent.com/pod-product-compliance
Lightning Source LLC
Chambersburg PA
CBHW051508250626
47156CB00001B/17